Desert Lost

Books by Betty Webb

The Lena Jones Mysteries
Desert Noir
Desert Wives
Desert Shadows
Desert Run
Desert Cut
Desert Lost

The Gunn Zoo Mysteries
The Anteater of Death
The Koala of Death

Desert Lost

A Lena Jones Mystery

Betty Webb

Poisoned Pen Press

Copyright © 2009 by Betty Webb

First Trade Paperback Edition 2011

10 9 8 7 6 5 4 3 2 1

Library of Congress Catalog Card Number: 2009924196

ISBN: 978-1-59058-863-5   Trade Paperback

Poisoned Pen Press
6962 E. First Ave., Ste. 103
Scottsdale, AZ 85251
www.poisonedpenpress.com
info@poisonedpenpress.com

Printed in the United States of America

For Flora Jessop,
who's been there and knows what happens

Acknowledgments

My thanks and admiration go out to Dennis DeFrain and Flora Jessop, of the Child Protection Project, for their tireless work in saving young girls from forced polygamist marriages, and for keeping me up to date on changes in Arizona polygamy law. I also thank the Sheridan Street Irregulars for their suggestions in the preparation of this manuscript; they made it better. Also helpful was Sergeant Mark Clark, of the Scottsdale Police Department, who, among other pieces of advice about police procedure, was kind enough to tell me where abandoned Jeeps wind up. Any errors in procedure are mine. But a very special thanks goes out to Lake Angelus, MI Police Chief James Webb (retired) for his many years of patience with his mystery novelist cousin—even though she did throw rocks at him when they were kids. Thanks for not throwing back, Jimmy!

Chapter One

Thumb out, shoulders hunched against the wet Phoenix night, eighteen-year-old Jonah King stood at the curb trying to catch drivers' eyes as they stopped for the light. Most ignored him. A cool wind was blowing the rain sideways and they were in a hurry to get home.

Home.

Jonah tracked his mind away from the word. Better not think about home. Looking like you were about to cry wouldn't help business.

There. The silver Mercedes with the dark tinted windshield. It had passed him earlier, blazing through the yellow-lit intersection, but had returned, the driver checking him out with a slow curb crawl. Encouraged, Jonah puffed out his chest, straightened his shoulders and ran his hand through his wet blond hair, confident he still looked good. He'd managed to keep his weight up and his teeth hadn't yet eroded. Nothing wrong with his skin, either, that a little borrowed Cover Girl couldn't hide.

All things considered, he was a bargain.

The Mercedes stopped, its tires hissing like snakes against the wet pavement. The automatic window hummed down. "Need a ride, son? Or...?" The voice hesitant, as if the driver hadn't done this often.

Jonah phonied a smile. "Looking for a party, dude. How 'bout you?" When the Mercedes didn't pull away, he approached the window and looked inside. Big car, little man; the standard.

The guy wasn't too bad, though. Fifty-plus, balding, soft around the middle. Jonah didn't mind. Preferred it, even. The athletes, they were the ones you had to watch out for because they could catch you if things went bad. Mr. Softie would be easy to handle.

Sensing it was time, Jonah took control. "Hey, man, like I said, I'm just out here looking for a party. You want some fun, I'm your boy. If not, leave me alone and let me do my thing."

An exhale from the Mercedes. "How much?"

At Jonah's answer, the man opened the passenger's side door. "Climb in."

Not for the last time that night, Jonah did as he was told.

Chapter Two

Stake-outs are boring, which is why I tend to avoid them. But there I was at midnight, lurking in an RV parked in a friend's south Scottsdale storage yard, waiting for taggers to swarm over the wall and spray paint nasty things about snowbirds on the sides of mothballed Winnebagos. At least, thanks to the RV's in-service potty, I wasn't wearing diapers.

The rest of Scottsdale liked to pretend this area of town didn't exist. Instead of the trendy condos and palatial homes further north, the neighborhood consisted of a series of heavy equipment storage yards semi-protected by cyclone fencing topped with loops of razor wire. No one lived here. No one wanted to.

I had been sitting in the RV for six hours, drinking coffee to keep me warm, killing time with stomach crunches and push-ups. I was just congratulating myself that the storm which had blown through Phoenix earlier in the evening had skipped Scottsdale altogether when a car pulled up near the fence. Grunts and shoe-shuffling floated toward me on the crisp March air. The taggers, out for another night of ageist vandalism? Grateful that my boring vigil was about to end, I grabbed my Mag-Lite and camera, and tiptoed to the half-open door.

Although security lights bathed much of the storage yard in weak green florescence, pockets of black dotted the gaps between the RVs. To add to my sightline problems, the cyclone fencing around the yard was ringed by a thick row of eight-foot-high oleander bushes, the Arizona remedy for ugly.

So I waited.

More grunts, more shoe shuffling. Then a thud, followed by quick steps and a car door closing. A few seconds later, the car rolled away as silently as it had arrived.

Not taggers.

Curious, I stepped out of the RV and approached the fence. Doves, awakened by the bustle, cooed briefly, then went back to sleep. A soft wind scraped oleander leaves together. Florescent lights hummed. The only other sounds came from cars rushing along the freeway and the lonely yip of a coyote on the nearby Salt River Pima/Maricopa Indian Reservation

With the keys the yard's owner had loaned me, I unlocked the front gate and peered out. As my eyes became accustomed to the shadows, I saw something wedged between the gap in the oleander hedge fronting a boat storage yard across the street. A wee hours garbage drop from a nearby business whose Dumpster was already full? Such bad-neighbor practices were not uncommon in this area of the city, but experience had shown me that objects other than garbage were sometimes dumped, too.

Conscious of the sounds of my own footsteps, I crossed the street for a better look. At first the bundle appeared to be little more than thick wrappings of cloth holding together a red-splotched tarp, but when I switched on my Mag-Lite, I saw the terrible reality.

A woman. She looked dead.

The faraway coyote howled again. Another answered. When I drew in my breath, the doves rustled once more, then flew away.

The breeze on my face felt like cold fingers.

No. It couldn't be. Not here.

I fought back the surge of sorrow that threatened to render me useless and knelt down to check for a pulse. My initial impression had been correct. Although the woman's skin was still warm, her carotid artery didn't pulse, and her glazed blue eyes stared sightlessly into the merciless night. The wounds on the left side of her head had leaked onto her single braid. More blood had spread onto her calico dress, a garment so long it covered everything except her hands and feet.

As I gazed into those dead eyes, I realized that she looked vaguely familiar.

I didn't know her, but I'd seen her on a hundred other faces, pale Nordic features made almost identical by generations of incest. The prairie-type dress, designed to hide a woman's shameful body from lustful eyes, sealed the deal.

Not possible. Not in Scottsdale.

But the truth lay before me, cooling in the night.

The dead woman was a polygamist.

"Isn't this neighborhood a bit low rent for you, Ms. Jones?" Lieutenant Dagny Ulrich, of the Scottsdale Police Department, stared at me. In the normal course of business I kept out of her way, but murder changes everything. What was she doing here? Lieutenants usually stayed in the cop shop, shuffling paperwork and playing politics.

I motioned toward the nearby RV storage yard, now strobe-lit by blue police flashers. "There've been some break-ins at The RV Corral, tagging and stuff, so Henny Allgood, the owner, asked me to run surveillance for a few nights. When I heard suspicious sounds coming from here, I walked over to investigate and found…this. Like any good citizen, I immediately phoned it in." Especially like any good citizen who was an ex-cop.

Dagny had taken charge as soon as she arrived, and now a fleet of police cruisers blocked both ends of the street. Yellow crime scene tape glowed under portable spotlights. Dozens of officers walked back and forth mumbling into their radios, while from another nearby storage yard, an irritated Rottweiler barked a warning. Car exhaust and male sweat buried the perfume of the desert.

Without taking her eyes off the dead woman, Dagny asked, "Do you know her?"

I pretended not to understand. "Who? Henny? She's an old friend, but we don't hang out much any more. The usual scheduling problems."

Dagny frowned, not that she had been smiling earlier. "Don't get smart with me, Lena. Do you know the vic?"

"No."

"You sure?"

Crime scene techs bustled around the body, taking pictures, picking up detritus, looking for any leavings which might identify the woman's attacker. Official time of death would be determined when she arrived at the medical examiner's office, but to my experienced eyes, the beginning of rigor in her extremities meant she'd been killed only three or four hours earlier. Yet the closest polygamy compound remained a six-hour-drive north, near the Utah border.

"I never saw her before." Technically, it was the truth.

Dagny finally looked at me. Her hazel eyes held no warmth. "Are you sure?"

"Of course I'm sure."

"And, *of course*, you wouldn't tell me if you did, would you? Being helpful was never your strong suit."

Dagny wasn't the type to let bygones be bygones. Several years earlier, the report I had handed in after getting shot in the botched drug raid she'd scheduled without adequate prior surveillance stalled her climb up the Scottsdale PD career ladder. She'd contested the report, but in the end, my version—backed up by two other officers on the scene—won out. Still, she blamed me alone for her subsequent career troubles, especially her bust from captain to lieutenant, and since then she'd done what she could to sabotage my P.I. business.

I bore my own grudge. Thanks to Dagny's ambition-fueled impatience, I still carried around a bullet in my hip and it hurt like hell on rainy days. Good thing I lived in the desert.

With difficulty, I kept my voice neutral. "I'm helping as much as possible, Dagny, but like I said, I just heard the car. I couldn't actually see it because the oleander hedge obstructed the view. I heard the killer dump her, but couldn't see him."

"You sure?"

"What, you think I bashed her head in myself and somehow avoided covering myself in blood spatter?"

A faint smile. "You could have covered yourself in plastic."

"*Plastic?*"

The smile disappeared, or maybe I'd imagined it in the first place. "Take a little trip back through time, Lena, say, seven years ago. To that case where the insurance salesman drove home during his lunch break, wrapped himself in garbage bags, beat his wife to death, then went back to his office clean as a whistle. No blood spatter."

The Moss Hayward case, the second-to last one I'd worked under Dagny's supervision. Hayward had beat his wife to death for the insurance money, then tried to make it look like a botched burglary. In his rush to discard the garbage bags, the homicidal hubby had neglected to wash his hair, and a bright crime tech discovered one almost-invisible drop of blood underneath Hayward's comb-over. Hayward was now doing twenty-five to life in the state prison.

"Dagny, you can't possibly suspect that I…"

She waved my protest away. "Of course not. But you've always been a loose cannon."

"Not that loose."

The smile returned. "Really? Then tell me, how's the anger management therapy going?"

Without answering, I turned on my heel and headed back to The RV Corral.

Certain that Henny's taggers had been scared away by the police presence, I spent the rest of the night with my feet up against the RV's console, staring at the pictures of the dead woman I'd taken with my digital camera before the police arrived. What had she been doing so far from home? Her single blond braid, balanced by a slight pompadour over her forehead, proclaimed that she was a "sister-wife," a woman who shared her man with numerous other women. She appeared to be somewhere in her forties but might easily have been younger since the lifestyle, with its non-stop child-bearing, aged women before their time.

I forced my memory back to the miserable weeks spent working undercover in Purity, one of the many polygamy compounds clustered around the Arizona/Utah border. Plenty of motives for murder there. Simple jealousy, battering that escalated beyond the standard wife-controlling punch, and money. Always money.

Polygamy was rife with welfare fraud. Since multiple marriages weren't legal, the great majority of its children were illegitimate, and like most illegitimate children, each received a monthly welfare check. If there were fifty children in a household—not uncommon—the haul could run to several thousand dollars per month per family. The money was obediently turned over to the compound's prophet for "investments," while the women and their children continued on in poverty. Although in recent years the Feds had instituted some welfare modifications, payouts continued to make their way into the compounds. Polygamy wasn't merely a religion in Arizona; it was big business. Sister-wives weren't just pawns; they were cash cows.

The women seldom protested their lives' difficulties—they knew better—but every now and then one broke the silence when an unusual greedy prophet left her with hardly enough money to feed her children. Still, even if the dead woman had been killed for challenging her prophet's financial practices, the question remained: why kill her, then drive past three hundred miles of empty desert to dump her in south Scottsdale, and by doing so, insure a police investigation? Given the sect's penchant for secretiveness, it didn't make sense.

I stared at the woman's face again, wondering how many children would wake in the morning to find their mother gone.

That face. That familiar face.

Maybe I couldn't identify her, but I knew someone who probably could.

Chapter Three

I slept in the next morning, which created no problem because Jimmy Sisiwan, my Pima Indian partner at Desert Investigations, always beat me to the office. But I showered, dressed, and breakfasted quickly just the same, hoping the routine of the day would chase away last night's grim memories.

When I finally did make it downstairs to our two-desk front office, Jimmy looked up from his computer, his curved tribal tattoo gleaming against his dark forehead. Orphaned at an early age, he'd been adopted by a Mormon family and raised in that faith. By the time he'd graduated from Brigham Young University with a degree in computer science, however, he'd begun delving into his Pima Indian heritage. Following the genetic call, he moved back to the reservation, learned the old language, and tatted himself up like an eighteenth-century Pima warrior.

His soul may have been Indian, but his computer skills were pure Techno-Wizardry.

"Catch any taggers last night?" White teeth flashed from his handsome, reddish-brown face. A glance at his computer screen showed me he was in the middle of another batch of background checks for Southwest MicroSystems.

"A murder victim got in the way." I filled him in on the dead woman and my suspicions.

"Polygamists? In Scottsdale? Doesn't sound plausible to me."

"She had all the signs, Jimmy. Clothing, hair, the whole bit."

He shook his head, more in sorrow than doubt. "Wonder what she was doing all the way down here."

When I brought out my digital camera and showed him the pictures, he widened his eyes. "Either I'm imagining things, or she looks an awful lot like Rosella!"

Rosella Borden, one of my closest friends, was a former sister-wife who'd escaped from one of the compounds fifteen years earlier, taking her baby daughter with her. She now used her knowledge to help vulnerable girls escape before they could be forced into becoming the plural wives of elderly men. "Don't worry, that's not Rosella. But she could easily be a relation."

"No kidding. A half-sister, maybe, or a cousin."

"The problem is, since so many of these polygamists look alike, the victim might be only distantly related. Maybe she's even from a different compound, one of those satellite things Prophet Hiram Shupe keeps setting up, so it's possible Rosella and the dead woman didn't know each other at all." Which is what I hoped, since most murder victims were killed by their nearest and dearest, and when threatened—even by her relatives—Rosella could play rough.

"You'd better call her, Lena. She'll want to know."

And she could help with the I.D. "Right. But yesterday she called and told me she was headed toward Second Zion to pick up a couple of runaways, that if I don't hear from her within twenty-four hours, to alert DPS."

Rosella wasn't being paranoid. Prophet Shupe didn't appreciate people who helped his cash cows break out of the pasture. The God Squad, his private police force, obeyed his every command, and it was rumored that he wanted my friend dead.

I did some quick math. If Rosella left Scottsdale before six and cheated the speed limit all the way to Second Zion, she could have arrived around midnight. The girls would be waiting for her in some agreed-upon desert canyon. It would take around a half hour to hike them out and get back on the road, six ticket-risking hours for the drive back, then another hour to get them settled in a Phoenix safe house. If the rescue went according to schedule, Rosella could possibly be in her own bed by nine a.m. I checked my watch. Nine-thirty. Waving a hovering Jimmy away, I dialed her home number, but it switched over to voice mail. I left a quick message, then tried her cell. Same thing.

"She's probably sleeping," Jimmy said. "Try again in a few minutes. Or if you want, I can drive to her house right now and roust her."

In case the victim was Rosella's sister—she had at least thirty—I wanted my friend to get as much rest as possible before confronting grief. "I'll go over there in a couple of hours." That said, I began returning phone calls from the lame, the halt, and the heartbroken.

I'd started Desert Investigations right after leaving Scottsdale PD, having learned the hard way that following a superior officer's orders could be dangerous to my health. Running a P. I. business had turned out not to be the safest profession, either, but at least I was my own boss.

In the beginning, Jimmy had brought in the bulk of Desert Investigation's income via his pre-employment background checks for various corporations. But due to my involvement in a murder investigation that took place on an Arizona film set, I'd been hired as a consultant for a television series. *Desert Eagle*, so-named for the big handgun its Cherokee private detective carried, was partially filmed here, necessitating that I attend only one Los Angeles production meeting a week. While I disliked the travel, the retainer was so exorbitant that my contributions to Desert Investigations' coffers now topped Jimmy's. Ordinarily, I would fly to Los Angeles every Friday morning for a production meeting, but due to the current writers' strike, the series was on hiatus. In the meantime, I busied myself with the standard P.I. cases.

My first client call of the morning was to Emily Glendenning, a wealthy, fiftyish widow who wanted to believe she'd met the man of her dreams on the tennis court at one of the local resorts. After doing a basic background check and then following her

European heartthrob around town for a few days, I needed to deliver some bad news. Werner Emil Hoffman, supposedly born in East Berlin, where as a teenager he had heroically braved Soviet guns while leading an escape party over the Berlin Wall, was a phony. Actually born in the Red Hook section of Brooklyn, his real name was Antonio Nezniacu, and he made a living by fleecing women like Emily. He did, however, have an ear for languages, and during his various scams, had picked up enough German to fool non-German speakers.

Emily's reaction was straightforward, if sad. "I'll give him his walking papers tonight."

I felt a spike of alarm. "Maybe I'd better be there when you do." Although Nezniacu's background revealed no propensity for violence, in this crazy world a woman could never be too careful.

"No need. Baby Brian's coming over."

Having met her son, the youngest of five, I had to smile. Her twenty-seven-year-old "baby" was six-foot-four with the build of a Hollywood action hero, and one look at him would scare the much-shorter Nezniacu into submission. "Just make sure Baby Brian plays nice."

A laugh, welcome under the circumstances. "I'll try, but you know how kids are these days. Can't tell 'em a damned thing."

The rest of the morning passed in much the same way, delivering a mixture of bad news and good. Henny was disappointed that I hadn't caught the taggers who'd been plaguing The RV Corral, but sensible as always, she understood that a murder victim trumped messed-up RVs. When she asked if I planned to resume my vigil that night, I told her the taggers probably wouldn't come back.

"Now that the area has become a higher-profile crime scene, the kids will move on to safer territory."

"You really think so?" Her voice sounded jagged from living too many years spent smoking too many cartons of unfiltered Camels.

I reaffirmed there was an eighty to eight-five percent chance they were gone for good, and with that, we parted on friendly terms. Before I could place my next call, the phone rang in my hand: Warren, calling from the real estate office.

"The lease is signed, and Beth says we can move into the house tomorrow, if we wish. You finished packing yet?"

I'd met Warren when he was filming *Escape Across the Desert*, a documentary about the Phoenix prisoner of war camp for German U-Boat crewmen during World War II. With his blond, surfer-boy looks, he was handsome enough to be an actor, but after a few minor roles, he'd found he preferred the other side of the camera. And, eventually, fact to fiction. The latter decision had worked well for him. One of his documentaries, *Native Peoples, Foreign Chains*, about the near-extermination of American Indians, had won an Oscar. The son and grandson of movie directors, he was as Hollywood as they come, yet we were moving in together. Because he disliked being separated from his eight-year-old twin daughters who lived in Beverly Hills with his actress ex-wife, he'd kept his home there so he could be within shouting distance of them for at least one week every month. Except, of course, when he was filming in some exotic location: Saudi Arabia, Mozambique, New York.

Just hearing his voice made my heart smile, but I tried to disguise it. Unabashed adoration isn't good for anyone, especially handsome men. "Packing? I'm getting there."

Actually, I hadn't packed so much as one carton. Now in my mid-thirties, I had not lived with anyone since turning eighteen. A childhood spent in foster homes was probably responsible for that, but to be honest, I knew other ex-fosters who had no trouble forming permanent relationships. Most, though, hadn't been raped repeatedly by a foster father at the age of nine.

"Exactly how many boxes have you packed?" Warren was clearly suspicious.

"I can't remember."

"You do intend to move in with me, don't you?"

I took a deep breath. "Of course I do. I'm halfway packed."

"Tell me the truth, Lena."

Counting to ten, I exhaled slowly. "It's just that I haven't done anything like this before." *And it's scaring the hell out of me.*

His voice softened. "Why don't we handle it like this, then? Go ahead and keep your apartment. If at any point you feel our situation isn't working, your place will still be there for you."

"Maybe I'll do that." No point in revealing that from the start, I'd planned to keep my apartment upstairs from my office. Changing lifestyles was one thing, burning bridges was another.

"Now remember, I'm picking you up at the office at three o'clock so we can take some measurements at the house. Beth will meet us there."

"You don't have to keep reminding me."

"Could have fooled me."

We talked for a little while longer, but when I hung up, Jimmy was giving me the Evil Eye.

"What?" I asked.

"Nothing."

"Say it."

"I'm smarter than that," he muttered, turning back to his keyboard.

Jimmy didn't think Warren was right for me. Even worse, he thought I was wrong for Warren. *Oil and water*, he'd once said. *Cactus and neon.* On my good days, I believed Jimmy was just being petty; on bad days, I agreed with him. But this wasn't the time to start worrying about relationship complications, so I dialed Rosella again. To my relief, she picked up.

In a voice fogged with exhaustion, she said, "Jesus, woman. You coulda let me sleep. I didn't get to bed 'til after eight this morning."

"Have you seen the newspaper?"

"Brought it in, didn't look at it. Reading the comics isn't on my to do list. Last night I delivered those Second Zion runaways to that safe house on the west side. Prophet Shupe was goin' to give them to his four-hundred-pound uncle, and the kids were so grossed out they'd made a suicide pact. Hell, they already had the gun! I took it away from them, so now I've got another firearm for my collection. Now let me get back to sleep, okay? I had myself a pretty good dream goin' there. Prophet Shupe dead, with a stake through his heart."

A good dream by any sane person's standards. Since inheriting leadership of Second Zion from his father, Hiram Shupe—who just happened to be Rosella's ex-husband—had issued increasingly bizarre prophecies, most of them concerning the End of Days. Six times he'd led his followers out into the desert after convincing them he knew the exact day and minute God would "rapture" them up to Heaven. Each time God let him down, and Shupe herded his dehydrated flock back to Second Zion. Following God's continued no-shows, Shupe arrived at the conclusion that the inhabitants of Second Zion were too sinful for rapture. After several months of pondering the problem, he discovered a novel way to cleanse his followers' souls. Their chief sin, he'd decided, was idolatry. His followers cared too much for each other and not enough for him. After all, wasn't he, Prophet Hiram Shupe, The Living Presence of God on Earth, the only rightful object of anyone's affection?

So several years ago, Shupe, The Living Presence of God on Earth, began breaking up families. He moved the women and children into dormitories, and the men into smaller bachelors' quarters. Breeding rights changed, too. Brother James now had sex with Brother Silas' harem, and Brother Silas took on Brother Peter's women, so on and so on, until every family unit in the compound had been dissolved. There had been some grumbling, but on the whole, Shupe's brainwashed followers obeyed. Those that didn't were never seen again.

When God still didn't rapture Second Zion up to Heaven, Shupe discovered yet another solution. He ordered the compound's pets—puppies, kittens, hamsters, goldfish, whatever—killed. God had told him, he claimed, that the children used their pets as false idols, giving them the devotion that was rightfully due The Living Presence of God on Earth. After the roar of guns stopped, my informants told me, the only sounds you could hear were children sobbing.

But I didn't see how Prophet Shupe, crazy as he might be, could have anything to do with the dead woman, Second Zion being three hundred-plus miles north of Scottsdale.

Rosella might have heard something, though. Out of sheer self-defense, she kept an eye on her ex-husband's whereabouts.

"The newspaper, Rosella. Read the story on page three, bottom of the fold. They managed to get it in just before deadline."

After a few mumbled curses, I heard paper rustling, a brief silence, then, "All I see's some blurb about a woman's body bein' dumped in south Scottsdale. Is that what you mean? Since you woke me up, you gotta think there's a connection between me and the, what do you call it, the DB, the dead body? Hell, Lena, if I ever kill anyone, it'll be Prophet Shupe, the bastard."

"Rosella, the woman was a polygamist."

"What makes you think that?" Suddenly she sounded wide awake.

"Her hair. Her clothes. Her resemblance to you."

Rosella was tall, her big-boned frame harkening back to the immigrant Scandinavians who had joined Brigham Young on his trek across the American prairie to the Great Salt Lake. Her face, with features too blunt for true beauty, was a face so common on the compounds that the women could have been cloned. That kind of similarity happened when people interbred with close relatives for more than a hundred years. Frequently, they also shared the same birth defects. Born with all her fingers and toes, Rosella was one of the lucky ones.

"Lena, you sure about this? I mean, how could one of those women wind up down here?"

"*You're* here, aren't you?"

"That's different. After the last beating, I scooped up the baby and ran like hell. I'd never have made it, except Celeste, one of my sister-wives, helped us get out."

In polygamy parlance, a sister-wife was one of your husband's other wives—if you counted such "marriages" as legal, which they weren't. "Helped how?"

"It was supposed to be my night to spend with the Prophet, but she, uh..." Rosella fell silent. For all her toughness, Rosella was like most ex-sister-wives; uncomfortable talking about sex. Also like the rest of them, she had never been allowed to call him by his given name, not even during their most intimate moments.

"Celeste convinced him to change his mind?"

After clearing her throat, Rosella answered, "Yeah. She knew I wanted to run, so she made sure she was wearing some dress he especially liked. Blue calico with red flowers. And she kind of, well, wiggled her hips when he came over to...Anyway, she got him thinkin' about her instead of me. That's when I ran."

It was rare for one sister-wife to help another escape, but not unknown. "Have you heard any rumors lately about Shupe's activities? Other than those armaments caches he's supposedly bunkered near the Utah border?"

I could almost hear Rosella's head shake through the phone. "Nope. The kids I pick up aren't much in the mood for talkin' and I'm too busy drivin' to cross-examine them."

Chances were the runaways would know little about Shupe's expansion plans, but I still had to ask. "Do you know anything about new satellite compounds he's started? I've heard he's been setting them up all over the place—Texas, Colorado, Missouri, Canada. Think he might try for Scottsdale?"

She laughed. "*Scottsdale?* C'mon, Lena, that's nuts."

I wasn't so sure. When Rosella ran, she had changed from her long-skirted dress into baggy jeans, the better to navigate the rough desert terrain around Second Zion. Most of the runaways did the same, leaving their cumbersome dresses at the compound. The dead woman had still been wearing hers. The woman was no teenager, either. By their late twenties, most sister-wives had already accepted their fate and were trying to make the best of it. Even if they still wanted to run, they had borne too many children to carry across the desert, and couldn't bring themselves to leave them behind.

When I shared my thoughts with Rosella, the laughter stopped. "Okay, so the dead woman probably wasn't a runner. But as for there bein' some sort of satellite compound in Scottsdale, where would Prophet Shupe hide it? Up at Grayhawk, near the book club ladies? Over at the Boulders, so the golfers could gawk? When he sets up satellite compounds, they're always in the boonies. He may have been getting crazier these past few years, but I'm sure he still understands that he can't get by with his shit in Scottsdale. Too public."

A vision of razor-wired fencing fronted by thick plantings of eight-foot-tall oleanders flashed across my mind.

Chapter Four

After emailing the woman's picture to Rosella's computer, I called my old friend Sergeant Vic Falcone at Scottsdale PD headquarters. Vic's quick action had kept me from bleeding to death after I was shot in that ill-fated drug raid. Someone had once told me an old American Indian belief held that when you saved a person's life, you became responsible for that person ever after. Vic might have originally hailed from Jersey City, but when it came to me he acted mighty Indian.

"I hear you had a run-in with Dagny Ulrich over a DB last night," he said. "Better watch yourself, kid."

Still *kid*, after all these years. I pictured Vic's sharp-featured Sicilian face, gentled by soft brown eyes. "What was she doing at the crime scene, anyway?"

"You don't know?"

"That wasn't a rhetorical question."

"She was there because she's left orders to be alerted whenever you turn up connected to something. Anything. Homicide, parking ticket, whatever. When you called in that body dump, she couldn't get out the door fast enough. Like I said, watch yourself."

"Thanks for the warning. Now about that DB. Any info yet on the woman's identity?" I already knew *what* she was, but the specific *who* remained in question. Rosella would sleep for another couple of hours, then fire up the computer to look at the photo I'd just emailed her. In the meantime I wanted to know what Scottsdale PD knew.

Vic lowered his voice, which probably meant that Dagny was near. "Nothing so far. The woman had no ID on her, and AFIS doesn't have her prints on file. The buzz around the station is that she might be some kind of actress."

Ah, because of the woman's nineteenth-century "prairie" dress. Almost fifty small theater groups were sprinkled throughout the Phoenix/Scottsdale metroplex, and the surrounding county boasted a couple of Old West theme parks featuring OK Corral reenactments. There were also a few Scottsdale shopkeepers who, during high tourist season, dressed in Western drag. To believe the dead woman was one of them made more sense than the truth. Besides, Scottsdale PD had zilch experience with polygamists. Lucky them.

"Dagny's going to have her cleaned up so she can post a photo online, right?" I asked. *After she'd had the woman's tell-tale hairdo washed and re-arranged to hide that big dent in her skull.*

"Already done. You know how efficient the lieutenant is."

We chatted for a few more minutes, then I let him go and checked my watch. Noon. Leaving Jimmy to the culinary joys of his brown bag lunch, I took the stairs up to my apartment.

When I'd moved in several years earlier, everything had been beige, from carpet to paint to furniture. The only spots of color had been a yellow-and-black clown Kachina doll lounging on the window sill and the black satin toss pillow with red embroidered lettering that said, "Welcome to the Philippines." I'd stolen the pillow from my fourth foster home because they were nice people and I wanted something to remember them by.

Last year, after finally accepting that this was my home, I'd tricked out the place in neo-Cowgirl, adding a saguaro-rib sofa upholstered in a bright Navajo print, a red Lone Ranger and Tonto bedspread, and two turquoise-shaded lamps with bases shaped like horses' heads. The Philippines pillow was still there, though. I don't let go of the past. Which is, my therapist never tires of telling me, part of my problem.

I sidestepped a pyramid of empty packing crates and went into the kitchen to nuke a Styrofoam container of ramen noodles. That done, I slid an old blues album on the turntable. The vinyl was one of my favorites: Fred McDowell, his hair-raising slide guitar work audio-taped in his own living room by musicologist Chris Strachwitz. While the old master growled his way through "You Gotta Move," I slurped down ramen and thought about polygamy.

Most people didn't know that more than fifty thousand polygamists currently live in the Southwest. Every now and then their self-styled prophets, most of them every bit as crazy as Prophet Hiram Shupe, made the six o'clock news when they got caught performing forced underage marriages, but normally the prophets shunned publicity. Their lifestyles were illegal, of course, as were their common practices of child rape, battering, welfare fraud, and witness intimidation. But, hey, God was on their side, right? The very thought that these Taliban-types might be moving their mess to Scottsdale put me off my ramen.

I was standing in the bedroom, surveying the packing cartons and wondering where to start, when my cell rang.

"Better get over here." Rosella. Fully awake.

"You know who she is?"

"Not on the phone." With that, she hung up.

Rosella lived in the Garfield Historical District of Phoenix, an in-transition neighborhood where gentrified homes hunkered next to dilapidated cottages too far gone to be anything but tear-downs. After establishing a successful in-home medical transcription business, she'd bought a two-bedroom adobe at a bargain basement price, and after five years, was still renovating. As I exited my Jeep, I noted the house's slow Hyde-into-Jekyll transformation. Old siding, new doors and windows, two sparkling brass carriage lamps flanking a crumbling cement porch.

Before I could raise my hand to knock, the new oak door opened. "Come in. Quick."

Stymied by her paranoia, I darted a quick look around but saw only several African-American children playing hopscotch, and a homeless Hispanic pushing his garbage bag-filled cart down the sidewalk. As soon as I was inside, Rosella slammed and double-locked the door behind me.

"What's going on, Rosella?"

She shoved the printout of the dead woman's photo into my hand. "That's Celeste King, my cousin, my former sister-wife. She's the one who helped me escape from Second Zion."

In that community, it was common for cousins—mothers and daughters, even—to marry the same man, but since the "marriages" were legally nonexistent, they kept their maiden names. "Are you telling me the dead woman is one of Shupe's wives?"

"She was the last time I saw her, but if she's down here, he's probably reassigned her to someone else." I noticed for the first time the redness of her eyes. She'd known the woman, and loved her. "Oh, Lena. I owe everything to Celeste, *everything*. My freedom. My sanity. Celeste getting killed in Scottsdale means something downright strange is happenin'. Men like Prophet Shupe don't let their women leave the compounds on their own, not ever. And if she ever decided to sneak off, well, I would have been the one to pick her up. I mean, damn, that's what I *do!*"

From somewhere in the back of the house, a girl's voice rose in song: KariAnn, Rosella's sixteen-year-old daughter, home from the Arizona School for the Deaf and Blind on spring break. Despite the tension of the moment, I smiled. Her voice was a sweet soprano, but flat. The deaf often have trouble hitting the right notes.

Seeing the direction of my glance, Rosella managed a smile, too.

"That latest poem, she get it published?" I asked.

"In *Highlights Magazine*, no less. Now she's settin' it to music using some kinda mathematical formula she found on that website for people in the beginning stages of Usher's. Who'd a thunk music is math."

KariAnn suffered from Usher's Syndrome, a common product of generations of incest. Like profound mental retardation, this particular genetic combination of deafness and blindness was endemic on the polygamy compounds. The prophets loved it because the handicap guaranteed the sufferer SSI payments for life, yet the disease left the girls fertile enough to breed more Usher's kids. Cash cows squared.

Rosella closed the door to her daughter's room, then led me into the living room, which was further along in the renovation process than the house's exterior. Pale yellow walls contrasted with polished oak floorboards, and bright patterned throws covered the reupholstered sofa and armchair Jimmy and I had helped her lug home from Goodwill. The lemony scent of furniture polish filled the small room.

As I settled myself on the chair, she said, "One of us has to tell the cops."

"Right."

"But, uh, as you know, I try and stay away from them."

"Right."

"Because of any kidnap charges that might be pendin'."

"Right." One of the problems with helping young women escape was that they were so often minors, therefore still legally under their parents' control. Under Arizona statutes, helping a minor hide from his or her lawful custodial parent was custodial interference at best, kidnapping at worst. Since Rosella had been implicated in dozens of "custodial interference" cases, the county attorney, who boasted polygamists in his own family tree, had set his sights on the more serious charge. For the same reasons, the state attorney general didn't like Rosella, either. My friend was one warrant away from a jail cell. Add to this the numerous death threats that had been leveled against her by Hiram Shupe's God Squad, and Rosella's paranoia wasn't merely understandable, it was smart.

"How about an anonymous phone tip? There's a pay phone over by the Ranch Market."

"Two blocks from my house? The cops ain't dumb. Look, all they need is Celeste's name, then they can do the rest. There's some phones outside that Circle K on Forty-Fourth Street. Call on your way back to Scottsdale and disguise your voice."

A pointless caution in the day of voice recognition systems, not to mention the fact that my retrofitted 1946 Jeep, painted front bumper to back with Pima Indian symbols, was memorable. Still, I could see little harm in calling in the tip. Celeste King's life had been cruel enough without letting her lie unidentified in the cool room down at the county morgue.

"Give me a dollar, Rosella."

She grabbed her purse and pulled one out. "This means I'm your client?"

"For what it's worth."

Down the hall, her daughter's tuneless singing continued. Something about aspens trembling in the wind.

After making the call from the Circle K, I drove back to the office on surface streets, along the Hispanic neighborhood on eastern McDowell with its used furniture stores and payday loan rip-offs, past the National Guard Armory at the western edge of Papago Park, then cruised through the big sandstone buttes into Scottsdale proper.

Here's the thing about Scottsdale: it really is beautiful, an oasis in the middle of a harsh land. But being surrounded daily by beauty can scald your eyes blind. Our City Council's aesthetic shortcomings prove this.

Lined with lofty palms and blooming flowers, Scottsdale city center is called Old Town, a determinedly Old West neighborhood which has sung its siren song to Minnesota and Canadian tourists for decades. Jammed up against the art galleries and Indian jewelry boutiques were a full assortment of upscale bars and restaurants. Walking Old Town's streets—where Desert Investigations happens to be located—can be a joy because this oddball conglomeration of the old and the new somehow works. However, just before you turn north off McDowell and head into

Old Town, you have to confront SkySong, the City Council's current financial darling. A one-point-two million-square-foot cathedral dedicated to the combined religions of modern technology and gimmee-gimmee retail, this architectural sour note looked more like two huge caskets fronted by four equally-huge, upside-down toilet plungers.

This is what can happen when you let beauty-blind politicians make artistic decisions.

I winced my way past SkySong and headed toward Desert Investigations. There I found Jimmy still working his way through background checks for Southwest MicroSystems. He switched gears the moment I asked him to look up Prophet Hiram Shupe. Having once loved a polygamy runaway and experienced firsthand the damage that had been done to her, he hated the prophets as much as I did.

Less than a half hour later, he slapped a thick printout of articles on my desk.

It made for grim reading.

According to some compound escapees, Prophet Shupe had recently stepped up blood atonement enforcement for anyone sinning against him personally or against compound rules. Those rules encompassed everything from diet (meat no more than once a week, except for Shupe and his God Squad); sexual behavior (missionary position only, husband on top of wives); to financial misdeeds (men attempting to hang onto their salaries, women to their welfare checks). Blood atonement meant death, but since Second Zion was surrounded by vast, empty desert, no bodies had ever been found.

As I read on, I grew more and more alarmed.

Not content with ruling over the intimidated citizens of Second Zion, Shupe had stepped up the establishment of new compounds, and was even rumored to be in the planning stages of yet another in central Arizona. Supposedly, a senior member of his God Squad had been dispatched to help. This flurry of expansion was necessary, one newspaper article claimed, because given Second Zion's high birth rate, it was bursting at the seams.

"Jimmy? Did you read this stuff before you printed it?"

"That last line's the kicker, isn't it? A satellite compound in Central Arizona could mean anywhere from Wickenburg to Casa Grande. Or any place in between."

"Like Scottsdale."

I couldn't let that happen.

I was still studying Jimmy's printout when the door opened and Warren walked in carrying a clipboard. As always, he looked good. Honey-colored hair, sky-blue eyes, and a fit, nervy build. Even on close inspection he appeared closer to thirty than the forty-one he admitted to.

"Ready, Lena?"

"Ready for what?"

His perfect mouth twisted into a wry smile as he tapped the clipboard. "It's three o'clock. Time for our appointment with the realtor to take measurements at the house. Don't tell me you forgot."

It's possible that *forgot* wasn't the right word. Somehow I just couldn't seem to wrap my mind around the fact that I was moving in with him. "Can we do this tomorrow, instead?"

The smile disappeared. "Apparently you've also forgotten that I'm flying back to L.A. tonight to spend a long weekend with the twins. It's their birthday. You promised you'd use the time to get things organized."

I took care not to let my discomfort show. "Me? Get organized? I can hardly organize an apartment, let alone an entire house. What if I put the coffee pot in the toaster oven?"

My poor joke seemed to work, because his mouth curved into a smile again. "It wouldn't fit. C'mon, Lena. Let's get going before Beth thinks we've stood her up again."

Moving was such a bitch. Packing, measurements, life changes. Fighting to quell a growing sense of panic, I followed him to his Mercedes and buckled myself in. After patting me on the shoulder much as a cowhand would soothe a nervous horse, he pulled away from the curb and turned north up Scottsdale Road.

For a long time, Scottsdale had been the toniest town in Arizona. Not anymore. Home prices in Paradise Valley—a partial misnomer since the town was as much mountain as valley—topped Scottsdale's. The higher the home, the higher the price. Warren drove west on Lincoln Drive, past big resorts hiding behind oleander hedges identical to those in south Scottsdale. The edifices behind these hedges, though, were vastly different. No storage yards, just sparkling fountains that fronted sprawling marble exteriors, cool tile lobbies, and uniformed attendants eager to cater to a guest's every need. Across the road, on the mountain north of the resorts, film and rap stars' homes dotted the slope, their designs ranging from Southwest Modern to Hollywood Horrible. After living for years in my one-bedroom apartment over Desert Investigations, I felt wildly out of place.

I felt even more so in the house Warren had leased. By Beverly Hills standards, it was small, a mere thirty-nine-hundred square feet encompassing four bedrooms, four baths, formal dining room, den, media room with stadium seating for twelve, and a pool that would have daunted Michael Phelps. The adobe-and-glass edifice perched on the south side of Mummy Mountain as if readying itself for a dive into the neighbor's swimming pool below, but I had to admit it was a stunning property. Another upside was that Warren would be there to share it with me. If he loved the house, I'd learn to love it, too.

Beth Lugar, the realtor, waited in front of the massive front door, her own clipboard at the ready. Bottle brunette and face-lifted, she was clad in a casual lilac pantsuit, the cost of which probably equaled the average person's monthly mortgage payment. As we stepped from the car, she pulled artificially plump lips away from expensive orthodontia into a grimace that vaguely resembled a smile.

"On time today, I see. Good! Let's get started. I have an appointment in Carefree at six. A nice little starter home for an adorable young couple."

Knowing the exorbitant real estate prices in Carefree, it was all I could do not to harrumph. While she escorted us through the empty rooms, our footsteps echoed across the terrazzo tile floor and the smell of fresh paint assailed my nostrils. The house was ten years old, but rubbed and scrubbed into a sterility that unsettled me. Still, as Warren had repeatedly stressed, this was only a lease. If things didn't work out between us, then no harm, no foul.

"How's that sound to you, Lena?"

"Fine." What had they been talking about?

Warren sighed. "I asked if you'd rather have the sofa sideways to that long glass wall or facing it."

Shielding my eyes against the afternoon glare, I looked southwest toward the smog of downtown Phoenix. "Facing it, I guess. Why get a crick in the neck from looking sideways all the time?"

"I just thought you might prefer to face the fireplace."

Fireplaces in the Phoenix metroplex were pointless, the weather usually being too hot. When the weather did cooperate, the county's Clean Air Initiative often kept the fires unlit. Still, hearths looked pretty filled with flowers.

"Like I said, either way's fine with me."

Warren sighed again, then went back to measuring the wall. "Thirty-four feet, eight inches," he called.

Beth made purring noises, mostly aimed in Warren's direction. He had that effect on women.

I turned away from the smog and looked east toward Scottsdale. In the distance, I could see the curve of the Pima Freeway where it spanned the dry Salt River. At the freeway's edge, near a narrow strip of untouched desert, lay a dark green feathering of trees and oleander bushes. Squinting, I could see the storage yard where I'd found Celeste King's body.

"Magnificent view." Beth stood at my elbow.

"You could say that."

"There aren't many lease-option-to-buys available with a one-eighty-degree view of the Valley."

I said nothing, knowing that sometimes the more you see, the more you wish you didn't.

By the time Warren finished taking measurements, it was almost five, and Beth had started making polite hurry-up noises. "Get everything you need?"

He checked his clipboard again. "Looks like it. How about you, Lena? Any questions?"

"I'm fine."

He smacked the clipboard against his muscular thigh. "That's it, then. Beth, thanks for taking the time for this. Have a safe trip to Carefree."

She was already out the door.

Unlike Beth, Warren didn't seem to be in any hurry to drive away from the house. He stood at the edge of the property, looking from one hill-climbing house to another. "I can breathe here," he said.

"That's Arizona for you." But not for long, I worried. Too many houses dotted too many hillsides, and our famous cobalt sky had already grown yellow around the edges.

"Lena, are you happy?"

The question startled me. "Why do you ask?"

Warren turned away from the view and looked me straight in the eye. "Because you don't seem to be."

"Occupational hazard, I guess." At least that's what I hoped it was.

"Maybe we should…" He looked out at the hills again, and his mood—which had been darkening—seemed to shift. "Oh, hell. Let's get something to eat."

"So early?"

"Why not? Jimmy will have closed the office by now, so there's no point in you opening it back up. Or is there something else calling out for your attention, something more important than me?"

"Don't be silly."

"You sure?"

I bit him gently on the shoulder. "Absolutely."

He didn't look like he believed me, but didn't press the issue. "That's good, then. So how about a nice quiet dinner at one of those new sample menu restaurants on Camelback? The *Journal's* review of Rene Marceau's place gave it three-and-a-half stars out of four. You get a little of everything, from duck comfit to sweetbreads glacée."

A serious foodie, Warren had been taking cooking classes at the Scottsdale Culinary Institute, which was one of the major reasons why the new house, with its state-of-the-art double kitchen, appealed to him. He had already bought cases of copper pots, food processors, pasta rollers, and other kitchen contraptions I couldn't identify. They looked like torture devices.

"Aren't sweetbreads sheep's stomachs or something? How about a plain old steak? Bloody rare. And a baked potato stuffed with sour cream and chives, cheese crumbles and bacon bits on top." Real, artery-clogging food.

He tried unsuccessfully to hide his disappointment. "Okay, forget the sweetbreads. McDuffy's has good steaks. Baked potatoes, too."

We were soon ensconced in a booth, our early arrival guaranteeing that we had our corner of the restaurant to ourselves. Service was proportionately quick, our rare steaks arriving less than ten minutes after we sat down. During a lull in the chewing, Warren said, "I meant to ask you before we got started measuring, how are things at the office? Any interesting cases lately?"

Caught off guard—had he done that on purpose?—I made the mistake of telling him about Celeste, Rosella, and the possibility that Prophet Shupe might have started a satellite compound in Scottsdale.

He put his fork down, a piece of steak still speared on the tines. "Please don't take that case."

I pretended to be too busy cutting my own steak to answer.

"Those polygamists are dangerous, Lena. Especially Shupe and his toadies in Second Zion. They're even worse than the polygamists in Purity, and you almost got killed working *that* case."

"Life is dangerous."

He gave me a look. "It doesn't have to be."

"I could get killed crossing the street. Fall off a ladder and break my neck. Have a heart attack." Especially after eating a McDuffy's steak.

"I worry about you."

Warren worried about me and I worried about him worrying about me. "I'll be okay, Warren."

He stared down at his plate. "I can't believe I used to believe your job was sexy. Now it just scares me."

Me, too, sometimes. Eager to change the subject, I said, "Listen, I'm really sorry about acting so distracted lately. Tell you what. Leave me a key to the house, and I promise to get everything ship-shape before you get back from L.A. Dishes in cabinets, sheets on beds."

"Your clothes in the closet?"

"And I'll leave plenty of room for yours." Smiling, I picked up his abandoned fork and lifted it to his mouth. "Open wide, baby."

Chapter Five

That night, after Warren left my bed to take the redeye to Los Angeles, I lay awake staring at the ceiling. As reflected lights from the cars on Scottsdale road threw horizontal stripes across the shadows, I thought about Celeste and the way she'd stared up at a sky she could no longer see.

They tell me there was a night when I, too, looked up at the stars and couldn't see them, the night my mother shot me and I almost died. I don't remember any of that, just a slow rise from blackness to a white hospital room two months later. The nurses were asking questions. Did I know my name? Did I know what had happened? Did I like the new Teddy bear the nice social worker left for me?

Slowly, over the years, a few memories had returned. A white bus, a clearing in the woods, children crying, my father's stricken face as he said goodbye. But every time, just as I was almost there, just about to grasp the missing pieces of my life, I would see my mother's horror-stricken face, hear the gunshot, and then…

Nothing.

Maybe I didn't want to remember.

March is an iffy month in Scottsdale. Usually the sun is out—we are in the middle of the Sonoran Desert, after all—but on occasion it goes missing in action. This morning was one of those days. As I sat looking out the window from my desk at Desert

Investigations, I saw gray clouds scuttle back and forth so low to the ground it seemed I could reach right up and touch them. Even the ever-present tourists dimmed their smiles as they strolled along the art galleries along Main Street.

I was about to brew myself something hot and jittery when Sergeant Vic Falcone called and told me that a telephone tip had come in, identifying the dead woman I'd found.

I pretended surprise. "Really? Who was she?"

"The caller or the DB?" That Vic, you couldn't put anything past him. "The caller's name—a female, by the way—remains a mystery, but the DB's name is Celeste King, last known address Second Zion, in Beehive County. We're thinking she might have been mixed up with those polygamists."

"Polygamists?"

Vic grunted. "Officially, we don't care what those people are doing as long as they stay away from Scottsdale. Anyway, Dagny reached out to the Beehive County Sheriff's Office and they're sending a couple of deputies to ask around. Not that they'll learn anything, Second Zion being what it is."

He was right. Polygamists seldom cooperated with the police. As far as the polygamists were concerned, the only law enforcement organization that held any legal or moral weight was Prophet Shupe's God Squad, which communicated only to The Living Presence of God on Earth. Those sheriff's deputies would be lucky if they were even allowed onto the compound's grounds.

Vic's gruff voice rolled on. "We don't know what Ms. King was doing in Scottsdale, but the cause of death was six blows to the head from some wooden object. The M.E. found splinters and they might have come from a two-by-four. The first blow was fatal, but the killer kept right on swinging. You know what they say about overkill."

"A crime of passion."

"Especially since she was four months pregnant."

I sat up straight. "Are you sure?"

"That's what the medical examiner says. A boy. Or would have been, except his mama died."

"Was murdered, you mean."

"Whatever. The M.E. took DNA samples, but you know how that goes. With the backlog over there, we'll be lucky if we get the results back by Christmas."

Despite what we see on television cop dramas, most police departments have to wait months, or at least several weeks for DNA results. This was partially because the process itself was so slow, and partially because so many states, Arizona included, had enacted laws requiring DNA samples to be taken from anyone booked on suspicion of a felony. In this case, the DNA results should prove immaterial, the father of Celeste's baby most probably being Prophet Shupe. Sister-wives rarely fooled around on their husbands, because the sentence for a woman's adultery was death. Not by stoning—the polygamists weren't *that* fundamentalist—just a gunshot in the back of the head as Blood Atonement.

But Celeste had been beaten to death.

I thanked Vic and hung up. After a few minutes of thinking about women and the various forms of trouble they could run into, I said to Jimmy, "I'm going out for awhile. If anyone calls for me, say I'll be back in a couple of hours."

Without taking his eyes from his computer screen, he waggled his fingers, and I walked out the door.

A chill wind blew down from the north, making me grateful I was wearing the heavy vest I'd found at Tempe Camera. Designed for photographers, it had eight pockets for various lenses and filters, but which came in handy for the tools of my own trade: disposable latex gloves, digital tape recorder, handcuffs, snub-nosed .38 revolver.

The neighborhood where I'd found Celeste's body was less than two miles from my office, so within minutes I was pulling into The RV Corral. Henny Allgood met me at the gate, her dyed red hair brighter than the oleander blossoms ringing the storage yard. Eighty if she was a day, Henny was one of those crusty old desert rats Arizona specialized in, with a rail-thin body and weathered face that had suffered through decades of droughts. Too stubborn to pay attention to the Surgeon General's warnings, she took a long drag of a Camel. Coughed. Flashed nicotine-stained dentures.

"Looks like you were right about them taggers, Lena. They didn't come back."

"A police presence will do that for you."

"Ha. 'Bout the only thing cops ever done for me." Behind her, a fleet of stored RVs stretched all the way to the back fence. Winnebagos, Fleetwoods, Skylines, Monacos, the entire gas-guzzling species. The driveways of most Scottsdale homes didn't have large enough parking areas, so their owners left them with Henny when they weren't wallowing down the highway. But other RVs belonged to snowbirds, who stored them when they returned home to less scalding summers.

Henny took another drag off her cigarette. Coughed again. "Thinkin' 'bout getting me a dog. Something big and mean."

"Like that Chihuahua you keep in your office, Pedro something or other?"

"Señor Pedro de las Cruces de las Sunnyfield Farms de las Sonora. Little shit cost me a fortune. No, not another one like him, couldn't afford it. Rottweiler, maybe. Or a pit bull."

"Then you better make sure Mr. Big-and-Mean doesn't eat Señor Pedro de las Cruces de las whatever."

"What you doing back here anyway, Lena? Come to deliver an invoice?" A grin.

Because of a big favor Henny had once done me, I never invoiced her for anything. "Just stopped by to ask if you've seen anything unusual lately."

The grin disappeared as compassion flickered across her hard face. "Like a dead woman? I been reading the papers. What's this crap I hear about her being some sort of actress?"

"They know better now. Here's the thing, Henny. Have you seen any new folks in the neighborhood? New businesses that seem a bit out of place? Unusual activity, especially at night? Women in long skirts?"

"Long skirts? Make me laugh, why don't you? Women today, the skirts they wear, you can see their asses. Birth canals, even, now that underwear's gone outta style. As for unusual activity, we're zoned for light industry down here so something strange's always goin' on. Those self-storage places that have been going up all over the place, hell, you know what they're like. People driving back and forth day and night with trailers and trucks and I don't know what all. Buncha dealers in stolen goods, I'll bet. Meth cookers, too, probably. Neighborhood's gonna blow sky high some day, them with it. No loss."

"Depends on your point of view." Five years earlier, Henny had lost a grandson to crystal meth and she still pretended it didn't hurt.

"You ask me, Lena, you oughta do some snooping around."

As they say, great minds think alike.

After leaving Henny to her dreams of pit bulls and Rottweilers, I walked over to the crime scene. Except for a one-inch strip of yellow crime scene tape snagged on a prickly pear cactus thorn, the area appeared to have been picked clean by locusts. Looking down the street, I studied the slight curve that made the dump spot invisible from any intersection. At what point had the killer noticed the same thing? The night of the crime, when he was driving around with the body? Or had he already been familiar with the neighborhood?

There was nothing left to do but visit other nearby busi-nesses, so the next couple of hours found me showing Celeste's photograph around the neighborhood, asking people the same questions I'd asked Henny. The answers were in the negative until I arrived at Little Rick's You-Store-It.

The tiny office, hardly bigger than some of the storage units it fronted, was furnished in the style known as South Scottsdale Gloomy, with dark, faux-paneled walls, a faux Navajo blanket-covered sofa, and more plastic ashtrays than should have been legal. But the room looked spiffier than Little Rick himself, a middle-aged man who topped six feet and weighed a hundred pounds more than he should have. His nose and eyes were red; not an uncommon sight around here during early March. We desert rats get rheumy when the temperature drops below eighty.

Little Rick squinted at the photograph through thick bifocals. "She looks like one of those weird gals who shops at Frugal Foods, the one on Hayden Road."

"You sure?"

He wiped his runny nose with a grungy hand. "Don't let these glasses fool you, Miss Jones. I'm a long way from being blind. Yeah, I'm sure. There's usually three of them shopping together. They..." He cleared his throat. "They look a lot alike, so I'm figuring two sisters and their mother. Or grandmother. It's getting harder and harder to tell these days, what with cosmetic surgery and all."

"How often is 'usually'?"

"I make my grocery run about ten on Tuesday nights, 'cause that's when you can get through checkout the fastest. That's when I see them."

"Every week?"

"Yeah, and that's what makes it so odd about the amount of stuff they load up on, enough to feed the whole Chinese Army."

Or an entire polygamy compound. "When's the last time you saw them?"

"Like I said, last Tuesday."

"All three?"

"Yeah." He wiped his nose again.

"You called them 'weird.' Why?"

"The way they act, the way they dress. All the time in real dowdy stuff, skirts down to their ankles, big bulky sweaters just about as long as their skirts. You ain't gonna see their pictures in that magazine my wife reads, *Scottsdale Style*."

"Have you talked to the police about this yet?"

"Couple of detectives came by yesterday, showed me a different picture. Same woman, though. I told them the same thing I'm telling you. Not that it's any of my business or anything, but I heard she was beat up something awful." He tapped the photograph before handing it back. "Is that true? I mean, you can kinda tell she's dead here, but other than that, she doesn't look too bad. Almost pretty, actually."

The miracles of PhotoShop. When I'd told Jimmy I planned to show the picture around, he insisted on removing the blood and inserting a lifelike highlight into Celeste's dead eyes. When further questioning of Little Rick elicited no new information, I went back to my Jeep, planning to hit Frugal Foods next Tuesday. I was running low on ramen noodles, anyway.

After a quick burger at Mickey D's, I headed back to my office, but before I arrived, my cell played the opening bars of John Lee Hooker's "Boogie Chillun." Pulling over to take the call, I found myself listening to Rosella.

"Lena, I'm on my way to pick up another kid from one of the compounds. Feel like ridin' shotgun?"

My hands clenched on the Jeep's steering wheel as Rosella continued. "Justa couple a minutes ago I got this call from a woman up in St. George sayin' there's a girl who walked in over the ridge from Second Zion. If you come with me and the kid's not too bad off, you can question her about Prophet Shupe and any possible satellite compound down here. Maybe she's heard something."

The small town of St. George, Utah, was separated from Second Zion, Arizona, by ten miles of sand, rock, and a state line. Sympathetic residents of the Utah town sometimes harbored compound runaways until they could be picked up by anti-polygamy organizations and delivered to safe houses in Phoenix. Considering they were a mere stone's throw from Prophet Shupe's wrath, such compassion took courage.

"Do I have time to stop by my office for a wig?" I asked Rosella. "I'm *persona non grata* around the compounds, myself."

"Borrow one of mine. You want brunette or red?"

"Brunette. I'm on my way."

When I arrived at Rosella's house, she'd donned the red wig. It made her look like a stripper. KariAnn stood next to her, carrying an overnight bag.

"The School for the Deaf and Blind's still on spring break and I don't want her stayin' here alone while we're gone, so we're droppin' her off at a friend's house," Rosella explained.

"Aw, Mom." Although almost blind, KariAnn, was perfectly capable of taking care of herself. But her mother worried that in our absence, Prophet Shupe might somehow find a way to reclaim what he saw as his "property." Especially ready-to-be-bred property.

After parking my Jeep in her garage, Rosella hustled us into her aged Santa Fe, which despite its bulk, could move fast when necessary. With a final, paranoid glance out the rear view mirror, we pulled onto the street. Fortunately, Rosella's friend lived near I-17, so by one p.m., after dropping KariAnn off, we were headed north.

Traffic wasn't too bad once we passed the north Phoenix suburb of Anthem, and cleared even more at Cordes Junction, where we gassed up at the big truck stop. When we climbed in altitude—pushing eighty all the way—the desert gave way to lush pine forests and snow-capped mountains. By the time we exited I-17 just north of Flagstaff to turn onto SR-89, the slight chill we'd left behind in Phoenix had morphed into near-freezing temperatures. As the sun dipped lower in the sky, the mountains dropped behind us and we entered desert flats again. High desert, this time, even more lonely and windswept. Perfect terrain for keeping secrets.

At Fredonia we gassed up the SUV again and turned west on the narrow blacktop paralleling the Vermillion Cliffs, a border-hugging stretch of red rock that had become home to the California condors released by wildlife sanctuaries. But more dangerous creatures than the near-extinct birds lived in the cliffs' shadows.

The last time I'd been in polygamy country was to help a woman accused of murder and rescue her thirteen-year-old daughter from a forced marriage to a sixty-eight-year-old man. By disguising myself as the second "wife" of a disillusioned polygamist, I had been able to experience the lifestyle's sins firsthand: arrogant prophets, young girls battered into submission, genetically-damaged babies, and—unbelievably—the collusion of women who served as capos for their masters.

A shadow, perhaps of a condor flying between us and the dimming sun, passed over the Santa Fe.

"Lena, haven't you been listenin'?"

I started. "Huh?"

"You were a million miles away." Rosella flashed a sympathetic smile. "I was tellin' you about Celeste and all she did for me."

Giving her my full attention, I said, "Back in Phoenix you said she'd helped you escape the compound. Why would she do that? What would have been her motivation?"

"She just wanted to help, that's all."

"Are you sure she didn't have an ulterior motive?" If so, it probably wouldn't have been jealousy. The few photographs taken of Prophet Hiram Shupe showed a near-anorexic scarecrow with the height of a basketball player but none of the grace. His cavernous face was devoid of any hint of compassion. His pale eyes, which his followers believed could look straight through the clouds to God himself, revealed madness. Just thinking about him gave me the willies; heaven only knew how he'd terrified the young Rosella. Or for that matter, poor, murdered Celeste.

"She knew I was miserable so she helped me escape, and yeah, she did it out of the goodness of her heart. Stop bein' so damned cynical."

"You actually confided in a sister-wife?" A dangerous thing to do in the compounds, where information could be used as ammunition.

"Celeste was the kind of person you could tell anything to. Maybe she was only two years older than me, but she was real motherly. More than Prophet Shupe's other wives, anyway. The morning after, um, after my wedding night, she helped clean me up. When I stopped crying, she told me it would get better, to stop trying to fight him off because that kind of thing just made him rougher. She promised that as soon as I got pregnant, he'd start leavin' me alone."

I thought about that for a minute, one woman counseling another to lie back and submit to repeated rape. "How long did it take for you to get pregnant?"

A trembly sigh. "Almost a year. But I stopped fightin', and she was right. He wasn't so rough after that, and at least he was quick. After a while I learned to think of other stuff while he was...Well, it got almost bearable."

"Almost?"

The hard edge returned to her voice. "Prophet Shupe was a pig. *Is* a pig. If it hadn't been for Celeste, I don't know how I woulda survived. Celeste had a way of, oh, I don't know, making me see the lighter side of things."

The lighter side of rape?

"I helped her take care of her babies, and when KariAnn was born, she helped me, too. And the both of us, we helped with all the other kids. I never saw a woman who loved children more than Celeste did, so it wasn't all bad. We had ourselves some laughs, me and her."

Just one big, happy, dysfunctional family.

"Prophet Shupe really liked her," Rosella continued. "Not me, so much. It took me too long to get pregnant."

I remembered Celeste's dead face. She'd been pretty enough, although not as pretty as Rosella. But physical attractiveness wasn't the most prized quality on a polygamy compound. Fertility was what really mattered.

Brushing a stray hair from my black wig out of my face, I said, "You said she was two years older than you. She already had several kids when you left?"

"Four, includin' a set of twins. And she was pregnant again."

Celeste would have been sixteen, which meant that she'd begun having children at the age of twelve or thirteen.

"She was lucky in another way, too. Most of her kids was girls."

Bouncing baby boys grew into adult problems on polygamy compounds. When they entered their mid-teens, the boys learned the flip side of polygamy: if one man had ten wives, nine men would go without. The few young men chosen by the prophet to receive multiple wives were among the lucky minority. The prophet ordered the others—almost always undefended by their mothers—bussed out of the compounds no later than their eighteenth birthdays, when they were no longer eligible for welfare payments and their use to the community was at its end. Undereducated and unfit for modern life, boys as young as sixteen were dumped in Salt Lake City, Flagstaff, even Phoenix. A few were lucky enough to make their way to rescue missions; the majority endured short and brutal lives on the street.

Celeste had been pregnant with a boy when she'd been murdered, which made me wonder how many boys she'd previously produced. I started to ask, but my question was cut short when Rosella veered the Santa Fe so sharply onto a gravel road that I had to brace myself against the dashboard.

"Just about two miles down here is where we're supposed to pick the girl up," Rosella said. "At that deserted mining camp up against the cliffs."

By now it had grown so dark I couldn't see her face. "I thought you said the call came from St. George? We haven't crossed the Utah border yet."

"We can't make the pickup at her house 'cause the caller's got kids of her own and doesn't want to endanger them. She said she'd be waitin' with the girl at the camp. No problemo, because that's the same place I just picked up those two runaways, Patience and True, on Tuesday night. Maybe it ain't the greatest location, but at least it's not one of the canyons. Those things scare the crap out of me."

When I'd rescued a runaway from one of the area's steep-sided canyons, it had necessitated picking my way between boulders and rattlesnakes, so I understood her fear. Nodding my agreement, I settled back against the seat. The sky was inky, and now that Rosella was using running lights only, the gravel road barely visible.

"You sure you can see where you're going?"

"I was raised here, remember? Second Zion is three miles north. As the crow flies."

"No crows out tonight," I observed, steeling myself for yet another jerk as she steered the Santa Fe through a washout. "For God's sake, Rosella, slow down. One more bump like that and I'll lose a filling."

"Whiner."

But she eased off on the gas pedal and we sat in companionable silence until we reached the camp, a ragtag collection of falling-down buildings and rusted machinery that loomed like ghosts against the night. When she turned off the Santa Fe's running lights, I saw no car, no nervous woman, no runaway. Just the flitting shadows of bats diving at insects.

"You sure this is the place?"

"It ain't quite seven, and I told the woman I'd get here sometime between seven and eight."

I have nothing against bats, but the idea of spending another hour in their company didn't thrill me. Especially not with Prophet Shupe's armed-to-the-teeth God Squad headquartered so close by. Plus, up here in the higher desert, the temperature was probably in the low thirties, and my vest wasn't doing a very good job of keeping me warm. But I sat back against the seat, prepared to wait it out.

"Wanna stretch your legs?" Rosella smiled at me through the dark, her long wig draped around her face like a blood-red shawl. But she still looked like Rosella, as pretty as she was tough.

"No. And you shouldn't either. You don't know what's out there. We need to stay in the car until they show up."

Ignoring my advice, Rosella opened the car door and stepped out, her breath misting white against the night. "Come on, Lena. The air's great. Fresh. Not like that Phoenix sludge. Up here you can really smell the desert."

The note of sadness in her voice revealed that she sometimes missed her former life, the wide open spaces speckled with wildflowers and sage, the Vermillion Cliffs marching across the state line, the eagles, the condors. To me, all that beauty had been irrevocably stained by vicious prophets and their brainwashed followers.

"Get back in the car, Rosella."

A low laugh, caught by the wind and carried toward the Utah border. "Nothing out here but the night. I'm walkin' over to that shed. I used to play here with my brothers. It looks like somebody's boarded it up, but not real good. C'mon. Come see."

Uncomfortable with her wandering off alone, I hopped down from the SUV, but only after patting my vest pocket to make double-certain my .38 revolver was still there. The night, although cold, was stunning. Out here, miles from any city lights, the stars blazed, and the Milky Way created a speckled white sky road. As I gazed in admiration, a meteor dove toward the horizon, then disappeared into the badlands. Would it smash into the earth near us, or was it still hundreds of thousands of miles away, fooling our eyes as it passed on the other side of the Vermillion Cliffs?

I pulled my vest closer, not that it did much good. The wind was brisk, making the mining camp's old boards creak and clatter. Usually this far from civilization, coyotes would be calling to one another, but not tonight. It seemed as if they themselves had declared the area off limits.

Which was odd, because coyotes loved to sniff and paw through ruins like this, where mice and other small prey could hide. So why…?

"Rosella," I whispered. "We need to get back to the car."

She either didn't hear me or pretended not to, just kept walking toward the rickety shed that blocked the mine's entrance.

"Rosella! Now!"

I hurried forward and grabbed her by the arm, prepared to force her into the SUV. As I spun her around, the door to the shack exploded outwards, followed immediately by the stench of sulfur, the sound of a shotgun blast.

Rosella pitched forward.

Chapter Six

Men's voices raised in triumph. More than one. Two, maybe three.

"Got the bitch!"

"Don't let that other one get away!"

"God's will be done!"

Ignoring the rapidly-approaching shadows, I dove toward Rosella. Her wig had fallen off and lay sprawled near her outstretched hand. Not bothering to check out the extent of her injuries, I grabbed her by the collar and began dragging her toward the Santa Fe. She wasn't a small woman, so the trip, peppered with the blasts of shotguns and rifles, seemed to take forever. When a streak of fire raced across my arm I knew I'd been hit, but there was no time to cry out in pain, no time to do anything other than switch hands and get her to the shelter of the bulky vehicle.

Fortunately, I'd left the passenger door open, and strengthened by an adrenaline rush, tumbled Rosella inside. I pulled the door shut, then climbed over her into the driver's compartment, where I saw she'd left the keys dangling in the ignition. Head low, I started up the Santa Fe and slammed it into reverse, desperate to put as much distance between us and the gunmen before I needed to stop and turn around. The continued twang of gunshot against metal alerted me that the car was being hit, but the average vehicle can endure a lot of firepower before a lucky hit ruptured the gas tank. Even then, a car might not blow.

Then again, it just might.

When I'd reversed far enough away, I shifted into drive and spun around. I hadn't yet heard a car, but common sense told me that our attackers hadn't hoofed it from Second Zion to the mine. With all need for secrecy gone, I flipped on the Santa Fe's brights, spewed a hailstorm of gravel, and barreled back down the road the same way we'd come. With Rosella hurt, even the most reckless speed meant relative safety. I had to get her to a doctor. The hospital at St. George was her best bet, and it had the added benefit of lying in the opposite direction of Second Zion. And maybe, just maybe, on the way we might encounter a patrolling DPS officer who would see me driving like an idiot and pull us over.

Prophet Shupe's God Squad hated real cops, but they were too cowardly to pull their guns on one.

Just as I began to think we might make it to the highway without further incident, a pair of headlights appeared in our rearview mirror. Then another pair. Two vehicles. The God Squad, gaining fast. I pressed harder on the accelerator only to be rewarded by a fishtail spin as the Santa Fe left the road. While we bumped over a scattering of rocks and brush, I forced myself to ease up enough to straighten the car out, then steered it, one-armed, back onto gravel.

How far was that damned highway?

Distance is easy to gauge in the city. At night, stoplights mark off intersections, and the reflected glow from store windows makes even the darkest asphalt glimmer. It's different in the badlands, where the only light comes from the moon and stars. Every now and then a creosote bush, caught by our headlights, appeared to move toward us, but it was merely an optical illusion. What *was* moving toward us—and fast—were the headlights in our rear view mirror.

"Rosella? Speak to me."

Nothing. A quick glance to the side proved that she remained in the same position I'd dumped her in. Was she still alive? I bit back a sob. If necessary, there would be time for tears later, but for now I had to reach that hospital. Then…

Well, then whatever would happen would happen.

I drove on into the darkness, thinking about Rosella, about KariAnn, about all the terrified girls who'd fled Second Zion on foot hoping to elude their pursuers. Some had made it. Some hadn't.

"Rosella?"

Still nothing.

Just as I was about to call to her again, the highway abruptly appeared at the top of a rise less than a hundred yards ahead, lit by a slow-moving sedan. I blasted onto the blacktop, horn wailing, and hooked a hard left around the car. Too focused to make the call myself, I flashed my headlights on and off, hoping the driver would grab his cell phone and alert 9-1-1 that some crazy was loose on the road.

As the car's headlights dwindled behind us, I tried rousing Rosella again. "Speak to me, woman!"

Finally, a groan. She was still alive.

Almost gibbering with glee, I said, "We're headed to the hospital at St. George, so hang in there." I couldn't see any blood, but that meant nothing; the Santa Fe's interior was too dark. My brief flicker of happiness disappeared even further when another check in the rearview mirror revealed two pair of headlights careening around the sedan. Our attackers remained in full pursuit.

But I knew this highway well. Clear blacktop to the Utah border, over the ridge, then a smooth descent into St. George and at the edge of town, the Dixie Regional Medical Center with its fully-staffed and well-guarded emergency room. Even Prophet Shupe's God Squad wasn't crazy enough to follow us there. Praying that no coyote or antelope would wander onto the blacktop ahead of us, I hit the accelerator again until we topped ninety and the old Santa Fe began to vibrate. The sedan's headlights dropped back, but our pursuers stayed with us as we crossed the Arizona/Utah border. Mere yards on the Utah side, I saw a flash, then heard another shotgun blast.

The Santa Fe's rear window shattered and a snowstorm of powdered safety glass brushed my face.

Not bothering to look back, I stomped on the gas pedal again until my foot could go no further and, despite the Santa Fe's shuddering, the speedometer nudged past one hundred. Our speed remained constant until, at the top of a hill, we went airborne. I muttered a prayer the tires wouldn't blow when we landed, but somehow they held. After a brief hesitation, the Santa Fe lurched forward again, miraculously still facing into the general direction of St. George. I steadied the steering wheel and finally chanced a look in the rear view mirror. Our pursuers still dogged us but the Santa Fe couldn't go any faster.

Almost as much for my comfort as hers, I started talking to Rosella again, even though I doubted she could hear me above the road noise and wind. "Just another couple of miles, girlfriend, and we'll be there. A cakewalk. Hey, I see lights! Houses! A gas station. More cars. Maybe *real* cops!"

Rosella groaned again. "Uhn, Lena?"

"Present and accounted for," I gabbled. *Was the God Squad gaining?*

More groaning. Then a curse scalded my ears. Ignoring the headlights in my rear view mirror, I chanced another glance at Rosella. She was trying to sit up.

"Jesus, what happened?"

"We got shot. And Shupe's God Squad is right on our ass, so get the hell back down."

No dummy, she ducked her head. "Was that...? Yeah. I heard a noise and then I remember fallin'. If you're taking me to the doctor, don't bother. Nothing wrong with me that an aspirin can't cure."

"The whole rescue operation was a set-up, Rosella. Prophet Shupe's God Squad was waiting for us, with guns." Another look in the mirror showed me that our pursuers were gaining. No point in telling her, though. "We're making good time, no doubt about that. Flying. Literally." I stifled a giggle, because the Santa Fe *had* flown for a moment. But it wasn't built for this kind of rough riding, and I was pushing the old heap far beyond its capacity.

I slowed to take a turn, hoping the other vehicles would slow, too. They didn't, and the space between us closed dramatically.

"We're almost there. I can even see the hospital in the valley. Big, bright parking lot. Ambulances. People."

"Hospital? Are you nuts? Like I told you, I got me one hell of a headache, but that's all. I must've bumped my head when I fell."

"I took a bullet in the arm."

"And you're *drivin'*!?" As alarmed as she sounded, she didn't try to sit up again, just stayed hunched over. "For God's sake, how bad is it? You need me to fix a tourniquet? Here, I got a belt…"

I looked down at my left arm. No rivulets of red, just a few spatters against my beige vest. My wound probably wasn't serious. "Not necessary."

"But *shot?* Damn, Lena!"

"I've experienced worse." I still carried that bullet in my hip, courtesy of the drug raid that ended my career as a police officer.

Our pursuers drew closer, then just as it appeared they planned to chase us down the hill right into town, the headlights dropped back and disappeared. Had they turned on one of the many side roads that led back to Second Zion? Or had the men switched off their lights and were running in the dark, waiting to sneak up on us if we slowed down? I took no chances. Never allowing the Santa Fe to drop below ninety, I sped all the way down the hill to the St. George city limits before easing up on the accelerator. As it was, I blew through a red light—narrowly avoiding getting T-boned by a Volkswagen—and took the next intersection on two wheels.

"You're gonna kill us both," Rosella muttered, scrunching even further down into her seat. "Then we'll need an undertaker, not a doctor."

"Think positive." Slowing even further, but not so fast as to propel her through the windshield, I rocketed into the hospital's parking lot.

As emergency rooms go, Dixie Regional's was relatively tame. A coughing child hovered over by a protective mother; a drunk with a bloody nose; a pregnant teen grimacing through either labor pains or a panic attack; and several people with assorted bumps and bruises, none seemingly serious. Amidst all this discomfort, nurses performed a relaxed triage, but when Rosella barreled through the door yelling, "My friend's been shot!" the tempo changed.

Two nurses rushed toward me at the same time a doctor stuck his head out of a green-curtained cubicle. "Put her in three!" he ordered.

Over my protests, the nurses hustled me down the hall and into another cubicle, Rosella following hard behind.

"This is nothing," I said. "She's hurt worse than I am. Look at her head."

The nurses ignored me. Before I could stop them, they hoisted me onto an examining table, slid off my vest, then cut away the bloodied remnants of my long-sleeved black tee shirt. After a brief look at my arm, the ER doc, an acne-scarred hulk who looked like he'd gone a few rounds with the pre-prison Mike Tyson, agreed with my own self-diagnosis.

"It's just a graze," he proclaimed. "You lucked out, lady."

He applied a topical anesthetic and some dressing, and the wound's fire died down. The scratches I'd received when the Santa Fe's rear window exploded inward weren't serious, either.

"Once those scratches heal, you'll still be prettier than me," the doc said. "But it looks like you've been shot before. That scar on your forehead…" At my expression, he changed tacks. "Mind telling me who used you for target practice this time?"

"I have no idea."

He gestured toward the opening in the curtains. "Maybe the deputies out there can jog your memory. In the meantime, a broken nose in the next cubicle is calling my name. But after that, I want to see your friend. These so-called 'bumps' can be more serious than they first appear."

With that, he pushed his way past two very large sheriff's deputies. Rosella, who had stayed by my side throughout the bandaging, cursed under her breath.

Here was the problem.

The law in Utah was pretty much the same as in Arizona: help a minor escape from one of the compounds and you were guilty of custodial interference and/or kidnapping. By driving to a Utah hospital, where the staff was mandated to report any gunshot wound to the authorities, I'd delivered Rosella into the lion's den. Although tonight we hadn't broken any Utah laws, after checking our Arizona I.D., the deputies might fax a copy of their report to Arizona. Given both states' animosity toward anyone who tried to help polygamy runaways, Rosella could find herself in big trouble.

ID check accomplished, the deputies began their interview.

At first I played dumb. The bright lights of the ER helped, as did the bustling of nurses, hurrying to wherever nurses hurry, doing whatever nurses do. But under the deputies' persistent questioning, the dumb act failed to work. So I began to lie.

After spinning a yarn that I hoped wasn't too outrageous, I finished, "Like I said, officers, we were just driving around sightseeing when some stupid hunter shot at us."

The taller deputy looked at me skeptically from under the brim of his Smoky Bear hat. "Sightseeing. After dark."

I shifted around on the examining table. Why did they make those things so uncomfortable? "Well, dark is when the bats come out. We love bats. The area's covered with them."

"Would that be *leptonycteris curaasoae* or *antrozous pallidus*?" asked the shorter deputy.

"Uh, both."

Deputy Tall's skepticism matched his partner's. "Did you have any teenage girls in your car when you and that Santa Fe outside got shot up by these so-called hunters?" He must have recognized Rosella's name, not that surprising a development, since she was infamous up here.

Rosella, whose relations with both Arizona and Utah officials had always been testy, spoke up in a tone that was snippier than was wise under the circumstances. "No we didn't have any under-age passengers. Like my friend here told you, the whole shooting thing happened in Arizona, anyway, *not* in your jurisdiction. Why give us a hard time?"

Deputy Short looked irritated, but Deputy Tall's frown eased up. "Does that mean you don't want to lodge a formal complaint?"

Rosella opened her mouth to answer, but when I nudged her with my knee—hard—she closed her mouth again.

"That's right, officer." My tone was more cordial. What could we testify to, anyway? That an unknown number of men fired an unknown number of rounds at us? And that, no, we couldn't identify our attackers?

Deputy Short put his notebook away. "We still have to file a report. Especially since we already checked out the Santa Fe and found a red wig on the floor. Your own black one's on crooked, by the way. Seeing as how it's not Halloween, it kinda looks like you two were in disguise. Any reason for that?"

Before I could stop her, Rosella sniped, "Sorry to cause you guys so much paperwork."

Deputy Short narrowed his eyes. Did he resent her smart mouth, or was he a polygamist sympathizer, as were so many men in the area, even cops?

I gave Rosella a stern look. "Sorry if my friend sounded rude, officer. She's in shock."

His eyes didn't soften. "She doesn't look shocky to me."

"Appearances can be deceiving."

After they'd asked more questions I declined to answer, the deputies finally gave up and headed for the door, but not before Deputy Short delivered his parting shot. "By the way, Miss Jones, you'd have more luck seeing *antrozous pallidus* in Arizona. *Southern* Arizona."

With that, he followed his partner into the cold night air.

Once they were gone, I jumped off the examining table, which brought a tired-looking nurse scurrying my side.

"Miss Jones, the doctor doesn't want you to leave yet!"

"I am anyway. And in case you're wondering, yes, I have insurance, so you won't get stuck with the bill."

"I'm an ER nurse, not an admitting clerk," she snapped. Then she relented. "Look, you need to take it easy with that arm. You're lucky the wound didn't involve major tissue damage, but the doctor still wants you to stay overnight for observation. He doesn't like that bump on your friend's head, either. You said she lost consciousness for a while?"

"My head's as fine as it's gonna get," Rosella said. "We need to drive back to Phoenix."

"*Not* advisable!" The nurse's jaw jutted forward in an expression that probably cowed most of her patients. But not us.

"Advisable or not, we're leaving." With that, I wrapped my blood-spattered vest around me in a tardy display of modesty, and headed out of the cubicle.

As we neared the exit, Rosella nudged me. "Is the Santa Fe still drivable?"

"As long as you don't mind a little breeze."

"Shit, Lena, you're as crazy as I am. But we'd better take care of some business first." Over the ER nurse's loud complaints, she veered toward the admitting desk, me behind her, waving an insurance card in my good hand.

It would have been foolish to take the same highway back, where Prophet Shupe's God Squad probably lay in wait, so Rosella plotted a different route. After brushing away most of the safety-glass-turned-powder, she slid into the driver's seat, and soon we were taking the long way back to Phoenix, detouring southwest on I-15 through Las Vegas, where, as everyone knows, nothing bad ever happens to anyone.

Just before noon, after making several stops to guzzle coffee and orange juice, and once, to buy me a new black tee shirt, we rolled into Phoenix. It was a good thing Rosella's bump hadn't turned out to be serious, because my arm had stiffened to the point it could hardly bend. Given the number of street lights in the city, I'd have a rough time driving the Jeep, with its standard transmission, back to Scottsdale.

As if reading my thoughts, Rosella asked, "You sure you're okay to drive?"

"Just creaky, that's all. A couple of hours with an ice pack and I'll be fine. Hey, didn't you just pass the house where KariAnn's staying?"

"I want to clean up the Santa Fe first."

Given our situation, such finicky behavior seemed odd, but then I remembered that as KariAnn's loss of vision increased, her sense of touch became more acute. Rosella didn't want to alarm her daughter. "You'll never get all that powdered glass in the back seat. And the new air-conditioning system from the blown rear window? Better borrow my Jeep. I can take a cab home."

She shook her head. "After you prove to me you're okay to drive, I'll pick her up in the Camaro. I finally got it runnin'."

Like her house, Rosella's beloved '76 Camaro was in the process of restoration. She'd rescued it from a wrecking yard somewhere back in the Stone Age and with the help of a couple of mechanically-minded neighbors, was giving it new life.

But as we turned onto Rosella's street, we discovered that the Camero was now beyond saving. So was her house.

Both had burned to the ground.

Chapter Seven

Rosella stared at the smoking ruins of her house, her Camaro. "They found me."

Why bother trying to convince her she was wrong? Beside the stench of burnt wood and scorched metal wafting to me on the cool morning air, I could smell gasoline.

Arson.

Incongruously, birds still sang and, in the playground at the end of the street, children still laughed. My Jeep, parked at the curb, although now several yards away from where I thought I'd left it, was untouched.

Rosella's neighbors stood in front of the one remaining fire truck. Upon seeing her step out of the Santa Fe, they rushed over to offer condolences, clothing, food, whatever she needed. One elderly Hispanic man, his hands trembling from Parkinson's, told her she could stay in the garage apartment behind his house. "For free, and for as long as you need it, you and KariAnn. My grandson, the one who normally lives there, he's interning at Chicago General."

Before Rosella could answer, a thirty-something man in a dark blue fire department tee shirt and matching turnout pants approached her, clipboard in hand. A fire inspector. "Folks over there say you're the owner?"

Rosella nodded.

He stretched out his hand to shake hers, but the dullness in her eyes showed that she wasn't aware of the offer, so he lowered his hand. "I'm Fire Inspector Nelson Vickers. First, I'm sorry about your house. Your neighbors called in the alarm at 4:06 a.m. By the time the trucks arrived, they were out in front with garden hoses, but as you can see, the house was too far gone. At least they managed to push that Jeep away and keep it from blistering in the heat. Again, I'm sorry, but I need to ask you some questions and have you sign some forms." Without pausing for breath, he began asking about enemies.

Rosella replied in a monotone.

After jotting down her answers, the inspector continued, "We've called Phoenix Restore. They're on their way over to board up what's left, but you'll need to contact a fencing company, too. The entire lot is a hazard."

"Hazard." Rosella's voice remained flat.

"You said you're insured, I believe?"

A flicker of spirit showed. "Maybe I take a risk or two but never with somethin' like that."

Inspector Vickers raised his eyebrows.

Wrong answer, Rosella.

He started to say something else but thought better of it and merely held the clipboard out. Rosella signed. He handed her his card. "The Red Cross can be of assistance. They'll find you temporary lodging, some clothes."

Rosella took the card, but shook her head. "I don't need help."

Crinkles of worry appeared around Vickers' eyes. "Ms. Borden, are you sure you're all right?"

"Never better."

Vickers cleared his throat. "Because of the nature of the fire and all, another inspector might come by. Several, actually. And the police. That's usual in situations like this. Do you have a number where you can be reached?"

After she gave him her cell number, he walked off, apologizing as he went.

I put my arm around her. "Why don't you and KariAnn stay with me?"

She managed a bleak smile. "Out of the fryin' pan and into another fire? The God Squad hates you almost as much as they do me. Thanks for the offer, but I have a half-sister in California. She got out of the compound a couple of years before I did, and she's been beggin' me and KariAnn to visit."

"California might not be a bad idea."

"Dip my toes in the ocean. Walk on the beach. Do the whole West Coast thing, maybe stay for a while. A long while."

"You'd give up your..." I searched for the word. "...your work? With the runaways?"

"Them bastards won't run me off permanent, but for now I gotta get KariAnn somewhere safe. I haveta...I haveta..." She fell silent again.

She needed time to get her thoughts together. "Listen, Rosella. You don't need to make a decision right away. If you're uncomfortable about staying at my place, I'll put you two up at the DoubleTree. You can get matching mother/daughter herbal massages. Plan things out."

She didn't answer, just took her cell phone out of her pocket and punched in a number. Whoever was on the other end must have picked up immediately. "Jo? Rosella. That offer still good?" Waited. Then, "KariAnn and me'll be there sometime tomorrow. But first I need to make me a few calls and get some glass replaced. Yeah. I'm drivin'. Right. I'll tell you about it when we get there. Thanks." She rang off and turned to me, her eyes still dry. "You're a good friend, Lena, but I want my baby out of this whole fuckin' state."

"I'm back," I said to Jimmy, when I walked into Desert Investigations. I'd already gone upstairs to my apartment and showered off all the smoke fumes, blood, and powdered glass. Then I'd chewed a few aspirin.

Jimmy sat hunkered over his keyboard, searching for red flags on résumés. He didn't look around. "Took you long enough. How'd it go?"

"I've had better trips." Turning around, he took in my swollen face and bandaged arm. "Got shot, but it's not much more than a scrape. Rosella has a bump on her head. And her house burned down, along with the Camaro. Other than that, we're fine."

Jimmy rose toward me, his arms out. Stopped. Lowered his arms. Bit his lip. "You didn't call me because...?"

Unnerved by his rare show of emotion, I filled him in on everything, the ambush at the old mining camp, the pursuit on the highway, the destruction of Rosella's house and car. "So you can see that I was a little too busy to make a phone call. Especially since I was all right."

"All right? Lena, you're a couple of shades whiter than the average Anglo right now, so you're not doing as well as you believe. I'm betting Rosella isn't, either. What the hell were you thinking, leaving her alone over there to clean up the mess?"

"Ever try to force Rosella to do anything? Anyway, she wasn't alone. When I left she sitting on a neighbor's porch, wrapped in a blanket, wolfing down doughnuts and coffee while talking on her cell with her insurance agent."

He shook his head. Whether in sympathy or disapproval, I couldn't tell. "You'd better call Warren."

"Why?"

"Don't you think he'll want to know you've been hurt?"

The thought of involving Warren made me queasy. Our relationship was strained enough already. "He's in L.A. visiting the twins. Even if he were here, he couldn't do anything, so why shake him up?"

Jimmy advanced toward me again, this time with a bullish look on his face. "Maybe I'm not the one who should be handing out relationship advice, but..."

He halted mid-stride as the office door opened and two Scottsdale PD detectives walked in. Back in the day, I'd worked with both. Neither commented on my scratched face, possibly out of professional courtesy.

"Sylvie. Bob. You guys here about the fire already? That was some fast paperwork by Phoenix Fire."

They looked at each other.

"Fire?" asked Bob Grossman, not meeting my eyes. His body language was as stiff as my arm felt.

Sylvie Perrins, always the more aggressive of the two, said, "We're not here about any fire, Lena. We'd like you to come over to the station for questioning."

"Questioning? On what matter?"

She gave me a phony smile. "Wouldn't it be more comfortable to talk about that at the station? Hey, it's Scottsdale. We have comfy chairs and a cappuccino machine. It can make espresso, too, if you'd rather."

I didn't like the sound of that at all. "My own chairs are even comfier; real down, harvested by virgins from eider ducks who died natural, painless deaths on balmy summer nights. Nothing's too good for my clients. Or my friends. Have a seat, take a load off." At Sylvie's head shake, I waved toward my own fancy Krups. "I'm all set up for brew, too. Want a cuppa? Any way you like it."

The phony smile took on a plaintive droop. "Come on, Lena. Let's go down to the station. We'd like to get the conversation on videotape."

And I'd rather star in a porno movie. "Maybe I'd better call my attorney."

"Might be a good idea." Bob, not meeting my eyes.

"In that case, what should I tell her that I'm being questioned about? That's *if* I consent to going down to the station? I don't have to, you know, unless you actually place me under arrest. How about a little hint before it comes down to that? For old times' sake."

"Conspiracy to kidnap," Bob blurted.

Jimmy, who had hurried back to his computer, looked up in alarm. But I indulged in the first laugh of the morning. "Who am I supposed to have kidnapped? The Easter Bunny?"

Bob waved his hand, as if the answer was of no consequence. "Two minors, names of Patience Goodwin and True Huffstedder."

The girls Rosella had spirited away from the polygamy compound Tuesday night. If the cops suspected me of involvement
in their escape, they'd soon be after her, too. I hoped she'd made
it off her neighbor's porch and down I-10 to California.

"When were these girls supposed to have been 'kidnapped'?"
As if I didn't know.

Sylvie, whose face had turned deep red during this exchange,
answered, "Somewhere between ten Tuesday night and four
Wednesday morning." She waited, standing straddle-legged, arms
crossed, trying hard for the don't-mess-with-me cop look.

"Where was this crime supposed to have taken place?"

"Beehive County, up near Second Zion."

"Which is something like three hundred miles from here,
right, Sylvie?"

"Amazing things, cars. They go so fast."

I took pity on her. "At the very time you say I was kidnapping
two girls, Lieutenant Dagny Ulrich was questioning me about that
dead woman found near the RV storage yard. I guess you didn't
check the department log sheets before you came over here?"

Relief replaced Sylvie's embarrassment. "Ah, shit. Anyway, we
got a tip and had to follow up." She looked over at her partner.
"Bob, you want to use our laptop to check out those log sheets
or shall I?"

"On my way." He headed out the door, toward the laptop
all Scottsdale cops carried in their vehicles.

Sylvie finally eased herself down on one of the white armchairs.
"You're right. These are fabulous. Must've cost you a bundle."

"The joys of private enterprise. Now, how about some hazelnut cappuccino?"

With her butt sunk lower than her knees, the hard line of
her body had softened. "Double-shot would do fine. Sure hope
you're telling the truth, Lena. I've always dreaded the prospect
of dragging your ass in."

"You know I never lie."

This time the smile was genuine.

By giving me a hard time the other night, Dagny had inadvertently done me a favor. She'd documented our entire conversation, time-tagged it, and within seconds of logging onto the laptop, Bob found it. Bemused, he announced that Dagny's report even described what I was wearing the night of Celeste's murder, right down to my black sox and black Reeboks.

"That Dagny, such a fashionista."

Relieved at the opportunity to turn their visit into a social occasion, I walked over to the Krups and fiddled with the controls. Everything went fine until I had to hold the cup underneath the froth spout, or whatever that thing was called. The clumsy angle made me wince.

Behind me, Sylvie asked, "What's wrong with your arm? And your face? You really look like shit."

So much for professional courtesy. "Banged into a door. You know me. Two left feet." Finishing up the double-shot-cafs, I returned to my chair and sat back in my chair as if I didn't have a care in the world.

After a steely-eyed look at my arm, which showed she wasn't fooled, Sylvie said, "Seems to me that somebody's out to get you. *And* your pal Rosella. Is there anything you two are involved in that could get you in legal hot water?"

"Nothing."

"Why don't I believe you?"

"Because you've been on the job too long. You wouldn't believe your mother if she said she'd given birth to you."

A dry smile. "Yeah, I'm still searching for those adoption papers."

As soon at the two ambled out with their hazelnut cappuccinos, I called Rosella's cell. When she picked up, I said, "Sure hope you're headed west on I-10."

"Not yet. I'm reading an old copy of *Road and Track* at Gifford's Auto Glass, waiting for a new back window."

"Is KariAnn with you?"

"Sure. Why do you ask?"

I relayed the information that the long, polygamous arm of Prophet Shupe was reaching out for her. "You need to get out of town immediately. As in yesterday. Is there a friend who could loan you a different vehicle, because the cops will be looking for the Santa Fe? I'd offer you my Jeep, but it's too noticeable."

"She can borrow my Toyota!" Jimmy called out.

Rosella, who'd heard his generous offer, laughed. "Tell that handsome devil thanks, but I got me another source, one that won't lead straight to Desert Investigations. Hey, here comes the poor old Santa Fe, lookin' as good as new. Too bad I won't be usin' it."

Before she could ring off, I told her one more thing. "Don't use your cell phone anymore. Burn it. Chop it up with an ax. Run over it with a steamroller. Do whatever you have to do, just get rid of it."

"Gotcha. But I need a favor."

I didn't have to think twice. "Anything, Rosella."

"Don't leave it to Scottsdale PD to find Celeste's killer. Do it yourself."

"Well, sure, but with Scottsdale PD on the case, anything I do will just be..."

She cut me off. "They don't know enough about polygamy to solve squat. But you do. You can get to the bottom of this whole thing, maybe save some other women from that Scottsdale compound before they get murdered, too. So please, Lena. *Promise me!*" A note of desperation, one I'd never heard from her before, entered her voice.

Sighing, I promised.

Unless my ears tricked me, she was crying. "Don't forget, I'm countin' on you. Well, see you around, girlfriend. Somewhere. Sometime."

With that, she hung up.

Chapter Eight

Four good nights in a row, couldn't get much better than that. Jonah exited the Lexus fifty dollars richer, but after he made his connection, he was broke again.

The meth tucked safely inside his jacket, he hurried through the cloudless night to the abandoned building where he'd been squatting for the past couple of weeks. So far, the cops hadn't noticed that the plywood covering a ground floor rear window had been pried loose at the corner, but once they did, he and the other boys would have to move on again. For now, though, it sure beat a cardboard box.

After crawling through the window, he scurried through a litter of paper to his regular corner, knocked a few empty cans aside, and wrapped the blankets around him. The old office must have had something to do with travel, because big pictures of places he'd never even heard of hung on the dusty walls. Hawaii. Tahiti. New Zealand. Easter Island. *Easter Island,* where was that? Off the coast of Oregon? He had cousins in Oregon, supposedly, maybe even half-brothers and sisters. Maybe they'd seen those big stone faces and knew what they were all about. Maybe Easter Island was a place where they celebrated Easter every day, maybe prayed all the time. Maybe, as soon as he made a big enough score, Jonah would go there and get right with the Prophet again.

Maybe, maybe, maybe.

All those maybes scared him, so he readied his glass pipe. Lit up and inhaled the magic. Watched as the darkness brightened around him and the dusty walls gleamed.

Easter Island!

Easter, a time when the dead came back to life.

"You do all right tonight?" Meshach sidled up beside him and reached for the pipe.

Jonah looked around, his eyes now accustomed to the dark. None of the other boys were back yet, just his cousin.

"Good enough. You?" Jonah passed the pipe but kept his hand on the stem.

Meshach took a deep drag. "Nothing. So why bother hangin' around for more nothing?"

Even through Meshach was six months younger than Jonah, he looked twenty years older. Teeth pretty much gone, yellow hair dry as stable straw, paler-than-pale skin marred by spreading sores. On the street, he was a bargain basement boy. Sometimes not even that.

Jonah tugged at the pipe. Gently, at first. Didn't want to break it.

Meshach tightened his grip. "Once more. Please."

Feeling momentary pity, Jonah allowed him one more hit. Then he snatched the pipe from Meshach's mouth. "Go earn your own."

After all, kinship only went so far.

Hadn't they both learned that the hard way?

Chapter Nine

Another Tuesday night, another stakeout, another wig.

Since I conducted this surveillance in Jimmy's small pickup instead of a fully-furnished Winnebago, it was hard to get comfortable. And truth be told, Henny's RV storage yard had been considerably more attractive than Frugal Foods' crowded parking lot.

Clusters of stressed-looking people wheeled baskets of discount staples out of the market and unloaded them into the trunks of their luxury cars. When times grew hard in Scottsdale, people kept up their glitzy fronts but modified their shopping habits. No more strolling around the gourmet stores with their pastel-colored shopping baskets; just sneaked trips to Costco, Sam's Club, and Frugal Foods.

The owner of Little Rick's You-Store-It had told me that the women seldom showed earlier than ten o'clock, but in need of my own foodstuffs, I'd arrived at nine and checked the place out while doing my own shopping. About half the size of the Scottsdale Costco, this super-discount store specialized in family-sized containers of off-brand products, mostly from Mexico or China. I'd loaded up on enough ramen noodles to keep me fed for a month, along with two cases of generic diet soda, and several pounds of "ultra-dark, slow-roasted, genuine Arabica beans." The store also boasted a no-frills deli, so I'd filled my thermos.

Now back in the truck, I took a few sips of coffee, which brought beads of perspiration to my brow. In one of March's quick turnarounds, the temperature hovered in the low seventies, and I would have been better off with a Diet Coke. The unusually warm night turned out to be helpful, too, because it made the three women who exited the silver Aerostar van the next parking lane over stand out from the rest of the crowd.

Covered from chin to toe in blousy calico dresses and polyester sweaters, each face bore a striking resemblance to Rosella's. The gray-haired woman, tall and broad enough for two women, appeared to be in charge, driving two younger women before her like a Border collie herding sheep. There *was* something almost sheep-like in those two's expressions, a dutiful acquiescence I'd observed many times on the Arizona/Utah border.

"Half an hour, no more," Top Dog barked.

"Yes, Opal," said the younger of the other two women, a petite blond probably still in her teens. The vacancy in her face made me suspect mental retardation.

Before the women could catch sight of me, I lowered myself in my seat. The older woman had been called "Opal," and if I remembered correctly, Rosella had told me Prophet Shupe's first wife—before he'd added dozens more to his collection—was named Opal. Because of her title as first wife, she was the most powerful of the women, if you could call any blind follower "powerful." What was she doing in Scottsdale? Being a mere woman, Shupe wouldn't have chosen her to run a satellite compound; only men carried out such important functions. But was she still a member of his harem? Just because she'd been his first wife meant little to him. The Living Presence of God on Earth was notorious for pawning off used wives to other men; he preferred fresh meat.

When the three women entered Frugal Foods, I eased my sore arm into a more comfortable position, my mind exploring Opal's spousal possibilities. Ezra Shupe, Prophet Hiram Shupe's brother, was Second Zion's enforcer, the overseer of the God Squad. If anyone had the power to set up a new compound,

Ezra sure did. And this probably meant that the Prophet had handed Opal down to his brother.

Along with Celeste King, the murder victim.

I checked my Timex Indiglo: ten o'clock. The women had been right on time. I settled myself for a half-hour wait.

One of the bad things about running surveillance is that you can't indulge in the usual distractions. You can't read, play music, make phone calls, or watch TV. All you can do is sit there. And, sometimes, think about your screw-ups.

I wasn't supposed to be sitting in the Frugal Foods parking lot tonight; I was supposed to be over at the Paradise Valley house getting things ready for Warren's return early the next morning. But I hadn't even begun to pack my own clothes yet, let alone organize his dishes and sheets. My idle mind kept replaying the many voice mail messages Warren had left on my cell, beginning at ten-thirty that morning.

"Miss you, Lena. Call me."

Twelve-fifteen: "Lena, can't wait for tomorrow. We'll go out and celebrate."

Twelve-forty: "Lena, are you all right?"

One-oh-six: "Lena, this isn't funny. *Call me.*"

One-forty-two: "I just called your office but Jimmy claims he doesn't know where you are. Is something wrong?"

At that point I'd stopped checking my messages.

What was wrong with me? In Warren I had a man who was everything any sane woman could want: talented, good-looking, an unselfish lover. I couldn't possibly expect more.

But God, I was so scared.

I forced my mind back to the business at hand. By now it was ten-twenty-two, and only four other vehicles remained in Frugal Foods' parking lot, including the polygamists' silver Aerostar. How long could shopping take? The answer came a few minutes later when the three appeared, pushing six filled-to-the-brim shopping carts. Little Rick was right; they looked like they'd shopped for an army. Lowering my head again, I listened as they maneuvered to their Aerostar and began loading the grocery bags inside. They didn't say much, just puffed and panted as they positioned everything carefully.

"Josie, don't you squash those hamburger buns," Top Dog/ Opal snapped. "They're only one day old."

The blonde mumbled a subservient reply, then said something that shivered me. "When is Celeste coming back?"

In my shock, I almost blew my cover by sitting up straight.

"Shut up about her, I told you!" Opal hissed.

"But I miss our sister-wife. When's she...?"

Our sister-wife. For Josie to use that phrase meant that all three women probably belonged to one man. Ezra Shupe, the prophet's brother?

Another voice interrupted Josie's wistful plaints about Celeste. "Opal, I sure wish you'd let us get that Crisco. That other stuff we bought's not as good. It tastes like medicine."

Opal was having none of it. "I'll determine what's good and what isn't, Darnelle. In the meantime, you need to get a handle on that pride of yours. Thinking you know what's best for others is a sin."

Darnelle, the dark-haired woman I'd seen earlier, said nothing. I wondered if she was thinking the same thing I did, that Opal seemed to have no problem committing that particular sin herself, if the right to make a nutritional choice *was* a sin.

Opal continued to bark orders until the groceries were loaded, then I heard doors slam shut and the Aerostar's engine start up. It sounded a lot like the engine I'd heard the night of Celeste's murder, but Scottsdale PD would never be able to obtain a search warrant based on such flimsy evidence. Perhaps once I followed the women to their destination, I'd come up with something more concrete.

Minutes later the Aerostar's tail lights disappeared down a small dead end street about a half-mile from where I'd found Celeste's body. This area, too, was commercially zoned, with a variety of small electrical firms, janitorial services, and other businesses unidentifiable by their names. At the end of the street, the van turned into the driveway of a heavy equipment yard. The sign, only faintly illuminated, read TEN SPOT CONSTRUCTION.

Cutting the Toyota's lights, I coasted to a stop in front of the self-storage facility next door. With my window open and the dark street quiet except for a few sleepy birds, I was able to hear a gate at the back of the yard clatter open. When it closed again, I heard the crunch of tires across gravel, the squeak of brakes, doors opening and closing. Then the scent of something cooking. Beans, maybe, with pork. More women's voices drifted to me, different timbres than the three from the Aerostar.

Suddenly a man's deep bass rumbled through the night air. "You girls bring me somethin' nice?"

I'd head that voice only once, but I'd never forget it.

Ezra Shupe.

The leader of the Prophet's God Squad had taken up residence in Scottsdale.

Chapter Ten

The next morning found me renting a unit at Kachina 24-Hour Storage. By happy coincidence, I was able to get an air-conditioned and well-ventilated ten-by-ten at the rear of the complex, on the side closest to Ten Spot Construction. A razor-wired fence fronted by ten-foot-high oleanders rendered the construction yard almost invisible, but that didn't bother me. I was interested in the house behind it.

Now I finally had a use for those empty cartons stacked all over my apartment. Wearing a bubble-cut brunette wig and a pink polyester pantsuit from my collection of disguises, I spent the rest of the morning shuttling back and forth between Desert Investigations and the storage company in a rented panel van, moving in what appeared to be a small house full of furniture. Actually, the only real piece of furniture was the cheap aluminum chaise lounge I'd purchased at Wal-Mart. As I toted cartons into my key pad-protected unit, I could hear children playing on the other side of the fence, a baby crying, women conversing in low voices. There was little snooping I could do in the daytime, but that made no difference since Kachina 24-Hour Storage was, as its name proclaimed, always open. Well-lit, and with an abundance of security cameras to ensure the safety of its patrons and their possessions, the complex even provided a public restroom at the back of the facility. The restroom's location, just a few steps away from my unit, was an added bonus.

One of the things I loved about Arizona was its liberal audio taping laws, which allowed any form of taping as long as one party to a conversation knew it was being taped, an ironic distinction since the *taper* was always one up on the usually ignorant *tapee*.

Sometimes the law actually works in your favor.

The weather being mild and sunny, the Kachina bustled with entrepreneur-ish activity. Two units away, a woman turned a pot on a foot-controlled potter's wheel; in the corner unit, a photographer hot-mounted black-and-white prints on stiff board; not far enough away, a garage band floundered its way through a Papa Roach rip-off. But the usual self-storage crowd was out and about, too. An elderly couple stuffed stacks of *National Geographic* and *Arizona Highways* magazines into the unit next to mine, and the pregnant woman across from me scrambled through her piled-high unit, heaping baby blankets and toys into a bassinet. As far as I was concerned, the more the merrier. The constant din from the storage units had probably inured the polygamists next door to unusual noises, while disguising their own.

Such as the screams of beaten women and children.

My job at Kachina 24-Hour Storage finished for the present, I locked up my unit and returned the panel van to Enterprise. There I picked up my own ride and drove off to Paradise Valley to mend some fences.

The day was cloudless, but a hint of yellow spoiled the western horizon. Smog riding the sky highway from Los Angeles, or Phoenix's home-grown variety? Turning up the narrow blacktop that led to the house, I saw Mummy Mountain rising steeply into that questionable sky, the mountain itself a ruined patchwork of gray rock and bad architecture. Twitching movements of brown hinted at roaming wildlife, but this peaceful panorama was spoiled by a radio blasting Green Day from a raucous poolside party below. Plop down seven figures for real estate and this was what you got: somebody else's noise. In comparison, Kachina 24-Hour Storage was a pocket of tranquility.

When I pulled into the driveway I saw Warren stuffing flattened shipping boxes into a commercial-sized recycle bin.

"Looks like you're making progress," I said, alighting from the Jeep.

He didn't turn his head.

As it always did when I saw him, my heart gave a little flutter. His scruffy jeans fit tightly around his ass and his bare torso glistened with sweat. He looked more like a movie star than most of the surgically-altered actors he'd directed.

"I'm sorry. I just… I just got busy."

"Too busy to return my calls?"

Maybe it was time to tell him the truth. After taking a deep breath, I said, "I'm scared, Warren."

"Of what?"

"Of me. Of us. Of having everything go wrong and being left alone to pick up the pieces." As had happened to me so many times.

When he turned to look at me, his handsome face was pinched with hurt. "You think I'd do that to you?"

I swallowed. "No, not really. It's just that, well, I haven't done anything like this before. Move in with someone."

"Make a commitment, you mean."

"But I'm trying now. So, how about I help with those boxes."

After a brief silence—during which I went through all kinds of hell—he said, "If you want."

We spent the next half hour working without conversation, stomping cardboard boxes flat, shoving them into the Dumpster. He'd made more headway than I would have believed possible, with the living room furniture positioned in the exact places he'd diagrammed, and an already-made bed in the master suite. The twins' room waited for the girls to move into, and even the large bath/sauna was finished, with sandalwood-scented soap in the dishes and gauze-soft toilet paper properly hung in an antique brass holder. In the kitchen, an espresso/cappuccino/coffee machine twice the size of the one at Desert Investigations awaited its master's command. The house had already begun to resemble a home.

His home.

I finally broke the uncomfortable silence we'd both been laboring under. "How'd you get so much done?"

"It's amazing how much work disappointment can produce." His eyes met mine for the first time.

I put down the box I had been about to toss into the Dumpster. "I said I'm sorry."

He held up his hand. "Apologies aren't necessary."

"If you..." This time I stopped myself before I finished with *if you want to call it off, I'll understand.*

"Real life's a lot different than screen romance, isn't it, Lena?"

I was afraid to ask him what he meant, but I figure it had something to do with happy endings.

"It's my own fault, because I know you better than you know yourself, and there've been no surprises. Now, are you ready to tell me what happened to your face? And your arm? Or are you under the impression my eyesight's going?"

"Car trouble."

"Lena. Stop it."

I told him.

Instead of renewing his pleas for me to quit the case, he stared off into the distance through the yellow sky. "And they say Los Angeles has smog."

"Ours isn't as bad."

"Give it time."

"It's blue, most days."

He finally looked at me through troubled eyes, and I knew it wasn't the smog he was worried about. But he just said, "Let's get the rest of this stuff unpacked, okay?"

By one o'clock, we had emptied the rest of the cartons except for those stacked in his office. Exhausted, I plopped myself down on the sleek leather sofa positioned to overlook the city.

He sank down next to me. "I'm keeping the bulk of my stuff at the Beverly Hills house. Probably a good thing, too, since it looks like I might be spending more time out there than I'd planned. But that's all right, seeing as how you don't have much time to spend with me these days." His tone was neutral, yet his words stung.

"Warren..."

He put a gentle hand over my mouth. "No more apologies. Your life is your life. My life, well, it'll be what it's going to be, with you or without you. I'd just hoped it would be with you."

I pressed his hand closer, kissed it. "It's not too late."

What with one thing and another, we wound up in bed, smearing our grungy, sweaty bodies all over fresh sheets.

Later, Warren asked, "When are you going to tell me you have to get back to the office?" His tanned chest gleamed against the white sheets.

Finally relaxed, I smiled. "I'm working nights this week. Running surveillance on the polygamists while Jimmy holds down the fort."

"Lena, those people..."

"We'd better not get started talking about them. I made a promise to Rosella."

"As if Scottsdale PD can't conduct a simple murder investigation. You used to be a cop, so you have to know better."

"Like I said, I made a promise."

He said nothing else for a while, then reached for me again.

We'd skipped lunch so we had an early dinner by the pool, with Warren doing chef's honors. Due to the Environmental Advisory, the second in a week, he didn't crank up the barbeque, just quick-seared two New York strips on the kitchen stove while I put together a salad.

"We'd make a good team, Lena," he said, his voice wistful.

I leaned over the table and gave him a quick kiss. "Because we both work in the film industry?"

I'd meant it as a joke, but his face grew serious. "Hardly. If anything, that's an impediment. But now that you bring it up, Angel's in trouble."

Angel—Angelique Grey, as she was known in her acting credits—was Warren's ex-wife and the mother of his twin girls. She was also the star of *Desert Eagle*, the private eye TV series I did consulting work for. Against all odds, we'd become friends. "What kind of trouble? And why hasn't she called me? She knows I'll help."

He frowned. "Don't you remember the last time you 'helped' her? Angel, along with an entire conference room full of people, wound up involved in a criminal case. None of them were happy about it, especially the writers. Thanks to you, they had to rewrite an entire season's worth of scripts."

"Oh. That."

"Yeah. *That.*"

Before I could remind him that my actions had halted a long-standing case of child abuse, he continued, "Be that as it may, her stalker's back."

"Nevitt's been released?"

"Apparently. I don't know what they did to him in that mental hospital, but something's changed big time and not for the better. He's sending her threatening letters now."

Dean Orval Nevitt had stalked Angel for years, and despite California's strengthened laws against stalking, she'd never been able to shake him. While he usually stayed just back of the one-hundred-fifty-foot boundary the courts had ordered, when he went off his meds he would still make his way to her front door. Sometimes he pretended to be a pizza deliveryman, sometimes the mailman. Sometimes he just showed up as himself. Last summer he'd arrived with a dozen long-stemmed roses to celebrate their fifth wedding anniversary. Delusional, yes, but he'd never before threatened to harm her.

Still, stalkers who appeared relatively harmless sometimes did turn dangerous, especially when thwarted over a long period of time. Such had been the case with Robert John Bardo, the man who shot and killed actress Rebecca Schaeffer because she wouldn't admit to their in-his-mind-only relationship. Suffering from a similar mental disorder, Nevitt was under the impression that he and Angel had been married in Mexico after her divorce from Warren. All Nevitt wanted, he swore in his several-times-daily letters, was to take up his rightful duties as husband and step-father to the twins.

I put my fork down. "He needs to be locked up again."

"The authorities can't find him. But Angel swore she saw him at the end of her street this morning, hiding behind a jasmine bush."

"Did she call the cops?"

"Of course. They came right out and conducted a search. No Nevitt."

Unlike me, gym-toned and karate-quick, Angel had a slight, almost too-delicate build. I couldn't see her fending off anyone, let alone a deranged fan. "Does she still have that big body guard?"

"The Black Monk? Sure, but he can't be around all the time. Even bodyguards have lives. Angel received another letter from Nevitt this morning and it has her so worried that she called and asked me to fly back and bring the girls here until the situation is resolved."

"But you were just out there! I thought we'd be able to spend some time together."

He raised his eyebrows. "That, coming from you?"

Sounds of the city below rose around us. Car horns. Dogs barking. A child crying. At least the noise from the nearby pool party had subsided, with Green Day's shrill lead singer replaced by the seductive tones of Barry White.

"Maybe I should go out there, too, see if I can do anything. Hey, we could even fly out together. What time's your flight?"

He gave me a look that started out grateful, then clouded over. "I'm just going to pick up the girls then head right back."

I noticed that he didn't give me a flight time.

I spent the evening in my unit at Kachina 24-Hour Storage, pushing my worries about Warren to the back of my mind while setting up surveillance equipment. I'd brought a directional mike connected to a recorder, but more importantly, a wireless remote-control camera equipped with a night vision lens so small that it would disappear into the oleanders. I didn't expect the polygamists to discuss Celeste's murder in the open air; they weren't that naive. But there was always the chance that I might capture evidence of a crime—even a lowly misdemeanor—which would provide Scottsdale PD with enough grounds for a search warrant. Although Arizona's attorney general deeply resented Rosella's so-called interference in "child custody" matters, he would never be able to ignore a local, non-Rosella-connected polygamy situation. Scottsdale's movers and shakers wouldn't allow it: the polygamists might scare the tourists.

I'd jumpstart that process tonight, then tomorrow morning, help Angel take care of the Dean Orval Nevitt situation. If tonight's efforts were successful, by the time I returned from L.A., the Scottsdale authorities might even have fingered Celeste's killer.

I waited until traffic at the storage facility died down and most of the tenants had gone home. On my row, the last to leave was the potter, who continued to pedal her wheel to the accompaniment of Vivaldi until almost nine o'clock. Then, to my relief, she finally called it a day. As soon as she'd shuttered her unit and disappeared into the night, I gathered up my equipment and crossed over to the fence.

The halogen lights illuminated the Kachina almost too well, and enough security cameras were stationed around the yard that I had to plan my route accordingly. In my earlier walk-through, I'd discovered that one area in the back of my locker had a blind spot, and that's where I planned to set up my own seeing-eye. The Kachina cameras would pick me up leaving my unit, see nothing for around forty-five seconds, then pick me up again as I emerged from the blind spot on my way to the ladies restroom. I'd need to work fast, but I was familiar enough with my equipment that hurry-up presented no problem.

The oleanders against the fence did their job well. Well enough, in fact, that it was necessary to trim away several branches to provide a sight line for my camera. After a quick peek inside the dark yard on the other side, I clipped the tiny lens to an oleander stalk, framed it with leaves, and repeated the same process for the mike. That accomplished, I trotted back into Kachina camera range, and strolled leisurely toward the john.

So far, so good.

Once back in my storage locker, with its metallic shutters rolled closed, I settled myself on the chaise lounge and clicked on the camera and backup recorder.

The monitor revealed that the house in back of Ten Spot Construction, your basic rectangular ranch-style, didn't appear large enough to serve as the usual polygamy dormitory. On closer inspection, I saw an extension at the rear that didn't match the rest of the house's architecture. I guesstimated that the addition brought the house's square footage up to around thirty-two-hundred square feet, still small for a polygamist enclave, but with enough space to house several wives and some of their children if they didn't mind being crowded. Not that they had any say in the matter. Toys littered the rest of the yard: a tricycle with missing spokes; a couple of plastic pails and shovels leaned against a sandbox; and near a swing set, a tattered Teddy bear. Most of the children would probably have remained in Second Zion. Not a happy situation for either the children or their mothers, but Prophet Shupe had never been known to consider the feelings of his followers, especially those of women and children. His brother Ezra cared even less.

Little happened at first. For a long time, the voice-activated recorder merely caught the plaintive yowls of a lovesick cat and the rumble of another Kachina renter's truck as it rolled along several lanes over, but the polygamy compound remained silent. Then, shortly after midnight, the monitor caught movement at the front of the house. A door opening, closing. Heavy feet cross-ing floorboards. At the sound of a cough, the recorder clicked on, conducting a deep voice into my earphones.

"...thought that would work."

I studied the man's image, reduced to a blue-gray ghost on the screen. Short and stocky; not Ezra.

"Sounds good to me." Taller and thinner, but also not Ezra.

"You still drivin' back up tomorrow?"

"Well, you know how it is when the Prophet needs you. I'm proud to be called. I think..."

The door opened again and a voice hissed out, "Ain't your business to think. Shut your mouths and get back in here before somebody hears you."

Ezra.

The other two men did as they were told, and the compound fell silent again. Obviously, the Prophet brother's kept a tight rein on his men. However, the toys in the yard proved that the children were allowed outside. Women would undoubtedly be out there with them, supervising.

And women tended to talk, even when they weren't sup-posed to.

Although I monitored the compound all night, nothing else happened. The men stayed in the house, as did the women.

When the indigo sky faded to gray, the Kachina renters began trickling in. By the time the sun was full up, so was the facility. Heavily-loaded rent-a-trucks trundled down the narrow lanes; shutters rolled up with metallic grumbles. In front of a unit close to mine, a man shouted "Easy, easy, don't let 'er drop!" but the answer to his good advice was a loud crash and a string of curses, both from the first man and his hapless pal. The potter arrived, whistling "Norwegian Wood," but when she cranked up her wheel, she dropped the Beatles for more Vivaldi.

Then Ten Spot Construction opened, and the sounds of heavy equipment being loaded onto truck trailers eclipsed even the Kachina's racket.

Directional mike or no, all that ambient noise interfered with the sound recording of the house next door, but I kept taping anyway, aware that the construction equipment would eventually vacate the yard and put me back in business. What the camera was capturing now, though, was interesting in itself. A man I didn't recognize led four jeans-clad boys—the youngest, barely twelve; the oldest, a weedy-looking teen—out of the house toward Ten Spot. Once they'd walked off-screen, I sat back and thought.

A construction company.

Of course.

Besides the usual welfare checks, construction companies were major sources of revenue for polygamists. The workers were drafted from the compounds and paid in a "script" redeemable only at polygamist-run stores. The actual salaries, tax write-offs, and profits were funneled to Prophet Hiram Shupe, who was rumored to hold several off-shore accounts. Rosella had told me that the boys seldom complained because they assumed that the combination of their free labor and welfare checks would ultimately earn them several young, pretty wives. Their dreams of glory seldom came true.

They became Arizona's Lost Boys.

Yet there were always younger, more gullible boys ready to step in and take their place on the construction gangs. The kids just didn't know any better.

Despite my outrage, I smiled.

Gotcha.

These minor children were living in Scottsdale now. And it was Thursday. Eight-fifteen in the morning. Spring break was over, so why weren't they in school, instead of flaunting Child Labor laws? I would not only show the video to Scottsdale PD and the Child Welfare people, but to school officials, too. Truancy was a crime. The polygamists would claim their boys were being home-schooled, but it would be up to them to prove it, and my evidence of the boys being led off to work instead of study would go a long way toward refuting those claims.

Triumphant, I ambled over to the restroom to freshen up.

When I returned to my unit, the monitor was displaying some interesting stuff. The lanky man I'd seen the night before exited the house escorted by his chunkier buddy and climbed into a pickup truck. Mr. Chunky leaned though the cab's window and said something I couldn't quite catch, then went back inside.

After the truck disappeared off-screen, I kept a steady eye on the house. The residents were probably having breakfast— this thought made me reach for the bag of Dunkin' Donuts Chocolate Sprinkles and the thermos of coffee I'd brought along—but unless I was mistaken, the women would soon bring the younger children outside to play. Kids needed their exercise.

At nine-thirty, my red-eyed patience was rewarded. The front door of the house opened and a swarm of children spewed forth, followed by two of the women I'd seen at Frugal Foods. I studied the children carefully, looking not only for evidence of abuse— polygamists were enthusiastic about corporal punishment—but also to see how many of them were of school age. Besides a grouping of toddlers, I saw several boys and girls, ages ranging from around five to ten. More fuel for my truancy fire.

A few minutes later, the door to the house opened again and Opal/Top Dog stepped onto the porch. She looked angry, and through my earphones, I could hear her speak sharply to one of the women.

"Darnelle! I need you in the house!"

Although Opal's voice came clearly through my mike, Darnelle didn't seem to hear, or at least pretended not to. I couldn't be certain, because when she bent her rangy form to pick up a toddler who'd fallen and scraped his knee, her chestnut-colored hair came loose from its braid and fell around her face, hiding her expression.

"There, there, little love," she murmured, clear as a bell. God bless directional mikes.

"Darnelle!" Opal stepped into the yard and strode toward the younger woman. "I've had about enough of this."

Again, Darnelle pretended not to hear.

Her ruse didn't work. As she clasped the boy to her breast, Opal jerked her around by the sleeve and gave her a hard slap across the face. Startled, Darnelle dropped the child, who then began to howl even louder.

Although his nose had begun to bleed, Opal ignored him, and tugged Darnelle toward the house. After one last, plaintive back look at him, Darnelle gave up her struggles and went with the older woman into the house. Fortunately, the small blonde who remained outside rushed toward the child and began to comfort him.

The fact that the camera had recorded the entire event— Opal's thoughtless disregard for the safety of a child and her casual cruelty toward Darnelle—didn't make me less angry. I tried to calm myself with the realization that Scottsdale PD, Child Protective Services, and the Scottsdale school system, would now have more than enough to begin an inquiry.

It didn't work.

My teeth were clenched in rage when I packed up and left.

Chapter Eleven

Next morning, after dropping off copies of my recordings to Vic Falcone at Scottsdale PD and a friendly CPS social worker, I called the Scottsdale School District and told them what I'd observed: approximately a dozen school-aged children, none of whom appeared to be attending school.

Confident that I'd blown enough whistles, I called Warren to see if we couldn't snag that flight to L.A. together, but he didn't pick up. Was he already in the air with his cell turned off? Or was he simply declining to answer? For a brief moment I thought about driving over to the Paradise Valley house, then decided against it.

I didn't bother to pack, just drove to Sky Harbor, less than a half-hour away. Once I'd parked the Jeep in the Short Term lot, I hurried across six lanes of taxies to Terminal Four, where the Southwest counter was located.

"Has Warren Quinn boarded yet?" I asked the ticket seller, a young woman with hair almost as blond as mine, but a lot less natural.

"Sorry, I can't give out that kind of information."

"We were going to fly to L.A. together…" I began, then noticed her eyes narrow. Of course. Thanks to the new anti-terrorism rules, who was taking what flight to where was no longer a matter of casual conversation. We were all looked upon as terrorists these days until we could prove we weren't.

Giving up, I bought my ticket, grabbed my boarding pass, and hurried up to the Departure Lounge. No Warren. He wasn't in Starbucks, either, or at CinnABon. I even looked for him in the bar, although he'd been in AA for ten years. Not finding him anywhere, I returned to the relative quiet of the Departure Lounge, where I tried his cell again. No answer. This time I left a long message about love and fear. I was still talking when the loudspeaker announced that my flight was about to board.

"Call me, please. We can still grab that lunch in L.A. With the twins." I thought about adding that I loved him, but considering the way we'd parted the evening before, decided that might come across as manipulative.

The late afternoon sun blazed a gaudy trail through the yellow-brown sky when I pulled my rental car into Angel's Beverly Hills driveway. The Black Monk, a huge ex-wrestler known for his shaved-at-the-top hairstyle and black monk's habit he'd substituted for a robe as his wrestling persona, met me at the door, dwarfing Maria, Angel's long-time housekeeper.

"You see that shithead Nevitt anywhere as you drove up?" His voice was surprisingly soft for a man so big.

"Sorry. And I looked."

The Black Monk grunted. "Too bad. I was hoping to have a word with him. Well, come on in. Angel's out by the pool."

"With the girls?"

Maria, standing at the big man's side, shook her head. The Nevitt problem must had taken a toll on her, too, because her face was more deeply lined than I remembered, her once-glossy black hair now streaked with white. "Mister Warren came by an hour ago and picked them up to take them to Arizona. Miss Angel, she's pretty upset about having to say goodbye to her babies."

So Warren hadn't waited for me. Somehow I wasn't surprised.

Maria retired to the kitchen as I followed the Black Monk through Angel's cream-on-cream living room, and out the sliding glass doors to the patio. The scent of chlorine and citrus trees did battle with the smoggy air as a waterfall tinkled itself into a large pool so irregularly shaped that it could pass for natural. Angel, gorgeous as ever with her long blond hair and flawless skin, sat at an umbrella table, staring into the pool. She wore sunglasses, but not, I suspected, because the sun was out. She clutched a tissue in one hand, a drink, probably lemonade, in the other. She never touched the hard stuff.

"Hi, Lena." A sniff. "It was kind of you to come to my rescue so quickly. Was your flight okay? I know how much you hate to fly. If you want to take the train back, I can get you a First Class ticket on the Sunset Limited."

Hollywood types have a reputation for being egotistical and self-obsessed. Perhaps that was true when it came to their careers, but where interpersonal relations went, I'd found most to be thoughtful, caring people. Like Angel. Like Warren. Sometimes beauty was more than skin deep; it went all the way through.

"The flight was fine, but I'll take a rain check on that Sunset Limited ticket." I took a chair across from her, while the Black Monk disappeared through the glass doors, probably to his apartment over the garage. "So Dean Orval Nevitt's on the loose again?"

Angel slid her sunglasses down to dab at her eyes. The whites around her blue irises were almost the same color as her manicured red nails. Eyes dabbed, she slipped the sunglasses back on. "Yes, but I don't understand it. Before, his letters were more pathetic than anything. I showed them to you the last time you were here. Remember all those little flowers and animals he drew around the edges? And the hearts? Lots and lots of hearts. Now…" She spread her hands in a gesture of helplessness. "How could such a lost soul turn so mean?"

Sympathy for the devil. "Better show me those letters."

"Otto's getting them."

By the time I remembered that the Black Monk's real name was Otto Beasley, and that he was a graduate of the University of Nebraska, not the Spanish Inquisition, he was walking toward us with one of those portable accordion files. His battered face, a souvenir of too many gone-awry spinning heel kicks in the wrestling ring, twitched like he'd smelled something bad.

"Two hundred-something Nevitt masterpieces in here, filed in reverse chronological order," he announced, plopping the box down on the table. "Color copies, of course. We gave the police the originals. So whataya want to see, Early Nevitt or Late Nevitt?"

"When he started threatening her."

As Angel looked determinedly at the pool, not the accordion file, Otto thumbed through the file, then handed me a letter. The outside of the envelope appeared the same as the stalker's usual attempts at art, with a clumsily-crayoned butterfly hovering over a daisy. Below the butterfly was a shaggy blur that might have been a groundhog, looking ready to pounce.

Otto cleared his throat. "When we opened the envelope, a dead butterfly fell out."

"Maybe it was alive when he put it in," I offered. "You know how muddled Nevitt's brain is. He could have thought it would live through the mailing process, and when Angel opened it up, the butterfly would fly out to wow her. If he's off his meds, that's the kind of boneheaded thing he might dream up."

Angel turned her gaze away from the pool, but only to look at me. "Read the letter."

I unfolded it.

ANGEL, YOU ARE MY BUTER FLY BUT YOU FLIT FROM FLOUR TO FLOUR. STOP THIS NOW OR EXPEERIENCE MY RATH, JUST LIK THIS STOOPID BUTER FLY DID.

XOXOXO

YUR LUVING HUZBEN, DEAN.

At least he could still spell his name. "Let me see the one that came yesterday."

Otto handed me another, the same type of envelope, the same block printing, the same Beverly Hills post mark. No cute drawings on this one, though. "It came this morning. Beverly Hills PD's already been by and scooped up the original. The postal inspectors are involved again, too."

This letter was more succinct than the previous one.

I WARRNED YOU, BITCH. NOW YULL PAY.

"Any enclosures?"

Angel flicked her eyes toward the letter. "Otto says no."

"You didn't see for yourself?"

"He won't let me open them any more."

Otto cleared his throat again. "They make her too upset. I'm afraid she'll get to the point where she won't be able to work."

This didn't jibe with the Angel I knew. Dean Orval Nevitt's letters and attempted visits had always bothered her—as did all the other head cases who believed they had a personal relationship with her—but when it came to taping her television series, she was the consummate professional. One season, against her doctor's explicit orders, she'd even continued to work after being diagnosed with pneumonia.

Which made me wonder. "Does the production company know about the threats?"

Angel shook her head. "Stuart's too protective of the talent. If he got wind of this, he'd post so many guards around the set none of us would be able to move. Otto's enough for me." She smiled up at him. To my amusement, the big man blushed.

Last season, Stuart Jenks had replaced Hamilton Speerstra as head producer of *Desert Eagle*. Jenks had proven to be more reasonable than Speerstra, but also less creative. At least he'd understood the improbability of the pale-haired, blue-eyed Angel playing a Cherokee private eye operating out of Phoenix, and had ordered his writers to insert a flashback storyline about an Anglo father. That segment, I knew, was due to be taped as soon as the writers' strike was over.

"When do you think you might get back to work?" I asked Angel.

She gave me a blank stare. "Does it matter?"

"It would get you away from this house. Give us time to track our boy down. After that..."

Well, after that, who knew? If the law worked the way the law was supposed to work, Nevitt would be carted off to the hospital again, the twins could fly back from Arizona, and taping could commence uninterrupted by a phalanx of bodyguards.

Just the Black Monk.

Dean Orval Nevitt's last known address before being committed to the state mental hospital had been a two-story Section Eight apartment building in South Pasadena, where the landlady, a hard-looking middle-aged woman wearing too much makeup, informed me that she'd seen nothing of him for months.

"He got sent away. Loony, you know." With her forefinger, she made a circular motion around her temple. "I rented out his apartment to someone else. I'll say this for him, he always paid his rent on time, unlike some tenants I could mention." While adding that last part, she stuck her head out the door and glared at an obese man of about thirty trying to make it up the staircase. He ignored her and kept on going, pulling himself along via the rickety handrail.

"Did you hear that, Freddy?" she yelled.

"You'll have it by the end of the week," he answered, pausing halfway up the flight. The bubbly sound of his breathing signaled serious pulmonary problems.

"If I don't get it, you'll be out, Section Eight or no Section Eight. And if you don't clean up that pigsty, the Health Department's going to close down this whole place and we'll all be out on our ears."

The man said nothing, just took another bubbly breath and continued up the stairs. When he'd let himself into his apartment, the landlady said, "Him and Nevitt, they were buddies, as much as a loony like Nevitt could have buddies. Maybe he can tell you something he didn't have time to tell the cops, they blew out of his place so fast."

"The police were here?"

"The other day. Nevitt was real hot for that TV star, Angelique what's-her-name, believed he was married to her or some nonsense like that. What a laugh. No woman would bother with a goofball like him, let alone a TV star. Although you can tell those big boobs aren't real."

Actually, Angel's boobs were every bit as real as mine, just more spectacular. But I let the error slide. "By 'goofball,' do you mean the stalking?"

"That, too. I meant the other stuff."

"Such as?"

"Ever see him?"

"Just pictures."

Her maroon-lipsticked mouth twisted into a superior sneer. "Then you saw that big red blotch on his cheek and his funny-looking mouth. Plus, he was all the time walking around mumbling to himself, not that you could understand a thing he said, with that weird mouth and all. Gave me the creeps, it did."

"The red mark is called a port wine stain, and his 'funny-looking mouth,' as you phrase it, was caused by an only partially-corrected cleft palate. So, yes, I can see why you had difficulty understanding him." Not that it would have helped if she could have; in addition to Nevitt's obvious physical challenges, he was a diagnosed schizophrenic who, when off his meds, hallucinated almost constantly. It was a miracle he could even get through the day, let alone stalk Angel.

The sneer never left the landlady's garish face. "Whatever. Anyway, I can't tell you any more than I told the cops. You want more, go talk to Fat Freddy."

With that, this paragon of political incorrectness shut the door.

At first Freddy—the label on his mailbox listed him as Fredrick Andrews—wouldn't open his door, but after several minutes of knocking and calling his proper name, he relented and squeaked the door back an inch. "What?" He'd left the chain on.

An aroma of rotting garbage, unwashed human flesh, and ripe cat box wafted through the opening. No wonder the cops hadn't stayed long.

"Mr. Andrews, I need to ask you a few questions about Dean Orval Nevitt." When he started to close the door, I added, "The quicker you answer me, the quicker I'll go away. Otherwise, I'll just stay out here, knocking and yelling. I warn you, I've got a lot of patience."

He thought about that for a moment, then unhooked the chain and opened the door. The smell intensified. Steeling myself, I walked through.

Freddy was a hoarder, one of those people who can't throw anything away no matter how useless or fetid. Newspapers stacked higher than my head lined the walls, blocking the one window and throwing the room into an early twilight. In front of the newspapers, empty cans of generic brand cat food and chili tumbled out of black plastic garbage bags filled to overflowing. Flies buzzed, cockroaches scurried. I couldn't tell where Freddy slept, because I couldn't see a bed. For that matter, I couldn't see the cat. Maybe it had died and was buried under the rubble.

"Ask your questions and get out," Fred mumbled. An acrid, unwashed odor emanated from him, competing with the heady perfume of the apartment.

I stepped back and breathed through my mouth, like I'd been trained to do at crime scenes where the victim had been dead for several days. "Do you know where Dean Nevitt might be living now?"

"No." Freddy's eyes looked glassy. At least he was on *his* meds, not that they seemed to have helped him much.

"Does he have any friends he could be staying with?"

"No friends. Like me."

"Relatives?"

"His mother died a long time ago. Don't think he had anybody else."

"Did he ever mention a place he liked to hang out?"

This time Freddy surprised me. "The park."

"Which park?"

"Arroyo Seco."

That took in a lot of real estate, since Arroyo Seco, where Warren and I had once picnicked, ran all the way from the San Gabriel Mountains to downtown Los Angeles. While I was worrying about that, something rustled behind me. I turned, expecting to see a family of rats coming out to bask in the late afternoon stench. Instead, I saw a ginger-colored cat settling itself on a stack of newspapers. The cat was as obese as Freddy.

I returned to my questioning. "Do you know which part of the park he liked to hang out at?"

"Down by the skate park. He used to be a skater before the medication screwed him up. He could do all sorts of tricks—Ollie kickflips, grinders, darksides…" His eyes lost their glassy stare and truly focused on me for the first time. "I used to skate, too. Bet you didn't know that. I even came in third in the Freestyle at the Santa Barbara Championship one year."

An image of a leaner, happier Freddy soaring through the air flashed through my mind. "That must have been wonderful," I said, trying to keep the pity out of my voice.

Apparently I was unsuccessful, because his face closed in again. "That's all I know. You leave now."

I did.

As it turned out, Nevitt wasn't at the skate park, or if he was, I didn't spot him. None of the skaters admitted to seeing him, either. Since it was now too dark to continue my hunt, I called Beverly Hills PD, told the investigating officer assigned to Angel's case what I'd learned, then drove back to Beverly Hills. There I found the Black Monk and Angel sitting together by the pool, watching lit candles float around on fake lily pads. It looked pretty.

"The skate park at Arroyo Seco?" The expression on Otto's face made me wonder if I'd done the right thing in letting him know what I'd discovered.

"That's what my informant said. Otto, Beverly Hills PD promised to check. But in the meantime, you're not going to do anything foolish, are you?"

Angel answered for him. "Don't worry. He doesn't want to hurt Nevitt, just keep him from hurting me or the twins. Isn't that right, Otto?"

Otto grumbled something that sounded like a yes, and went back to watching the candles.

The worry lines between Angel's eyebrows disappeared. "I'm sure Beverly Hills PD will follow up, and quickly, too. Since Rebecca Schaeffer, they've been very good at working with other jurisdictions in cases like this." She gave me a movie star smile. "Oh, Lena, I can't tell you how grateful I am! You've done more in a half day than anyone else has been able to do in weeks. Listen, I know my troubles have taken you away from your own work, and that you're eager to go home, but it's pointless trying to fly back to Scottsdale tonight. I'll have Maria put fresh linens on the bed in the guest room. You like pasta, don't you? She makes a mean carbonara."

It sounded like she thought the Dean Orval Nevitt problem was solved. Remembering that all those threatening letters had Beverly Hills post marks, I wasn't so sure.

Filled with misgivings, the next morning I returned my rental to Avis and boarded an eight o'clock Southwest flight. Over the mountains we flew into turbulence so severe that some passengers reached for their barf bags. Me, I merely clutched the armrests and prayed until the plane slid through the clouds and floated to a soft landing at Phoenix Sky Harbor.

I'd just picked up my bag from the luggage carousel when someone tapped me on the shoulder.

"Lena Jones?"

I turned to face two uniformed sheriff's deputies. The glum looks on their faces signaled bad news. Had something happened to Jimmy? Warren? Rosella? Or had the walking insanity known as Dean Orval Nevitt caught up with Angel?

"Yes, I'm Lena Jones. What…?"

"Miss Jones, you're under arrest."

Chapter Twelve

"You know this whole thing is ridiculous, Dagny."

The look Lieutenant Ulrich gave me across the interview room table was unreadable. When the sheriff's deputies had turned me over to Scottsdale PD, she'd ordered my handcuffs removed, but that had been her last display of mercy. Now she'd reverted to her usual clam-cold persona.

"When my officers went out to confront Mr. Ezra Shupe about your claims, he denied them all. Then he made some pretty serious claims himself. Unlike yours, his were backed up by the statements of several witnesses."

The closed room smelled of sweat and fear. Not mine, I hoped. "You saw the tape."

"A tape which, as the complaint Mr. Shupe filed against you stated, was illegally obtained by trespass."

Just like a polygamist; fighting the law with the law. "That's a crock. I stayed on my side of the fence."

"After reviewing those tapes, our tech estimated that your camera lens could possibly have protruded into Mr. Shupe's property by about a quarter-inch, so yes, it appears that you might have trespassed. More seriously, you videotaped minors without their guardians' consent. Given your knowledge of police procedure, why'd you do that?"

"Two points. Number one, I don't believe what you're telling me about the lens protruding into the property, because as you say, given my knowledge of police procedure, I made certain it didn't. Point number two, you know damned well why I made that tape."

No expression. "Shupe claims that you and your friend Rosella Borden were planning to kidnap at least one, possibly several, of those minors. Ms. Borden does have a history of doing that."

"Never proven."

"Where is Ms. Borden, by the way? We've had no luck getting in touch with her."

"I'm certain you've already discovered that her house burned down recently, so she had to find new lodging. Exactly where, I don't know." Which was the truth, given the size of the great state of California. "As for Ezra Shupe, he filed those charges to deflect attention away from the fact that one of his so-called 'wives' was murdered. You and I both know that when a pregnant woman is beaten to death, who's usually guilty."

"You're accusing Mr. Shupe of murder, then?"

Her intransigence was getting to me. "The woman was beaten to death, Dagny. And Ezra's known for his violence, whether he carries it out himself, or by proxy." My arm still stung from the God Squad's shotgun blast.

"No charges have ever been filed against Mr. Shupe. Or his brother."

Rosella had been right. Scottsdale cops had no idea of the way polygamy worked. The very idea that one of the compound's women would press abuse charges against her man—especially when the man was head of Prophet Hiram Shupe's God Squad—was laughable. Such a foolhardy woman would never live to appear in court. Is that what had happened to Celeste? I voiced my suspicions to Dagny, but she shook her head.

"When my detectives entered his residence, and he didn't resist by the way, we saw no evidence of spousal abuse."

"Given those long dresses they wear, those women could be beaten black and blue and you wouldn't be able to tell." I took a deep breath and fought back my rising temper. "Okay, so you don't see Ezra as a viable suspect in Celeste King's death. It doesn't change the fact that there's a polygamy compound operating right here in Scottsdale, that they're using underage children to work construction, and that the kids aren't attending school. Do something, Dagny. *Anything!*"

"Those problems are the concerns of Child Protective Services, not Scottsdale PD. For your information, we did convey our concerns to CPS and other possibly interested organizations."

Which was the same as saying little would be done. When it came to crimes against women and children in the compounds, county, state, and federal folk had dismal records for looking the other way. These days they were all too busy rooting out undocumented workers and shipping them back to Mexico.

Disgusted, I said, "Dagny, are you going to book me on Ezra's trumped-up charges or not? If you are, I'm through talking. I want to call my attorney."

A slight flicker in those cold eyes. "You're refusing to cooperate?"

"As long as you refuse to investigate broken child labor laws, *and* truancy, *and* blatant polygamy—which, the last time I looked, was against the law in Arizona—yes, I'm refusing to cooperate. Now how about that attorney?"

For a moment she just stared at me, her expression no more revealing than before. Then, to my surprise, she stood and walked to the door. Before opening it, she said, "You're free to leave."

Whether my answers had satisfied her or not, Dagny knew Ezra's claims were groundless. But I was certain that with Ezra's secret fiefdom now out in the open, he would continue to use me as an excuse to redirect the cops' attention elsewhere. Given the political climate in Arizona, his efforts just might work.

I took out my cell phone, summoned a cab, and went home.

Without stopping at the office to tell Jimmy I was back, I walked upstairs to my apartment and showered off the stench of the interrogation room. I couldn't shower away, though, the unease

I'd felt about leaving Beverly Hills before the actual arrest of Dean Orval Nevitt. I also wasn't certain that I trusted the Black Monk not to hurt him when he followed up my footwork and located him at Arroyo Seco Skate Park. I hoped that the Pasadena cops got there first.

Sorry as I felt for Nevitt, Angel's welfare worried me even more. Those last letters signaled a serious downturn in Nevitt's mental health, and while he'd never been violent before, there was always a first time. Something else about the letters bothered me, too, but no matter how I tried, I couldn't pinpoint it. Yes, the Beverly Hills postmarks were troubling, and so was the dead butterfly, but something…

Trying to force memory never works, so I set that problem aside to revisit later and turned my mind to a more immediate situation: Celeste's murder. Stepping out of the shower, I hurriedly dried, then dressed in clean jeans and tee shirt, and went downstairs to Desert Investigations, where I found Jimmy deep in conversation with a woman wearing ripped jeans and a gaudy tie-died tee shirt.

She sat with her back to me, but something about the set of her shoulders looked familiar. The woman's hair, a Brittany Spears-pink wig, curved gracefully at mid-neck length, stopping just above a neck tattoo shaped like a folded pink ribbon. I'd seen that design before; it identified breast cancer survivors and the people who loved them.

Jimmy smiled up at me. "Lena, guess who's here?"

My heart knew even before the woman turned around.

Madeline.

The foster mother I'd thought was dead.

Chapter Thirteen

I was seven years old.

Earlier that morning, a male social worker had picked me up from a foster home that, because of my continued acting-out, refused to keep me. Like most foster children, my clothes were stuffed in the black plastic garbage bag at my feet. As the social worker explained the situation to a tall, dark-haired woman who smelled like turpentine, I looked around at her house. Messy. Gaudy. The walls appeared to be white, but it was hard to tell because they were covered by so many paintings. The paintings themselves seemed little more than bright splashes, representing nothing other than odd combinations of color that clashed not only with each other but even with themselves.

"Red doesn't go with pink," I said, interrupting the social worker's speech about the effects of brain damage on behavior.

Before he could tell me to be quiet and, for once, be good, the tall woman said, "Smart girl. That's exactly why I did it."

Smart? No one had ever called me that before. Bad, yes. Destructive, yes. But never smart.

I was certainly smart enough to recognize that her colors were all wrong. Or at least, I thought they were. "You shouldn't put things together that don't belong."

She waggled her eyebrows at me and grinned. "Awful, aren't I?"

This was something new, too, an adult calling herself awful and finding it funny. The social worker took her baffling statement as his cue to leave. "Contact me when..." A pause. "Ah, if there's trouble."

To me, he said, "Now, Lena, you mind Mrs. Grissom. Or..." He didn't finish. He didn't need to. Ever since I could remember, my life had been one foster home after another. I was a walking disaster and I knew it.

When the social worker closed the door behind him, the tall woman handed me the brush she'd been holding. Like her hand, it was smeared with yellow. When I took the brush, my hand turned yellow, too.

"Forget that 'Mrs. Grissom' crap, kid," she said. "Just call me Madeline. Follow me into the studio and let's see how much trouble we can get ourselves into."

As Madeline hugged me, I noted that either I'd grown a couple of feet, or she'd shrunk. Probably the former.

"I thought you were dead," I said, after I could finally speak. She was still crying, I was still trying not to. Jimmy, despite the old adage that Indians don't cry, also looked pretty damp-eyed as he hurried out the door to give us privacy.

"Almost happened, sweetie," Madeline replied. "But here I am. And here *you* are, beautiful as ever."

We blubbered at each other for a few minutes until, during yet another bone-crushing hug, I noticed her stomach growling. Once our mutual tears had dried—yes, my dam finally broke—I offered to take her to McDuffy's for a big steak, but she informed me that she didn't eat meat any more.

"You're a vegetarian? Since when?" I remembered the wonderful meatloaves she used to bake, the plump roast chickens, the Friday night steaks.

"Since my double mastectomy. Going through something like that makes you start thinking."

The double mastectomy was the reason CPS had removed me from Madeline's home after less than a two-year stay. The agency had considered her too ill to care for me, and her husband, Brian, too distracted by work and worry. CPS had probably been right, but children don't understand things like that. As a result, I never truly bonded with a foster family again.

"Most Chinese restaurants offer vegetarian dishes," she said. "I passed three Chinese buffets on the way over here."

"Buffet? No, we need some place quieter so we can talk." I remembered Fresh Mint, the vegan Scottsdale restaurant praised by one of my vegan clients. Within minutes we were both sitting in a quiet booth, surrounded by calm-seeming people eating dishes that actually looked appetizing. The female customers wore their hair long and unprocessed, and half the men had beards. Both sexes wore love beads, natural fiber clothing, and canvas—not leather—shoes. I felt about as at home here as I did at Warren's house.

Better call him, a little voice whispered. I nudged it back. *Later*.

Other than her pink wig, Madeline fit right in. She had aged, but had done little to disguise the march of time. Although I saw lines here, sags there, the imperfections gave her face a depth cosmetic surgery could never approach. Even her out-of-fashion jeans and tattered tee shirt—the front proclaimed THE GRATEFUL DEAD IS NOT DEAD, THEY'RE JUST NAPPING—looked good on her. A brief glance at her hands revealed no nail polish, just a thin strip of what appeared to be Prussian blue under one of her short nails, some chrome yellow under another.

"Still painting, Madeline?"

"I'll stop painting when they pry my brush from my cold dead hands." A sly smile, in recognition of what had almost happened to her.

"I thought you *were* dead," I repeated.

Her smile vanished. "As soon as I went into remission, I started looking for you, but of course, CPS wouldn't give me any information. By then Brian and I had bought a house in upstate New York, where my sister lives. Sickness makes you realize how important family is."

Perhaps in response to my stricken face, she reached out and took my hand again. "Shit. What a tactless thing to say. You'll always be my family, Lena. *Always*."

Afraid I'd get emotional again, I didn't respond.

From the very beginning, Madeline had accepted me as I was, not as she wanted me to be. Like many brain-damaged children, I'd been subject to seizures, which had me in and out of the hospital. Even worse were the violent rages that could be triggered by just about anything: a change in the weather, a meal I didn't like, a word or glance I misinterpreted. During those rages, I would strike out at whatever or whomever was closest and as a result, the path of my childhood lay littered with broken dishes, slashed sofas, and bruised care-givers. Although earlier foster parents had begun their work with me with high hopes, they'd all eventually run out of emotional resources.

Until Madeline.

We sat in silence until I recovered myself, then Madeline—alert as ever to my changes in mood—said, "Well. Speaking of family, have you found your biological parents yet?"

I shook my head. "The trail's cold. Which reminds me. If CPS wouldn't help you, how did you find me?"

"Last week the local newspaper ran a wire story about a child abuse case in Atlanta. This poor little girl…" She paused for a moment, then continued. "About midway down the story, it mentioned a similar case in Arizona, and gave the name of the private detective who helped rescue a child about to undergo…Well, you know. Anyway, after a quick search of the Internet, I wound up on Desert Investigation's web site and saw your picture."

Leaning over the table, she touched the scar on my forehead. "You never had it fixed?"

"It helps me remember."

Helps me remember the night I was shot, helps me remember my mother's screams, helps me remember my father saying goodbye.

The waiter's sudden voice interrupted my slide down the time tunnel. "What'll you ladies have?"

Madeline ordered something called Rainbow Wonder, while I, an unregenerate carnivore, settled on the soy spare ribs in citrus ginger sauce, hoping they'd remind me of meat. As soon as the waiter left, I summoned the strength to broach the subject I hadn't felt strong enough for earlier.

"You mentioned something about remission. Are you...?"

She touched her wig. "Just a fashion statement. I've been cancer-free for years, but it was one hell of a struggle. No one ever tells you how tough chemotherapy can be. It's like they're inserting fire into your veins. Then comes the nausea, but since we're about to eat, I won't describe that. Cannabis helps fight it, not that the government cares, the puritan pricks."

My Madeline, still feisty. I'd been so moved by seeing her again that I'd not thought to ask her about her husband. I'd been fond of Brian, but he'd worked such long hours I rarely saw him.

"Brian didn't come with you?" I asked. "I'd like to see him, too."

Her face changed. "He's dead. Huntington's Disease."

For a moment I stopped breathing. Brian, dead? It didn't seem possible. All that concern about Madeline's health, and then... Suddenly I had a vision of Brian hunched over his workshop in the garage, sander in hand. A cabinet-maker by trade, he was building a special-order hutch. The scent of male sweat and sawdust drifted down to me over the years, twisted my heart. I'd taken him for granted. But isn't that what we always do with people we love?

"When?" I finally managed to ask.

"Almost twenty years ago." She paused, then continued. "We always knew it was a strong possibility since both his father and paternal grandfather died from Huntington's, but when Brian turned forty and hadn't shown any symptoms, we fooled ourselves that he'd beat the odds. That's when we started adoption proceedings for you." She looked down at her lap, where her paint-stained fingers curled around each other, the knuckles white. "Then I got sick and everything changed." She managed a trembly smile. "You know all about that, don't you. Anyway, three years after Brian died I remarried."

That explained something. "You took your new husband's name." Once I turned eighteen and had been released from CPS custody, I'd tried to find Madeline, but her change of residence, coupled with a name change, had been too much for my then non-existent detecting skills. Believing she must have died, I consigned her to my past.

"Looking back," she continued, "I can see that I must have married out of grief because Jim and I had nothing in common. He thought art was a hobby, and I thought the same thing about his interest in sports. Did I mention that he was once a minor league baseball player, a pitcher? I must have been temporarily insane to think it would work out."

Warren's face emerged into my consciousness. "Opposites can attract."

"In the beginning, maybe. Not during the long haul."

The waiter saved me from replying by bringing Madeline's Rainbow Wonder and my vegetarian spare ribs. To my surprise, the "ribs" were delicious. Maybe there was something to this vegetarian business after all.

In between bites, Madeline asked me what cases I was working on now. Without naming names, I told her about the faux German and his dashed hopes to marry one of my wealthier clients. To keep my recital upbeat, I followed with funny stories about my work on the TV show *Desert Eagle*, including the eccentricities of the actors and the even more extreme eccentricities of the producers.

When Madeline finished laughing, she said, "I've seen that show. That actress doesn't look Cherokee."

"The writers are fixing the problem for the next season. If there is a next season."

We discussed the writers' strike and its impact on my own life. When we'd talked the subject to death, I moved on to Celeste King's murder and Scottsdale's new polygamy compound. Seeing the alarm grow in her eyes, I decided to skip Rosella's and my adventure in northern Arizona.

Madeline looked appalled. "Why do those so-called prophets get by with their behavior? It's out-and-out human slavery. Sex trafficking, too!"

"When people live in those kinds of closed communities, it's almost impossible to gather proof of forced 'marriage' and child sexual abuse. But proof is needed before CPS and the cops can go in."

"Sounds like a Catch 22."

"Exactly."

"Yet you still fight the good fight." She shook her head. "How can you continue when it just uncovers so much evil? Don't you ever feel overwhelmed?"

Most of my remembered life I'd felt overwhelmed, but she didn't need to know. "Good people, people like you and Brian, gave me the strength to carry on."

"We made that much difference? Oh, baby, I hope so. When you first came to us, you looked so lost."

Lost was the operative word. No mother. No father. Just a series of foster homes where I'd never fit in. I'd been lost, all right, and maybe I still was. Segueing away from this startling revelation, I steered the conversation onto a safer subject. "On the way over here, you mentioned you'd had a recent show just outside New York City. How'd that go?"

A rueful smile. "Same old, same old. Decent reviews, crappy sales. Art, you have to love it or leave it, because you sure as hell don't make much of a living at it."

After that pronouncement, I refused to let her stay in the cheap Phoenix motel she'd booked, so as soon as we finished lunch I drove her back to Desert Investigations and carried her suitcases upstairs to my apartment.

She stumbled her way through the packing cartons, listening to my explanation about Warren's new house, hardly commenting on my reluctance to move. But at the sight of the vivid oil painting on my living room wall, Madeline's jaw dropped. "Holy shit, what's that?"

"Apache Sunset, by George Haozous. According to him, it's a historically accurate rendition of an Apache village massacre by the U.S. Cavalry."

"Something tells me Haozous is Apache."

"Gee, how could you tell?"

"Because for a change, the Indians are the victims, not the cavalry." Madeline's smile was wry. "It's always good to see the other side of the story, cracked heads, trailing intestines, and the other bodily wonders. Besides, all that red looks great in your living room. Matches the Navajo print on your sofa."

I ushered her and her suitcases into the bedroom.

After taking a deep breath, she said, "Oh, my God. You re-created it."

I set the suitcases next to the bed. "What do you mean, 're-created'? I just bought this stuff from a Glendale antique shop because I thought it was cute."

A disbelieving look. "Don't you remember, Lena? You used to tell me that when you grew up you wanted to be a cowgirl, so I fixed up your bedroom just like this." She gestured around the room. "Those turquoise horse head lamps are like the ones you had. Maybe they actually are, since you found them in some antique shop. The bedspread? It's the same color as your old one and the same style, too. The only difference is that this one has the Lone Ranger and Tonto on it instead of Roy Rogers and Dale Evans. That's why you don't want to move; you'd be leaving your past, not just an apartment."

I didn't know what to say, so said nothing. How could I not have realized what I was doing?

She leaned over the bed and ran her hand thoughtfully across the Lone Ranger's face. "What does Warren think about it?"

It took me a few more moments to recover from my shock about the bedroom, but when I did, I said, "He doesn't understand. Maybe because I never really understood it myself. Before now, that is."

A sad smile. "It's common for kids raised in foster homes to experience relationship problems. They need people, yet push them away because they're too afraid of having their hearts broken again. Is that what's happening with you?"

As I stacked the empty boxes against the wall, I allowed that she might be right. "Warren once said something like that."

"Perceptive man. How are you, Lena. Don't give me any more of that 'everything's fine' crap. How much can you still remember?"

"Too much. Not enough."

I told her I remembered my parents boarding the white bus, the long ride, the laughter, the singing, the clearing in the woods where my father died, my mother's screams, the gunshot that changed my life. Then came a long period of nothingness until I regained consciousness in a Phoenix hospital. I almost told her that I'd had to say goodbye more often than my child's heart could stand, but then thought better of it. Madeline had done what she could to repair my shattered life; what happened after she got sick wasn't her fault. She'd experienced enough sorrow.

"So that's it," I finished.

She didn't say anything right away for a moment, just continued to stroke the Lone Ranger's face. "Still having those nightmares?"

I let my silence be her answer.

"The first few months you were with us, you woke up screaming every night. Then you stopped. Just like that. Stopped cold. Then you started talking in your sleep."

Madeline looked at me, her face expectant. When I didn't ask the question she apparently thought I'd ask, she smiled. "Where should I put my things?"

Later, as I tossed and turned on the sofa, I wondered about what Madeline had said. In the past few days I'd come up with one reason after another to slow the finality of moving in with Warren, and yet none of my reasons rang true. Could she have been right, that getting close to someone threatened my too-damaged heart? If she was, my relationship with Warren was in more trouble than I'd previously believed.

Chapter Fourteen

That night Jonah stopped the wrong car.

The too-standard Nissan, the john's too-neat haircut, the too-controlled voice—it all screamed "Cop," but in the throes of a major meth jones, Jonah had ignored the tells. Now here he was, sitting in a small room at the cop shop, trying to keep it together. He'd been busted before, but something about the questions this detective asked seemed off.

"Tuesday night? Gimme a break. How the hell can I remember what I was doing Tuesday night? Can't nobody remember that far back."

The detective, a moon-faced man with arcs of sweat staining the underarms of his blue shirt, gave him a smile. "As a matter of fact, I can. Tuesday night I was home watching *The Lion King* for the sixteenth time with my kids."

"Don't make me puke." Jonah folded his arms, signaling that as far as he was concerned, this interview was over, so take him back to the holding tank already. He'd wind up serving a couple of months in Tent City, that stupid outdoor jail the other boys on the street were always bitching about. He'd get his three squares, make new friends, do some business, then hit the streets again. Big fucking deal.

The detective tapped his thumb on the manila file folder he'd brought with him into the interrogation room. "Well, then, Mr. King, let me jog your memory. Tuesday night. A little on the cool side. It was raining."

"Thanks for the weather report, but I got nothing for you. Far as I'm concerned, one day, one night, what's the diff? Get up, get around, go to bed."

The detective looked down at the folder. "You have an attorney?"

What was with this shit? Of course he didn't have an attorney. Why would he need one? They both knew what the outcome of this conversation would be, so why jack around? "Like I said, Detective Sweet Ass, don't make me puke."

The detective's smile disappeared. He opened the manila folder, took out a photograph, and slid it across the table. "You know this woman?"

Jonah, who no longer knew any women, looked down.

Then he screamed.

"*Mommy!*"

Chapter Fifteen

Exhausted from her flight, Madeline slept late. My thoughts—and my sofa, which wasn't all that comfortable as a bed—had kept me awake most of the night. An hour after sunrise, I called Warren.

An early riser, he picked up immediately.

"How are the twins?" I asked him, after we'd exchanged empty pleasantries.

"Unsettled. Angel didn't tell them about her stalker, but they know something's wrong."

"Children can be perceptive."

"*Children* can, yes."

The stress on that first word seemed so odd that I almost asked him what he meant. But I didn't. "I told Beverly Hills PD where they could find Nevitt and I'm pretty confident they'll manage to pick him up in a day or two, which should take care of the problem. With the evidence of those letters and his past record of stalking, no judge will let him go this time."

"Hope you're right."

A long silence.

I steeled myself for a conversation that was long overdue. "Warren, we need to talk about our relationship. And, uh, the problem I've been having with it."

Another long silence, then, "I agree, but not now. The twins are up and clamoring for their breakfast."

"Why don't we get together later today? I could come over and we could…"

A heavy sigh. "Today's not the time for this, Lena. Angel wants the girls to stay with me until the Nevitt thing's wrapped up, and even if he's picked up right away, the legal process will take some time, a couple of weeks, maybe a month. So I'm spending today looking for a tutor. I don't want the girls to fall behind."

"Tomorrow, maybe?"

"I'll get back to you next week."

He hung up.

Madeline and I spent the rest of weekend catching up on old times. It could have been boring, but it wasn't, so when Monday morning rolled around, I was loathe to go downstairs to the office. My excuse, of course, was that I wanted to show her how much Scottsdale had changed since she'd left.

"I'm perfectly capable of finding that out for myself," she said. "In fact, I was thinking about visiting some galleries. Thanks to your location here, they're all within walking distance."

"Business or pleasure?"

"What, you think I'm nuts? Business of course. I brought along some slides of my work to flash around. You probably don't remember, but I used to show in that big gallery right down the street before I got sick."

She was wrong, I did remember. Years earlier, I'd checked to see if they'd heard from her; they hadn't. "Toulouse Fine Art. It's still there. Closed on Mondays, though."

"To walk-ins, yeah. But most galleries will see artists by appointment. And if I'm lucky, the good will I established while living here may still be in effect. Providing, of course, that everybody's still alive and doing business." She glanced toward the phone. "Do you mind?"

I handed over the spare key to my apartment and after wishing her good luck, left her sorting happily through her slides.

Downstairs, a note from Jimmy informed me that he'd be spending most of the day over at Southwest MicroSystems, so I found myself alone. While he wasn't the most talkative of men, the office seemed uncomfortably quiet in his absence. To keep myself company, I hummed a few bars of Muddy Waters' "Mean Red Spider," and brought in the weekend's newspapers, which lay in a stack outside the door. After I'd taken a Tab from the office refrigerator, I unfolded Sunday's *Scottsdale Journal* and began to read. I had just taken a big swig of soda when I saw a small item on B-3.

SON QUESTIONED IN MOTHER'S MURDER CASE

PHOENIX—A young transient is being held for questioning in the murder of Celeste King, 36, whose body was found late last Tuesday night in the 7800 block of Ambrosia, in south Scottsdale. An unnamed police source said that after being picked up Friday night in downtown Phoenix for solicitation, the victim's son, Jonah King, 18, made statements that linked him to the killing. He is currently in Phoenix's Fourth Avenue Jail, awaiting charges.

I spit out the soda. Not bothering to mop up the mess, I placed a call to my friend Vic, at Scottsdale PD. Fortunately, he was there.

Without bothering to identify myself, I blurted out, "Is it true, what I just read in the *Journal* about an arrest in the Scottsdale murder?"

"Pamela Anderson! Hi, baby. I see you've dumped that tattooed dork you been wasting your time with and decided to crawl back to me. Well, let me tell you, sweetheart, you're not the only woman hot for this ripped Italian bod. There's a whole line of chicks…"

I took a deep breath. "Sorry, Vic. Sometimes I get ahead of myself. Lena Jones here, your ex-partner. So how's things with you? The wife? The kiddies?" Vic's third wife had recently filed for divorce, and the kiddies—ages 24, 28, and 30, products of marriages No. 1 and 2—had long ago fled the scene.

"Bitch," he said, companionably. "Now that I've reminded you of your manners, here's the deal. Yeah, it's true. Jonah King propositioned an undercover cop in Phoenix, and when he was taken downtown, his name and face struck a chord with the homicide boys. Er, homicide *persons.* Anyway, when the detectives talked to him, he folded like origami, got downright hysterical. After he stopped screaming, Phoenix PD reached out to little ol' us, and Dagny sent Bob Grossman and Sylvie Perrins over there. Kid's already been charged with solicitation and possession of an illegal substance with intent to sell, but by the end of the week, he'll probably be hit with a homicide charge, too."

Bob and Sylvie would be careful enough to dot all the i's and cross all the t's, but I still needed to ask the obvious. "Did the kid actually confess to the murder?"

"Sylvie says not really."

"*Not really?* But you still expect him to be charged in the killing? What am I missing here?"

Some throat-clearing, then a muffled, "Morning, Lieutenant. Right. Just talking to one of my sources. Sure. I'll be in your office as soon as I've finished up. Definitely. Yeah, like, immediately. See ya in a sec."

Dagny's voice. More throat-clearing from Vic. A pause. Then, a whispered, "You heard that? I gotta go."

"C'mon, Vic. Just give me the highlights."

As rapidly as an auctioneer, he fired back, "He said had big fight. Said hit her. Said couldn't remember much else. Said too stoned. I say bye."

Dial tone.

I sat there staring at the mouthful of Tab I'd spit on the floor. Vic's rushed last words had conjured up the vision of a troubled young man, the usual polygamy throwaway. The image of a eighteen-year-old boy who could barely read or write wandering the unfriendly streets of downtown Phoenix, was a haunting one. Taught since birth to be paranoid about the outside world, Jonah would have avoided the rescue missions and instead, banded together with society's other lost children. For the kids, especially the good-looking ones, drugs and prostitution were the next logical step.

How long had Jonah been out there selling his ass for a high, wondering what he had done to deserve his torment? Weeks? Months? Had he, caught in a downward spiral of rage and despair, somehow made his way to the Scottsdale settlement and taken his revenge on the woman who'd allowed it to happen? And what about Celeste? Rosella had described her as a maternal woman, but had she, like so many sister-wives, abandoned her own son to the streets?

Unsettled, I just sat there for a while, staring at the pool of Tab on the floor. A new question nudged at me: if Jonah had truly killed his mother, where had he found the car he'd used to dump Celeste's body?

Jonah's street friends could have shown him how to hotwire a vehicle, but when I tried to picture that particular series of events, the images in my head began to dissolve. The typical meth user couldn't carry out such a complicated plan to save his life—or to end someone else's. Roll a john for extra cash, sure. Beat someone to death in a spontaneous, drug-induced brawl, sure. Shoot a Circle K clerk in the midst of a robbery, sure. But hotwire a car in advance in order to drive across Phoenix into Scottsdale, find his mother, beat her to death, roll her into the pre-stolen car, then drive around until he found a secluded spot to dump the body? And finally, leave the scene before I could make it from the RV storage yard into the street?

That scenario required too much forethought.

I continued sitting at my desk until the speckles of spilt Tab began to dry. Then, disgusted with myself, I reached into a drawer for a paper towel. By the time my mess was gone, I'd formulated my next step.

A visit to the Fourth Avenue Jail.

Cutting through the red tape wasn't easy, but after calling in an outstanding you-owe-me, a couple of hours later I found myself in the jail's stuffy visiting room. It being Monday, only a few other visitors were present, among them a thin black woman holding a fidgety baby as a corn-rowed inmate responded to her questions with monosyllables; and a much older white couple talking to an even older inmate covered with Aryan Brotherhood prison tats. Felonious Gramps? I'd always hated these rooms. They strip away the veneer of civilization we all rely on to get through the day.

After several minutes, an officer led a shackled Jonah King through the door. The boy's eyes were rimmed in red, whether from crying or withdrawal I couldn't yet tell. As the officer guided him to a chair, I noticed his hands twitch. Drugs, then. Probably meth.

"I'll be just outside the door if you need me," the officer said, and with that, left us alone.

Jonah looked exactly like what he was: a street kid going to seed. Unkempt hair, runny nose, small sores polka-dotting chin and cheeks. Otherwise, he resembled his dead mother; a tall, blue-eyed, blonde with features harkening back to the days of Viking raiders. I'd bet his mother never had his mouth, though.

"The fuck you want, bitch?"

That made it twice in the same day I'd been called a bitch and it wasn't even noon yet. "To help."

A dirty snigger from a kid who long ago stopped believing anyone wanted to help him. "What's in it for you? Gonna write an article and sell it for millions or something?"

It took me a moment to digest that odd question, and when I did, I realized that as a non-reader and non-television watcher, he didn't know the difference between a private investigator and a reporter. I explained my job to him in terms he could understand.

"Somebody's gotta be paying you." He sat back, his shoulders jerking. The long fingers on his manacled hands twitched as if they'd been plugged into a live electrical current.

After a few minutes of trying to explain the concept of *pro bono* and failing, he still didn't believe me. Frustrated, I segued into polygamy-speak, the one thing he knew a lot about. "I'm doing it to get right with God."

Another snigger, although due to his increased spasms, it emerged with a stutter. "You g-gentiles got no g-g-god."

To a polygamist, any non-polygamist was a "gentile," whether the person in question be atheist, Christian, Hindu, Buddhist, Jew, Muslim, Wiccan, or whatever. I decided to go with the flow. "Smart man. You caught me out."

He preened at the compliment, a positive stroke he rarely heard. Polygamists pride themselves on discipline, not love.

The story I fabricated would have been greeted with hoots of laughter by an ordinary teen, but Jonah wasn't ordinary. He might have been living on the streets, but his experiences probably hadn't yet overridden his upbringing under Hiram Shupe, a possible schizophrenic who believed in Blood Atonement and all the other Holy War claptrap that false prophets had spewed for decades. My new tactic would fight fire with fire, false prophet with false prophet.

I gave him a big smile. "The truth is, Jonah, a man hired me to come over here, a man who, like you, who was raised by polygamists and was eventually cast out. Just like you. This man made his way in the world and eventually became a millionaire. Now he..." I decided that my fictional prophet needed a name, so I pulled one from the Maricopa County Sheriff's Office. "Now Prophet Joe has started his own Army of God, an army devoted to the *true* religion, and he's recruiting strong young men like yourself who understand the concepts of obedience and loyalty. He needs faithful soldiers to help overthrow Hiram Shupe, whom he deems a false prophet. That's where I come in."

A few feet from us, the black woman's baby began to cry. When the woman began crying, too, her inmate made a disgusted sound and left, which only made her cry harder. The old Aryan Brotherhood inmate grinned; so did his visitors.

Jonah briefly eyed them all with contempt, then turned back to me. "W-why would P-Prophet Joe hire a woman? A woman can't do no good for anybody."

I resisted the urge to slap some sense into him. "We gentile women have powers you know nothing about." Not exactly hogwash, either, since polygamists believed women could achieve nothing on their own, not even conversation. In Jonah's undereducated and superstitious mind, the very fact that I was able to talk to him as an equal must have made me appear an alien creature.

"What kind of powers?"

"Prophet Joe ordered me not to divulge that information. Now let's get back to you and your troubles. Like I said, Prophet Joe wants you for his Army of God, but you can't do him any good as long as you're in here, can you?"

His tremors subsided slightly, enough that his stuttering stopped. "Will Prophet Joe make me one of his Select? Give me lots of girls? Pretty ones, not just the retards?"

I tried not to wince. "Dozens. Now, in order to get you out of jail, I'm going to need some information. You told the police that you visited your mother on the night she died, and that you two had a big fight. How did you get to Scottsdale from Phoenix?"

Jonah furrowed his blond eyebrows and his bloodshot eyes rolled up to the right, an indication he was either trying to remember or tell a lie. A few seconds later, while the weeping black woman and her baby were being ushered out by a sympathetic-looking female guard, he said, "Guy took me."

"A man named Guy? Or just some guy?"

"Some guy I picked up, fat little creep. Told him I'd do him free for the ride." He laughed. "Man, he couldn't drive fast enough. Thought he'd kill us both!"

Mystery number one cleared up. "Then what?"

More furrowing and eye-rolling. "I think...I think I just waited around. Yeah. That's what I did. It wasn't raining in Scottsdale. Is it always dry over there?"

"Prophet Joe ordained it. What were you waiting for?"

"To see her."

"Your mother?"

"Yeah."

"How'd you find out where your mother was living?"

"'Cause I lived there with her. Before, that is."

Judging from Jonah's current condition, he'd been ejected from Prophet Shupe's group at least several months back, perhaps as early as the morning of his eighteenth birthday. This meant that the compound had been there longer than I'd originally believed. How had that happened without someone noticing?

"You mean you waited for your mother to come out of the house? Or out of the compound itself?"

"I don't understand."

"What do you call the place in Scottsdale where your mother lived?"

"Ho's."

Somehow I managed not to laugh. *Ho's? As in 'whores'?* Probably not. "Are those initials?"

"Yeah, for Heaven's Obedient Servants." His shoulders gave another big twitch, or maybe it was a shrug. "I hung around near the gate for a couple a hours. Well, it worked out like I planned, 'cause she musta seen me from the house. Came sneaking out, ordering me to go away."

Planned, not a good word to use in jail, where every visit was videotaped and recorded. If Jonah had planned his mother's murder, he'd be indicted for Homicide One. The kid was a mess, but even the cynical ex-cop in me didn't see *killer* in his eyes, just misery, although he was trying desperately to hide it by acting tough. Even his contemptuous treatment of me didn't ring true.

"What did you expect to accomplish by going to see her?"

"I wanted her to intercede for me, to talk Brother Ezra into letting me stay there."

"Against the Prophet's orders?"

He shrugged.

It would be a cold day in hell when Ezra would allow a discarded male back into the compound. Once the Prophet banned a boy, he was forever banned, and nothing anyone could say—especially not a lowly woman—would make any difference. Celeste would have known that, too. But would she, urged on by mother love, have tried anyway?

This was my chance to clear something up. "Is Brother Ezra her new husband?"

"She got reassigned to him, yeah. Long time before we moved down here."

"How long?"

"Ten years, twelve? I can't remember exactly. What difference does it make?"

I didn't know yet, so I didn't answer. "Back to that conversation. After you asked her, did your mother promise to talk to Ezra?"

He ducked his head, but not before I saw a tear roll down his ruined face. "She just told me to go home. When I told her I d-d-didn't have one, she said 'That's your problem.' And then…and then she walked away. I, I think I screamed then. It made her turn around and…and come toward me. I didn't know what she was going to do, but I didn't like the look on her face, she looked real *mad*, so I…I pushed her away. Then…then she stumbled. And she fell down."

I couldn't see his face, but a tear splashed onto the table between us.

"That's it? She fell down?"

His head bobbed. "Hit her head on the sidewalk."

Jonah's story sounded more and more worrisome. I'd seen Celeste's wounds myself and knew they hadn't been put there by a mere fall. The woman had been struck about the head several times with a piece of wood hard enough to destroy her ear, hard enough and often enough to create a wide depression on the left side of her temple. The medical examiner thought the weapon might have been a two-by-four, not some stray rock lying on the sidewalk; he'd found splinters.

I told Jonah so, but he was still convinced he'd dealt the death blow. His shoulders heaved, a very different movement than his earlier withdrawal twitches. For all his bluster, this was a young man who loved his mother. I wanted to put my arms around him, comfort him, but the gesture would get me yanked out of the visiting room faster than if I'd shouted, "I have a bomb!"

"Listen to me, Jonah. You say that after you shoved her, she fell down and hit her head. Did you pick something up and hit her again?"

"Naw. I...I told her I was sorry."

"And?"

"Soon as she got up, she said nasty things. Then she slapped me."

I stiffened, an emotional tell you're never supposed to allow while interviewing a suspect. Fortunately, with his head drooped, he didn't notice. "So she didn't die right then, is that it?"

"Nah. She musta died later. After she went back into the compound."

"*She went back into the compound?* Did you tell the cops that?"

He shrugged. "I can't remember what I told them."

"Were you using when they interviewed you?"

"I guess so, since I usually am."

Which meant he had the typical addict's memory problems, remembering bits and pieces of an event, but never the whole. As for context, forget it. Addicts never really knew why they did anything, only that they had. Vic told me that Jonah had been interviewed by Sylvie Perrins and Bob Grossman. From personal experience, I trusted their judgment. Could they have slipped up? Jonah couldn't possibly have given them a credible confession, and a good defense attorney would realize that.

"Tell me, as much as you can remember, about those 'nasty things' your mother said after she stood up."

When he finally lifted his head, his eyes were bleak. "It's all so hazy, but I remember her telling me to go away and never come back, to just go live my life and not come bothering her again. She called me a 'useless piece of deadwood.' Then she slapped me and ran away. She musta died in the construction yard. Or in the house. And it was all my fault because I hit her." His shoulders began to shake with such ferocity I feared he might fall off the chair.

Before he became completely unglued, I said, "If your mother died inside, not on the street, how did her body wind up a half-mile away? You see, Jonah? You couldn't have killed her."

His eyes turned wild. "Don't remember, don't remember, don't remember! But I hit Mommy and she died. I killed her for my own purposes, out of my own weakness, not as a pure act of Blood Atonement. I'm unclean! I deserve the flames of Hell, not Prophet Joe's Army!"

With that, over the laughter of the Aryan Brotherhood folks, he shrieked for the guard.

Upon exiting from the jail, I took my cell phone from my vest and called Sylvie Perrins at Scottsdale PD. "Jonah's so-called 'confession' is full of holes, Sylvie, confabulated out of bits and pieces of half-memories. Hell, he didn't even hit her, she just fell down. The last time he saw her she was still alive and headed back into the compound."

An exasperated sigh. "That's not what he told us. He said he picked up a rock or some wood—he's not sure which, but the medical examiner says it was a piece of wood—and beat the shit out of her. His description was pretty graphic, too, detailed to the nth. Once she went down, he said, he grabbed her by the hair and kept slamming her until her head caved in. He even described the gurgling noise she made as she lay dying. Not only do we have his signed statement to that effect, but we've also got the whole interview on video. Before you ask, no coercion was involved. Hell, he couldn't wait to tell us all about it. You've been out of the department for several years, Lena, and it's obvious you've gone gullible, especially where screwed-up kids are concerned, but here's what's really happening. Now that the little punk has seen what a nasty place jail can be, he's had a change of heart and wants out. He's working you, girl."

"Jonah's not working me, Sylvie. He simply didn't kill his mother. And he couldn't have transported her body from the scene of the crime to where I found her, because he didn't have a car."

"That john who picked him up might have helped move the body."

"Shouldn't you be looking for the john, then?"

"We are. But unless the county attorney says otherwise, we've got enough to take to court even if we don't find the guy."

"Enough? Please. Where's the murder weapon, then? The one he can't seem to remember was vegetable or mineral?"

"We're looking for it."

When a cop's mind is made up, it's made up. Especially when she has a signed confession and videotape in hand. Further conversation being pointless, I murmured a polite goodbye and rang off.

Jonah was his own worst enemy. Neither Prophet Shupe, Ezra, nor even Celeste had thought him valuable enough to keep around, so the boy was doing his best to prove himself worthy of their low opinion. Sociologists had a name for it: the self-fulfilling prophecy. Unless someone intervened, the kid's downward spiral would continue until he was either shanked in custody or died on the streets.

In a way, Jonah almost reminded me of Dean Orval Nevitt, although on paper, the two couldn't be more different. Before being overwhelmed by schizophrenia, Nevitt had been a science major at UCLA, while Jonah, like so many church-schooled polygamy kids, probably had the equivalent of a sixth-grade education. Both young men dragged woundedness around with them like a ghost its chains. Their clumsy attempts to free themselves pushed others away. Nevitt's escape was to submerge himself in fantasies about Angel; Jonah escaped to drugs.

Earlier, Madeline had asked how, given such pain and evil in the world, I could continue on in my chosen profession. At the time, I'd given her the easy answer, but now that I'd stopped to think it through, the answer was obvious.

How could I not?

The traffic was fierce in downtown Phoenix, so I skipped the scenic route and rode the interchanges back to Desert Investigations. Instead of stopping by the office, I went upstairs to my apartment. Madeline wasn't there, but she'd left a note.

GONE TO ARTIFACTS.
TALK TO YOU WHEN I GET BACK.
LOVE, M

As I set the note down, Madeline walked through the door wearing a conservative black pantsuit and carrying a slide case. The only thing that screamed "artist" was the bronze and silver necklace hanging halfway to her belt. A close look revealed stylized rabbits doing what rabbits are famous for.

"Stacy Halford at ARTifacts, had opened for a private client, and after he left, she agreed to look at my slides," Madeline said. "She liked them a lot, so we might do some business. I also set up some appointments for later on in the week."

"Business with pleasure."

She gave me a hug. "Pleasure at seeing my little girl again comes first."

"Little? I've got two inches on you now!"

We chatted for a few more minutes, until I realized that despite her good news, she hadn't smiled once. "Madeline, is something wrong?"

Here came the smile, although it didn't make it all the way up to her eyes. "I don't know. I've just got a funny feeling."

"Funny how?"

"Like something's, well, off."

On my way home from the jail, an element of unease had nudged at the back of my own mind, too, but I hadn't been able to access its source. Normally when I felt this way, I'd either jog or go to the gym and work out until the hard exercise cleared my head enough for the problem to reveal itself. But for now, I hated to spend more time away from Madeline than absolutely necessary.

An idea came to me. "Come to the gym. I have a guest pass that's good for three visits, and you probably need some exercise after that long plane ride and then sitting around talking to me for the past couple of days. I can loan you some workout clothes."

"Gym? Workout clothes? Sorry, kid, but I share Woody Allen's feelings about exercise. When the urge hits, I sit down until it goes away. You forget that I've been walking around Scottsdale all morning. Other than that, the only muscles I'm really interested in exercising are those in my painting hand, and they're already in fine shape, thank you very much."

She then turned the conversation to the current state of art across America: the good, the bad, and the very, very ugly. Amused by her tales of art frauds and idiocies, I let myself be swept along. If I hadn't let her steer me away from the unease we were experiencing, things might have turned out differently.

For both of us.

Chapter Sixteen

After an hour or so regaling me with tales of her adventures in the art world, Madeline developed the itch to start drawing again. She followed me downstairs to Desert Investigations and positioned herself by the big plate glass window, the better to sketch the tourists strolling by. A few minutes later, however, she tossed her sketchbook aside.

"I can't get into this," she grumped. "They're all dressed like they buy their clothes at The Gap."

She herself wore a turquoise wig, paint-spattered cargo paints, and an orange shirt that proclaimed STOLEN FROM THE DEPARTMENT OF HOMELAND SECURITY.

"Sounds to me like a trip to one of the museums is in order," I said. "How about the Scottsdale Museum of Contemporary Art? It hadn't been built when you lived here before, and it shows plenty of weird stuff. Piles of dyed plant pollen surrounded by machine parts, that sort of thing. Should be right up your alley."

She shook her turquoise head. "My feet still burn from all that walking I did yesterday. Maybe I'll play a few video games on Jimmy's computer. Think he'll mind?"

"He's a sharer. The individual games aren't password protected, so if you log on with PIMAGAMZ, you'll get your choice of around fifty."

With that, she settled herself at his desk and fired the computer up. Within minutes, beeps, bangs, and war whoops muted her chuckles. While she was happily occupied, I turned to my own less happy thoughts: who killed Celeste?

Regardless of Jonah's obvious problems, I didn't believe he'd killed his mother, and I was determined to prove it. But how? In ordinary investigations, I would simply interview everyone involved in the case, but with the polygamists hiding behind locked gates, my usual modus operandi would be impossible. Then, remembering my stake-out at Frugal Foods, I wondered if it would be possible to get one of the women alone. If so, who should be my target? Big Dog Opal appeared happy with her place in the polygamy hierarchy, but Darnelle—who'd challenged her over the choice of cooking oil—probably wasn't. Josie, the petite blonde, had appeared the most tractable of the trio, but her probable retardation made her an unlikely candidate for serious questioning. In between fielding phone calls and sending out billing, I mulled over the problem until, just before five, Jimmy walked through the door, looking weary from his long day at Southwest MicroSystems.

I waved, but Madeline greeted him with, "Hey, Cutie!"

Okay, Jimmy was handsome enough with his mahogany skin, russet eyes, and well-defined features set off by the curved Pima tribal tattoo arching over his temple. But *Cutie*?

Jimmy wasn't much on nicknames, so I expected a scowl. Instead, a big smile spread across his face. "See you found my game stash."

Her smile matched his as she hit ENTER; an onscreen Sioux warrior swung his tomahawk at General George Armstrong Custer. "I didn't know there were such things as Native American video games."

"Indian kids have computers, too. Plus Game Boys, Xboxes, PlayStations, Wiis, and all the rest. By the way, it's *Indian*, not Native American. *Anyone* born in this country is a Native American, which includes you and probably Lena. Most of us red folks prefer the 'Indian' designation, regardless of Christopher Columbus' confusion."

"Consider me corrected." With a nod, Madeline hit ENTER again and Custer went kersplat. "Score one for the good guys."

"We scored considerably more than one that day." He proceeded to tell her the Indian side of the Battle of the Little Big Horn, which differed considerably from the U.S. Army version. Madeline responded with appropriate "oohs" and "aaah." Their relaxed camaraderie surprised me. She was so Bohemian, and Jimmy…Well, Jimmy was Jimmy. My business partner. My friend. My almost-brother. But Jimmy wasn't quite thirty, and Madeline was, what, almost sixty? What could they possibly have in common?

Fortunately, Madeline derailed this odd train of thought before it could get too far down the track. "Lena, Jimmy tells me he hasn't eaten since breakfast, and he's willing to pop for an early dinner. How about it?"

My carnivorous heart dropped. "Vegetarian cuisine?"

"How about Casino Arizona, over on the Rez?" Jimmy suggested. "Plenty of veggie dishes for the pure at heart, but for you and me, the whole barnyard."

Since my targets wouldn't show at Frugal Foods until ten, I readily agreed.

Casino Arizona was less than a ten minute drive from Desert Investigations, on the western edge of the Salt River Pima/Maricopa Indian Reservation. Designed to resemble the maze in an old Pima creation myth, the casino's exterior was circular. Inside, it contained the standard gaming offerings, but also a showplace theater, and a restaurant so esteemed by the gourmet magazines that even non-gamblers drove over from Phoenix to partake of its Indian/Southwestern fusion offerings.

With Madeline in mind, we opted for the enormous buffet. While she piled her plate with veggies, Jimmy and I snuck over to the roast beef on the cutting board, with a stop at the seafood bar along the way.

As we chatted over dinner, my earlier suspicions about the two proved wrong. My foster mother, never able to have children of her own, had such strong maternal leanings that she naturally gravitated to people decades younger than herself. While she sat next to me, her hand constantly touching mine, her eyes yearned after the small children in the dining room. Why was it that some women, brutal women, foolish women, even women who knowingly married violent felons and child molesters—like one of my other foster mothers had done, to my grief—could pop out one child after the next, while decent, loving women like Madeline could not?

Nature was pitiless.

While I nibbled on a fat shrimp, I asked, "Madeline, once you were cancer free, why didn't you adopt?"

"I tried a few times, but with my health history, the more trustworthy agencies turned me down," she said, matter-of-factly. "Since I didn't have the funds to go to China or Malawi or any of those other places people are adopting from now, I started doing volunteer work with children at the crisis nurseries. Sometimes art therapy, sometimes I just held them while they cried."

"Art mirrors life," Madeline had once told me, as she tried to coax me into painting away my nightmares. Perhaps if I'd been able to stay with her, that particular form of art therapy might have worked, and I'd be a more content woman today. As it was…

I remembered the way her canvasses had looked then, huge oils bursting with color and light. Madeline had never been a fan of realism, believing that with the invention of the camera, the purpose of art needed to evolve from the mere representational to visions less hindered by what was popularly perceived as "reality." The best contemporary art, she'd explained, portrayed an object's *inner* life, not confining itself to the object's outward shape. Her own bright canvasses revealed her own psyche: spontaneous explosions of pure joy.

"They're all about you, my pretty little Lena," she'd once said, while I gazed at them. But even then I knew that the paintings were about the great heart of Madeline.

I thought back to the slides she'd shown me yesterday. Blacks. Grays. Browns. The brightest color had been small smears of muddy ochre, as if shadows threatened to eclipse the light that struggled to break through.

Art mirrors life.

I put down my fork and hugged her.

"What was that for?" she asked, surprised.

"For saving my life."

Without my memories of her unconditional love and the belief that it might someday be found again, I might never have overcome the horrors that followed once I'd been removed from her home.

She hugged me back. "It was nothing."

"It was everything."

After dinner, Jimmy and I switched cars. He drove my too-recognizable Jeep home to his trailer on the Pima rez, while Madeline and I climbed into his Toyota and went back to my apartment. We spent the next couple of hours at the kitchen table, guzzling decaf and talking about the past, with me editing out the rougher segments of my life. She didn't need to carry that burden.

During one of my more edited tales, she interrupted me. "That's all very interesting, but I'd like to know if you're ever going to do anything about those nightmares of yours."

I looked toward the Mr. Coffee, wondering if I should fire up another pot of decaf. "What nightmares?"

She put down her cup. "Oh, sweetie, I could always tell when you were lying, because when you did, you looked away. Besides, last night I heard you crying and talking in your sleep. I got up to comfort you like I always did, but you stopped before I reached you. So I went back to bed and let you sleep."

With Madeline in the bedroom and me on the sofa, I'd thought she wouldn't be disturbed by my always-troubled dreams. Apparently I'd been wrong. "Could you understand what I was saying?"

"Mostly the same sorts of things as before. Riding on a white bus. Seeing your father in the woods surrounded by a group of crying children. Your mother, with the gun in a hand." For a moment she didn't meet my eyes. When she finally could, she asked, "Did you ever find out what really happened that night? It's hard for me to believe that a child as trusting and loving as you came from an abusive home."

Trusting and loving when she knew me, maybe, but the next foster home changed everything, possibly forever. Warren's face flickered briefly through my mind; I made him go away. "No, Madeline. I never did. My memory was probably clearer then than now."

She rose to pour herself another cup of decaf, bringing the pot—the evening's second—down to the halfway mark. Upon sitting back down, she said, "Not necessarily. Remember, you were still recovering from the damage your brain had suffered, and much of the time the things you said didn't make sense. Oddly enough, considering that your mother shot you, the worst of your dreams were centered around your father."

"What did I say about him?"

When she answered, her dark eyes were troubled. "That he was dead. That he'd been shot to death along with the rest of them."

The hairs rose along my arms. "*The rest of them?* What did I mean by that?"

"You were never specific. I contacted your social worker and he checked with the police, but there'd been no report of any unsolved killings that matched your descriptions. Not in Arizona, not in any other state." Her eyes shifted to the scar on my forehead. "But you'd been shot. No doubt about that."

When Jimmy and I had dug through years of Arizona newspaper microfiche, we'd struck out, too, which had made me wonder if whatever tragedy my dreams revealed might have happened somewhere else. And perhaps they'd happened in secret and were never reported. But that didn't make any sense. How could numerous people, most of them children, disappear off the face of the earth without someone noticing? It was so unbelievable that I was tempted to believe my nightmares were merely dreams, with no grounding in reality.

But I couldn't believe it. "Tell me exactly what I said. Don't leave anything out, even if it doesn't make sense." With a shock, I realized that I'd demanded the same thing from Jonah.

When she took another sip of her coffee, her hand shook; so much for the process of decaffeineation. "It all came in bits and pieces, you understand. You were only around four when you were shot, so your power of recall—even in dreams—was short on hard facts. For instance, you never mentioned where those shootings took place, or what time frame they happened in, so neither the social worker nor the police had anything to go on. You just talked about everyone being in the woods—your mother, your father, and all the other people, whoever they might have been. And you seemed to be describing a series of shootings, not just one event. There was the shooting on the white bus that almost killed you, but before that, several shootings in the woods. You mentioned something about bodies being dumped in a big hole, or maybe it was a quarry. I couldn't be sure. While you were mumbling about all this in your dreams, you'd cry about all the dead people." Her already-troubled eyes grew more so. "You cried the hardest over the children."

My god, what had I seen?

"Another thing."

"What?"

"One day, when Brian was playing some old '78s on my stereo, you began to sob. It was the first time I'd ever seen you cry while you were awake. In fact, you cried so hard that I had him put the album away."

"Which album was it?" Although I suspected the answer.

"Something by John Lee Hooker, you know, that blues guy. And the song was, 'Will the Circle Be Unbroken.' At first I thought the subject matter might have been the problem, you know, families separated by death. But before the album got to that particular cut, you'd already approached the turntable and were staring at it with the oddest expression on your face. Lena, could your father have been a musician?"

Not long ago I'd had a dream so real I knew it was an actual memory: my father stood near microphone, playing guitar, while to his side John Lee Hooker himself growled out "Will the Circle Be Unbroken?"

"Probably," I answered. "Maybe even a blues musician, a guitarist. Jimmy and I searched through Hooker's discography to see who John Lee's regular backup players were, but we never found anyone whose name meant anything to me. Looking through old pictures on the Internet didn't help, either, because most were publicity shots. The photos taken at the little dives John Lee played at earlier in his career tended to be of such poor quality that most of the musicians around him were little more than blurs. I'm guessing my father was just a local guy who sat in on a set for that one appearance, the one I remembered."

Her eyes lightened with hope. "But it gives you something to go on, right?"

"John Lee played all over the place, in the North, the South, the Midwest, on both coasts. Many of his gigs were spontaneous and never appeared on his official tour schedule. He's dead now, along with most of his original musicians."

"If it was a one-time deal, why do you keep calling him 'John Lee'? Not 'Hooker'? That sounds pretty familiar."

I shrugged. "I've got everything John Lee ever recorded, even copies of some unfinished demo tapes. So sure, I feel like I knew him, no surprise there. Jimmy's still trying to chase my father down through him, but he hasn't come up with anything so far."

A smile broke across her face. "Jimmy would do anything for you."

I smiled back. "And I would for him."

"Lena, did you know…" She stopped.

"Did I know what?"

"Nothing." She took another sip of decaf. "Is there anything else you've remembered that you haven't told me about yet?"

Plenty, but my sorrows weren't for her ears, she didn't need the burden, so I shook my head. "Just that the white bus we traveled on was driven by some big guy with dark hair. Mountain, they called him, but that probably wasn't his real name. And the same man, a handsome man, always sat right behind him. Most of my memories about him have to do with singing a particular song he'd written to the tune of that old children's song, "Jesus Loves Me." I guess it wasn't very original because the words weren't all that different."

Without thinking, I began to sing…

"Abraham loves me, this I know
All his writings tell me so,
Little ones to him belong,
We are weak, Abraham is strong…"

Madeline stiffened. "*Abraham*!"

Puzzled by her reaction, I asked, "What?"

"You don't remember that time in Sunday School?"

If it hadn't been for the expression on her face, I would have laughed. "You actually took me to *church*?"

A weak smile. "Just the once. It didn't turn out well because of the song about Abraham. The teacher came and got me, saying that when the class began to sing the damned thing, you grew hysterical. You really don't remember?"

Suddenly I was tired of this trip down memory lane. "No. I don't. Now quit pushing me, okay?"

Before I could apologize for my harsh tone, Madeline reached across the table and took my hand. "My poor, lost Lena."

At nine-thirty, I donned a mouse-brown wig and left for Frugal Foods.

The women arrived right on time, dressed in similar dowdy outfits, the only major differences being Darnelle's swollen nose and a bruise beneath her right eye. A more careful study revealed a satisfied smirk on Opal's face, fear in young Josie's eyes. Not looking forward to the next few minutes, I exited the truck.

Frugal Foods' bright lights revealed an angry scab on the tip of Darnelle's nose that looked like it was about to bleed at any moment. Someone had really worked her over, but who? Opal was big and strong enough, and certainly had malice enough, but I put my money on Ezra. The leader of the God Squad was known to be fast with his fists, especially where women were concerned. He demanded that his wives "keep sweet," which in polygamist-speak meant that they humbly submit to whatever bizarre request—sexual or otherwise—he made. What had Darnelle refused to do?

The store's tinny sound system was playing a violin-heavy version of the Beatles' "Let It Be" when I entered. An overhead fluorescent light flickered and hummed in accompaniment. After consulting a list, Opal headed toward the meat counter, directing Josie to the canned vegetables aisle, Darnelle to the baking products. I grabbed a cart and followed her. It wasn't easy to pretend that I was interested in the various brands of baking soda when I didn't even know the difference between baking powder and baking soda. All the while, I kept closing the gap between us, thinking that I might start a conversation by asking her advice about the two different products. My plan was interrupted when Darnelle sneezed, and out of reflex, dabbed her nose, inadvertently tearing off the scab. Her nose began to bleed.

Seeing her blood-smeared hand, she made a sound of distress, then rushed up the aisle toward the back of the store. I followed her into the store's restroom.

It was as frugal as the store's name. Lit only by one bare overhead light bulb, the restroom consisted of two stalls, plain white walls, a paper towel dispenser, and, above the wobbly sink, a black-framed sign exhorting employees to wash their hands. Drifting from one of the stalls, cherry-scented air freshener wrestled with a worse odor. As Opal leaned over the bare-bones sink, I ripped a paper towel from the container and handed it to her. "Here, Ma'am. For your nose. Wow, that's some shiner you have."

She said nothing, just took the towel, dampened it, and began to pat the blood away.

"I know it's none of my business, but who beat you up?"

No answer.

"You ought to report him to the police, get him jailed." Give the cops a reason to look more closely at the compound.

But at my suggestion, she headed for the door. To exit, she'd have to go through me, and I wasn't moving.

"Darnelle, let me help."

Her dark eyes opened wide at my use of her name. The whites were reddened from tears. "What makes you think I need help?"

"Your face. It's my guess that whoever's been beating you has done it more than once."

Her hand, chapped and reddened by hard work, flew to her face. "I don't know what you're talking about. I...I just fell down." As an actress, she wouldn't have convinced a child.

"Are you going to stay with Ezra until you're beaten to death like Celeste?"

She gasped. "What do you know about Celeste? Have you been following us?"

I pulled a business card from a vest pocket and shoved it into her hand. "Call me any time, day or night. I'll help you find a better life. Other women in your situation have escaped. Women like Rosella Borden."

At my mention of Rosella, Darnelle paled, making the torn scab on her nose stand out in stark relief. Before I could explain further, how Rosella had gone to college, started her own business, and bought her own house—I was going to leave out the part about the house being torched—the restroom door opened behind us and Opal strode though, her face taut with suspicion.

"What's going on?" she demanded.

"Nothing." Darnelle clenched her fingers around my card so that it couldn't be seen. "My nose was bleeding and this lady just helping."

Opal shouldered me aside so quickly I didn't have time to react and grabbed Darnelle by the arm. "Get out of here. Now." Wordlessly, Darnelle complied. Then the big woman turned to me. "As for you…" She raised her fist.

I narrowed my eyes. "Don't even think about it."

Faced with an aggression equal to her own, she backed down. But as she left the restroom, she said, "Even with that stupid wig on your head, I know who you are."

Then she smiled.

Chapter Seventeen

The unease I'd begun feeling after my run-in with Opal intensified to the point that the following morning I almost asked Madeline to cancel her gallery appointments and stay in the office with Jimmy and me. Guessing that she might resent my over-protectiveness, I didn't, so I just sat at my desk and worried as she left with her slides. Jimmy seemed oblivious to my discomfort.

Warren hadn't called me yet, either, which served to intensify my grim mood. Deciding to take the bull by the horns, I called his cell. He answered, but in a clipped voice told me he didn't have time to talk.

"Look, Lena, now that the girls are here, I'm going to be pretty busy for the next few days, so let's put off what ever kind of conversation we need to have until then."

He was withdrawing, but hadn't I been doing exactly the same thing myself? "Next week, maybe?"

"Oh, hell. I guess I might as well tell you. Because of the Nevitt thing, I've called my attorneys and we're going to petition for full custody. The twins will be safer with me."

I felt torn. In the year I'd been working as script consultant on *Desert Eagle*, I'd never doubted Angel's parenting skills. If Warren was successful, losing her children would break her heart. Maybe even the twins'.

<><><>

"Are you sure, Warren? She's a wonderful mother, very dedicated. Maybe you need to rethink this. For the twins' sakes."

"Now you're giving me parenting advice?"

He broke off the call.

Just before lunchtime my glum mood vanished when Rosella called me from a pay phone to assure me that she and KariAnn were safe, and on the road to a new location.

"Don't tell me where you're headed, okay?" I cautioned her. "Not even the state."

"Because who knows who's tappin' your phone these days, right? Big Brother never sleeps." She had to shout into the phone, because wherever she was calling from, traffic sounded heavy. Engines roared, horns blared. Behind all this, children's voices shrieked happily over the din, meaning that she was near a park or school. "What's happening back there, Lena? Are you any closer to findin' out what happened to Celeste? Talk fast because I've got less than five dollars worth of quarters."

I told her Jonah was about to be charged in Celeste's murder.

"No way," she huffed. "Granted, the kid was only about three when I escaped, but that was one sweet little boy."

"Most murderers were once sweet little boys."

"Yeah, and it snows in Phoenix every August. Jonah would never do anything to hurt anyone, especially not his mother."

"Jonah admitted that he shoved her."

"For God's sake, the kid's heart was breaking!"

I wasn't about to argue for Jonah's guilt, especially since I didn't believe in it myself, so I changed the subject and caught her up to date. Finishing, I said, "As far as I can tell, the authorities aren't doing anything, even though I gave them videotaped proof of various misdemeanors and possible felonies." I left out the part about Ezra's accusations of trespass.

"Arizona authorities talk big but never act," she responded. "Pretty soon they'll learn the error of their ways. Second Zion's so overpopulated that they're runnin' out of room. They got to spread somewhere, but some of the states, like Texas, are startin' to keep a close eye on them. Not Arizona, though. Hell, polyga- mists can get by with anything in Arizona."

The best estimates put the population of Second Zion popu- lation at almost five thousand and rising fast, with more than a hundred live births every year. That's what happened when a girl started her breeding life at thirteen and was ordered to continue having babies nonstop until she hit menopause. But since Rosella's supply of quarters was limited, I didn't let myself get sucked into a lengthy conversation about the resulting space problems when households averaged thirty to fifty children per.

Returning to the problem at hand, I said, "Here are some names. Judging from a conversation I overheard, they appear to be Ezra's wives. Opal. Josie. Darnelle. What do you know about them?"

"Opal? She's been handed over to Ezra? Ha! Serves the bitch right. That woman's a real piece of work, used to lord it over everyone else because she was the Prophet's first wife. She used to beat the crap out of any sister-wife she thought disrespected her or didn't do a more-than-equal share of work. You think Ezra's the enforcer? Hah! Ezra ain't nothing compared to her." Her voice became less outraged, more sad. "But that makes me think. Maybe Celeste washed dishes too slow one day, and Opal got carried away with the punishment and killed her. Opal's crazy enough to do anything, always has been. If she found out that Celeste helped me escape..."

I herded her off the Guilt Trip Trail. "That would have hap- pened at the time, not years later, so don't beat up on yourself. Do you consider Opal capable of murder?"

"Damn right I do. She's strong enough to drag a body around, too. I've seen her lift a fifty-pound sack of cornmeal over her shoulder like it was nothing." A truck backfired somewhere near Rosella. Or maybe someone got shot. Probably the former, because when the noise level returned to loud normal, Rosella continued unfazed. "Like I said, Opal was always beating up on people. Well, women and kids, anyway. But when either Prophet

Shupe or Ezra was around, she was the very picture of the 'still sweet' sister-wife. And they bought it. Then again, maybe they just didn't care what she did to anyone else, as long as she obeyed the men. Whatever you do, Lena, don't cross Opal. Not *ever*."

Too late for that bit of advice. "How about Josie? Blond, blue eyed, very petite. Pretty, although maybe a little low on the I.Q. scale. She looks like she could be around twenty, which would make her, what, five when you escaped from Second Zion?"

"Sounds like one of old Shiplee's granddaughters. He was Prophet Shupe's uncle. A few years before I took off with KariAnn, the Prophet gave Shiplee a batch of women, some of them real young, most of them a little slow, if you know what I'm sayin'. Their children tended to be the same way, not that anyone cared as long as the girls were good breeders. And they kept sweet, every last one of them. Never argued with a man, always did what they were told. If Josie's one of those girls, you can cross her off your list of suspects. I can't see any of Shiplee's grandkids killin' anyone. They wouldn't have either the spirit or the intelligence to cover it up."

"Wait a minute. If Shiplee was Hiram Shupe's uncle, wouldn't that make Josie his cousin or something like that?"

"We're talking polygamy, remember. Cousins is nothing. The Prophet had a revelation once that told him inbreeding kept the bloodline pure."

Ugh. "What about this guy Shiplee, then? Would he have any reason to kill Celeste?"

She vented her first true laugh of the conversation. "Now, that would be difficult, seeing how old Shiplee's been dead for years. Hell, he was already in his eighties when Prophet Shupe gave him those gals."

I shuddered. "How about Darnelle? She's around thirty…"

Rosella cut me off. "Darnelle Rumbaugh. Along with Celeste, she was one of my sister-wives when I was still with the Prophet. Nice woman, good mother. So she's Ezra's woman now? What a piece of crap compound life is, reassignin' her to that bastard. Anyway, she's only a couple years older than me, but when my daddy gave me to the Prophet—I was fourteen at the time—she'd already had three kids with him, all boys. By the time I escaped, she'd had a couple more. Boys again. The youngest was maybe around two, and if I remember correctly, seemed kinda sickly, but not sickly enough to collect SSI payments. He just caught whatever kinda bug was goin' around. Darnelle was always worried he'd be like so many of them other boys and die real early."

While working underground in another polygamy settlement, I'd noticed that boys seemed to have a higher death rate than girls. Genetic problems? I thought back to the boys I'd videotaped as they'd walked over to the construction yard. One of them, the straggler at the end, stood out in my mind because of his pale and weedy appearance. The man leading them had called him something. What was it?

I described him to Rosella, finishing with, "I think he was called Clay."

"Clayton, I'll bet. Clayton Rumbaugh, that boy of Darnelle's I was tellin' you about. Glad to hear he's still alive. I used to worry about him, but then she always took great care of her kids, made sure they got seconds at the table if they needed it. Especially that poor little guy."

"If Darnelle was one of your sister-wives, wouldn't Clayton be Prophet Shupe's son, then?"

The bitter laugh came back. "One of about seventy or eighty. The Prophet is still doing his godly duty, I hear, knockin' up little girls as fast as he can. Wonder if Darnelle had any more kids after he turned her over to Brother Ezra? 'Course, my sources don't tell me much about babies, just the gals who want to escape. Unless a kid's the Prophet's own child, another compound baby coming down the pike wouldn't blip their radar. Listen, I'm running out of quarters. Anything else?"

Hastily, I filled Rosella in on the scene in Frugal Foods' bathroom, and how rough Opal had been with Darnelle.

"What'd I tell you? Woman's a psychopath. Frankly, I'm surprised that Darnelle had the guts to stand up to her in the first place."

"It was only over cooking oil, nothing big."

"No rebellion is too minor for Opal's fists."

A mechanical voice intruded, demanding more quarters. This set off a round of cussing from Rosella, who by that time had run out. "Gotta go, I'll call in a couple more days. In the meantime, you help Jonah in any way you can, hear? And take care. Especially around Opal."

As it turned out, Rosella's wouldn't be the only payphone call I received that morning. I was walking out the door to grab some lunch at Malee's Thai on Main, the restaurant across the street, when the phone rang and Jimmy motioned me back. Covering the phone's receiver with his hand, he whispered, "It's someone named Darnelle. Isn't that...?"

"Sure is." My longing for Thai cuisine temporarily derailed, I hurried back to my desk and picked up the extension. "Lena Jones here. What can I do to help you, Darnelle?"

In a hurried voice, she explained she was calling from outside a discount yardage store where she'd been shopping with Opal. "When we got outside, she checked the receipt and said we'd been overcharged, so she left me to watch Sister Josie and went back to argue with the clerk. I saw this payphone outside and I had that card you gave me so I..."

I cut her off. "Is something wrong?"

"My son...he..." She began to cry.

"Are you talking about Clayton?"

She didn't sound surprised that I knew his name. "He's almost eighteen, and Sister Opal says they're going to..." She gasped. "Oh, no. I can see her leaving the checkout counter."

Before she could slam down the receiver, I told her to meet me that night by the compound fence, where it bordered the back of the self-storage yard. "I'll wait all night if that's what it takes. Darnelle?"

She'd hung up.

As I stood staring at the receiver, Jimmy's voice interrupted the dial tone. "Isn't Darnelle the name of one of those polygamist women?"

I replaced the receiver. "She wants to meet me at the compound fence tonight."

He frowned. "Could be a trap. You're not taking the bait, I hope."

"I don't have a choice." Not if I wanted justice for Celeste. And Jonah.

"Then I'm going with you."

The last thing I needed was Jimmy trailing me around Kachina 24-Hour Storage, but I decided to put off the inevitable showdown until after lunch, when I felt less edgy. "I'll pick you up something at the Thai."

"Didn't you hear me?"

"I'm having the lettuce wraps myself. As for you, how about that Spicy Basil Tofu thingy you're always ordering? With a large Diet Coke. Want some dessert, say, coconut ice cream? I might have some myself to cool off my mouth."

For once, usually mild-mannered Jimmy looked actually confrontational. "You're taking me with you whether you like it or not."

"I need a bodyguard to walk across the street to Malee's?"

He scowled. "Lena, sometimes I could…"

"Sometimes you could what?" Not waiting for his reply, I headed out the door. To my dismay, I heard the lock turn behind me, then the pitter-patter of not-so-little feet as Jimmy caught up with me.

"You're not walking away from me this time, Lena."

"*This* time? Since when have I made a habit of it?"

"Since always."

It was a perfect Scottsdale day. Still cool for March, but not uncomfortably so. Fleecy clouds lazed across an azure sky. As we jaywalked across the street, tourists flowed around us, hardly noticing we were there, although one woman stared at Jimmy as if she'd never seen an Indian before. Thirty or thereabouts, she looked very Midwestern, with pale, clear skin, sleek frosted hair, and tailored casuals that wouldn't have been out of place on a golf course. Her glossed smile, when she turned it on Jimmy, was singles-bar-ready, and for some reason that irritated me. My irritation increased when Jimmy smiled back. He was such a sucker where women were concerned.

"Pretty, isn't she?" he murmured.

"If you like the type."

"What type?"

The woman halted at the opposite curb, sending come-and-get-me messages to Jimmy from across the street.

"Which do you want, lunch or a date? Make up your mind, 'cause I'm starving." Leaving him to his fate, I walked into Malee's and fumbled my way through the relative darkness to a table by the window, where I had a clear view of the office. By the time my eyes adjusted to the gloom, Jimmy had rejoined me.

"What's that you just put in your shirt pocket?" I asked.

"Heather's phone number. We're going out tonight."

"Oh, for god's sake."

"She's from Chicago."

"And she's probably bat-shit crazy."

"Because she's from Chicago?"

"Because all the women you've ever been attracted to are nuts. Jimmy, you are so predictable."

"Am not." To the waitress, who'd just arrived and who also seemed smitten with his dark good looks, he said, "I'll have my usual, the Spicy Basil Tofu."

Point proved, I switched my own order from lettuce wraps to Evil Jungle Princess, whatever that was. Chicken, as it turned out, in a coconut cream-based sauce, topped with straw mushrooms and mint. Thanks to Warren's and Madeline's broadening influences, I'd become quite the gourmet as long as I didn't have to cook. Lunch would have been more enjoyable if Jimmy hadn't kept up his insistence that he accompany me to Kachina Storage that night and my fence-side meeting with Darnelle. Finally, more to shut him up than anything else, I relented.

"You'll have to stay inside the storage locker. Darnelle's probably paranoid about adult males, especially the dark-skinned kind." White supremacy remained a core tenet of polygamy culture, and from the alarmed look I'd seen Darnelle give Hispanic shoppers at Frugal Foods, I doubted she'd escaped the brain-washing. "I'll rig the camera so you can monitor our meeting. If she tries to strangle me through the fence, you can run out and rescue me."

I smiled.

He didn't.

My irritation with Jimmy grew when, just after sundown, he showed up at my apartment wearing a holster. Through the side slits I saw the dull gleam of metal. "What the hell's that?"

"Glock 29, ten-round magazine."

"Are you insane?"

"Just used to working with you. Speaking of pots calling kettles black, that's no water pistol in your vest pocket, either."

"Thirty-eight revolver, big deal. Besides, I know how to use a handgun. You don't."

"That's what you think."

Madeline, who'd been listening to this exchange while sifting through her slides in preparation for tomorrow's gallery appointments, said with alarm, "I can't believe you're both walking around with guns."

I tried to reassure her. "Everybody's packing in Arizona, don't you remember?"

"Not really."

Sensing another argument on its way, I turned to Jimmy. "You ready, cowboy?"

He slapped his holster. "As always."

We didn't talk much during the next couple of hours while we waited inside the storage unit for Darnelle to make her appearance. Around us, the Katchina activity continued as if the sun hadn't yet set. The potter peddled her foot-powered wheel and the garage band clanged away, as hopelessly out of tune as ever. The pregnant woman returned, and after spending half an hour shuffling through boxes in her unit, emerged with an armful of baby clothes.

I'd rigged up the camera and mike again, this time taking care they didn't protrude by so much as a hair into the compound. While I was reasonably certain that Darnelle wouldn't chance the meeting until everyone inside the house was fast asleep, I wanted to be prepared for anything. Maybe the camera would catch Ezra doing something he shouldn't, even though he knew spying eyes could be upon him; he was that arrogant.

The last light in the house flicked off around midnight, long after the Kachina activity had died down. Darnelle didn't make her appearance on the monitor until after almost two, but the full moon lit her image well enough for me to see her clearly. She clutched a tattered robe around her, which couldn't quite hide her lush figure; her unrestrained dark hair flowed almost to her waist. Before constant child-bearing had taken its toll on her body, she might even have been beautiful. Now the hint of a shadow at her jaw line made me wonder if Ezra liked his sex rough or if Opal's fists had been busy again. Relieved that Rosella and her daughter had escaped the strictures of compound life, I left a grumbling Jimmy to monitor the action and tiptoed over to the fence.

A soft breeze swept the compound yard, rattling through the oleander leaves. The family must have eaten a late dinner, because as I knelt down, I smelled hot grease and fried meat, a combination that clashed badly with the lingering taste of Malee's Evil Jungle Princess. Pushing aside the oleander stalks, I whispered, "Darnelle. Over here."

When she approached the fence, the silvery moonlight revealed tears on her bruised face. A new scent floated over to me. Sex. One of the men had recently used her.

"M...Miss Jones, p...please h...help my son." Her quaking voice was almost unintelligible.

"Who did that to you? Ezra? Or Opal?"

"P...Prophet Shupe."

I was so surprised it took me a moment to respond. "Hiram Shupe is here? In *Scottsdale*?" To my knowledge, the Prophet seldom came to the Phoenix area, preferring to confine his globe-trotting to his more isolated satellites, which were many. His private jet, supported by state money because of its supposed "educational purposes," allowed him to oversee his various satellites' finances and fertilize his dozens of wives.

"Answer me, Darnelle. Why is Prophet Shupe in Scottsdale?"

"I don't want to talk about him, just my son. Please. You gotta help my Clayton. He ain't got nowhere to go and he can't take care of himself and I've heard what happens to the boys who got to leave and..."

"Tell me about Prophet Shupe, Darnelle." But it was like telling the night to roll back.

"...make it on their own, terrible things happen to them boys, terrible things, oh I'd die if somethin' like that happened to him oh you got to help him I can't live without my sweet boy he's so helpless he won't last a week oh please..."

I let her continue her litany until she'd run down, but as soon as she'd exhausted herself, I tried again. "Help me help him, then. I can't do that unless..."

"All my boys are gone now except for Clayton he's all I got left oh Miss I'd...I'd...I'd die for my little Clayton."

"We'll talk about Clayton in a moment, but first, tell me why Hiram is here."

She gave me a stunned look. "Why d'you care about anythin' the Prophet does?"

Because I knew enough about Hiram Shupe to know that he wouldn't bother personally about the fate of one seventeen-going-on-eighteen-year-old boy. He'd make Ezra, the leader of his God Squad, take care of that problem. Something much bigger had to be happening in Scottsdale, something that Hiram Shupe believed needed his personal oversight.

"You tell me about Shupe and I'll help your boy. Deal?" I would help Clayton regardless, but she had no way of knowing that. "Now again, why is he here?"

"The Prophet...he..." She swallowed. "He says he's reassigning me and Josie again. That's why I got to get help for my boy *now*. Before I'm sent away!"

Reassignment. One of the more unsettling of polygamy practices. Since the women and girls were the property of whatever prophet happened to be reigning over them, they were used as barter. When a man pleased his prophet, he was rewarded with the prettiest women, even if they were already "married" to another man and had children by him. The practice operated in reverse when a man displeased the prophet; his wives and children were taken away and reassigned to the current prophet-pleaser. As always, the women's wishes were irrelevant; the same for their children, who were never allowed to speak to their biological fathers again.

"Was Opal reassigned?"

Darnelle shook her head. "She's stayin' with Brother Ezra."

The fact that Ezra was losing the two more attractive women and keeping only the sixty-something harridan, meant that he was being punished. Because he'd murdered Celeste? That made no sense. Beating a wife into submission was an accepted practice on the compounds, and if a man "corrected his wife too strenuously"—as beating deaths were defined—the woman was blamed, not the man. After all, if she'd been an obedient wife, the husband wouldn't have been forced to "correct" her in the first place.

For the first time, it occurred to me that Darnelle might not know that Celeste was dead.

"What's Ezra being punished for?"

Darnelle shook her head. "The men don't tell me nothing."

"You must have some idea."

"Maybe it had something to do with Celeste 'cause as I was washin' dishes I heard Prophet Shupe in the other room yellin' at Brother Ezra about something in the newspaper and he was blaming him for not controllin' his people and now we gotta do somethin' fast about Clayton 'cause..."

"That 'something in the paper.' Do you know what it was?"

"I ain't got time to read."

"Let me ask you this: when's the last time you saw Celeste?"

"A week ago? She musta got reassigned."

"Was anybody mad at her?"

"Opal was, 'cause she took her car keys away. Mine, too."

I'd already known that only Second Zion's most trusted sister-wives would have made the move to Scottsdale. It also followed that any woman thus trusted would have access to car keys, if only for shopping purposes. Rosella had never been that trusted; when she escaped Second Zion, she'd done it on foot.

"When did this happen? The business with the keys."

An exasperated sound. She was becoming impatient with this line of questioning. "'Couple a months ago. We used to take turns doin' the shopping, but Opal decided we were taking too long. Especially Celeste. So now Opal's the only one of us sister-wives allowed to drive the van. Why do you care?"

"Because someone beat Celeste to death."

A gasp. "I don't believe you!"

"I found the body, Darnelle."

She began to weep again, but not with the same urgency as the tears she'd cried over her son.

"Darnelle, do you think Ezra killed Celeste?"

"Don't know don't know don't know but she's dead and Clayton's gonna be too if they run him off so please..."

Her fingers reached through the chain link fence in supplication. Moved, I covered them with my own. Hers were cold. "Tell Clayton I'll help. That I'll..." I thought fast. "That I'll find a place where he'll be safe."

"When? Prophet Shupe says Josie and me got to go up with him to Second Zion next Monday and that's...that's the day before Clayton turns eighteen and if you can't do something before then..." Her voice rose to a wail.

I tried to shush her, but Darnelle was beyond caution. As her wails continued, frightened nightbirds took flight. It wouldn't be long before she woke the people in the house.

"Lower your voice," I cautioned. "I'll pick Clayton up tomorrow at the work site. What does he look like?"

"Dark-haired like me. And he…he's the smallest of them in the work gang, smaller even than those two fourteen-year olds."

"Tell him what I look like and to be on the alert for me, and to do whatever I say. And tell him, if he can, to be either the first or the last person to come out of the van when it gets to the work site. That'll give me the best chance of getting his attention without anyone noticing. Have him look for a white Toyota pickup. And I'll be wearing…" I thought for a moment. The polygamists had seen me as a blonde, and also in my mouse-brown wig. "I'll wear a red wig."

At this assurance, some vestige of sense crept back into Darnelle's panicked eyes and her sobs diminished. "But I don't know where Clayton's gonna be working. Like I was tellin' you, the men don't tell me nothing."

"I'll follow the work van."

In a sensible world, no one would mind if I took custody of a boy who was due to be dumped onto the streets, anyway, but the polygamists' world wasn't a sensible world; they were all about control. Sometimes there was a good reason for such control, too. Boys dumped too close to the compounds might find their way back. Look at what had happened to Jonah. Living in a city so near his mother had led to him being a murder suspect. Not that the polygamists cared about a lost boy's welfare, but Prophet Shupe probably cared plenty about the attention Celeste's death had garnered. It hit me then that Shupe was punishing Ezra because he'd been foolish enough to expel Jonah only a few miles from the Scottsdale compound instead of driving him up to Flagstaff or down to Tucson.

Ezra wouldn't make that mistake again. Clayton was probably destined for Flagstaff, or maybe even Salt Lake City. In the meantime, Prophet Shupe would pocket yet another paycheck for the boy's illegal labors.

My promise to save Clayton calmed Darnelle further, so I pressed her again about Ezra's possible role in Celeste's murder. "Did she do anything to anger Ezra? Besides the slow shopping problems?"

"I don't know."

But Rosella had told me that Celeste had frequently taken her side against the all-powerful Prophet so why would the woman act less rebellious against the less powerful Ezra? When I mentioned my doubts, Darnelle shook her head.

"Celeste always did everything Brother Ezra told her to do. Even that shopping thing, she said she didn't realize how long she was taking, that she'd just got caught up reading all those different labels. And that she was sorry. The only person who stayed mad over it was Opal."

I wasn't ready yet to narrow the suspects to Opal. "Is it possible something was going on between Celeste and Ezra that you didn't see?"

"Them walls is pretty thin, Miss Jones. If there was a fight, I'd know it. Besides, nobody fights with Brother Ezra. Not if they don't want to get beat up."

"It didn't have to be an actual fight, just something that might make Ezra lose his temper and maybe hit her harder than he usually did." According to Rosella, Celeste had been so sympathetic to her sister-wives she'd helped a few escape from Second Zion. A possibility occurred to me. "Did you confide your worries about Clayton to Celeste?"

She gave me an incredulous look. "Why would I do a crazy thing like that? Celeste woulda gone and tattled to Brother Ezra faster than you could say spit."

That didn't sound like the compassionate woman Rosella had described. "It's odd you would say that, because I was told that her sister-wives were always confiding to her."

"Where did you hear that? Look, Miss, maybe a long time ago, when Sister Celeste was still Prophet Shupe's wife, you could tell her stuff, but that ain't been true for years. After the

Prophet reassigned her to Ezra, she changed. She looked out only for herself. She didn't say much to anybody and nobody said much to her, because what little they did say got carried straight back to him."

"Why would she do that?"

"She was luckier than me and gave birth mainly to girls, but she's still got a fourteen-year-old son up there in Second Zion. She didn't want him dumped like her precious Jonah, so I'm guessin' she thought that if she made Brother Ezra happy, he'd ask the Prophet to keep the boy on once he turned eighteen, maybe even give him a couple of wives. That way she wouldn't lose him like I lost all my boys." With that, the floodgates opened again and her voice rose. "Oh, Miss, you gotta help Clayton, he's..."

A light snapped on in the house. I heard a man's angry voice.

Darnelle cast a frightened glace behind her. "I gotta go back. I'll...I'll tell him I was crying so loud I didn't want to wake him up." Her voice turned bitter. "And it'll be the truth. You wake up any man, you get real sorry real fast."

With that, she walked away from the fence.

"Did you catch all that?" I asked Jimmy, after I reached the storage unit.

He motioned to the monitor. "It's not over yet."

I leaned over to look. A tall man, half-undressed, had exited the house and was walking toward Darnelle. He had to be at least six-foot-six, and even through the night's shadows I could see his jutting brow and prognathous jaw: Prophet Hiram Shupe, AKA The Living Presence of God on Earth.

Darnelle bowed before him. "I'm sorry, Prophet. I...I was just..."

The Living Presence of God on Earth backhanded her across the face. "How dare you leave my bed before I'm done with you." With that, he dragged the weeping woman into the house.

As Jimmy took his earphones off, the monitor's glow revealed that his dark face had turned even darker with anger. "And they call this a free country."

I said nothing.

I didn't need to.

True to my promise, the rising sun found me in Jimmy's pickup truck, idling a hundred yards down the street from Ten Spot Construction. A little before eight, the van carrying the work crew left. I let it turn the corner before following. They didn't travel far, just a mere ten minutes' drive north to Indian Bend Wash, where the City of Scottsdale was dredging a large lake. As the van pulled into the parking lot at the southernmost edge of the lake, several blue herons flapped away in annoyance. But some wildlife welcomed their arrival. When the noisy work crew piled out of the van, a flock of Canadian geese taking a breakfast break from their migratory route, waddled over for a handout. They had no luck, so with empty beaks, the geese flew off in the same direction as the other birds.

The park was the perfect setting for a pickup. Dense vegetation, from Aleppo pines to olive trees and thickets of pampas grass furnished cover for whatever I needed to do to catch Clayton's attention. The work area around the lake was also shielded with the opaque, six-foot-high plastic sheeting required by Scottsdale City Ordinance to keep construction dust down. No one working the lake bed itself would be able to see beyond the barrier. Even better, four portable toilets sat partially hidden behind a clump of pampas grass. Boys have to tinkle and I doubted if they'd be escorted to the toilets.

The last boy finally clambered out of the van. In contrast to everyone else, his hair was dark—almost as dark as Darnelle's. He looked nervously around until he spotted Jimmy's pickup. He was less than a hundred yards from me, midway between the porta-potties and the truck.

Couldn't be better.

As the other boys trudged off after their leader, a brawny middle-aged man, I stepped out of the truck so Clayton could see my red wig. Then I motioned toward the porta-potties. He took a step toward them, but Brawny, who hadn't yet seen me, called out harshly. "Hold it, Clayton! We gotta report in first!"

I jumped back into the pickup before Brawny could see me.

"But I…" I heard the boy begin.

Brawny didn't let him finish. "Don't. Argue. With. Me."

"Sorry, Brother Steven."

A harsh grumble from Brawny warned against the public usage of "Brother," their standard form of address. Then I heard footsteps disappearing across the parking lot toward the lake.

I waited for a few more minutes, then raised my head again. No Clayton. He was probably signing in at the work site; hopefully, he was also reminding Brawny of his I-gotta-go condition. In order to facilitate a quick getaway, I started the ignition and turned the truck around to face the parking lot's exit, all the while keeping an eye on the fence's opening. In anticipation, I opened the passenger side door.

The wait wasn't long. Less than five minutes later Clayton exited the fenced area and trotted toward the porta-potties while Brawny watched from the gate. Once Clayton was almost to the porta-potties, he veered sharply toward the truck and sped up.

I kicked the passenger door open.

Clayton dashed across the parking lot with Brawny following. Putting on a burst of speed surprising in so slight a boy, Clayton closed the distance between us and jumped in the truck, locking the door behind him. But Brawny had shortened his lead, and was now so near that I could hear his labored breaths.

"Buckle up!" I yelled to Clayton, peeling rubber out of the lot with the door wide open.

"Yes, ma'am!" As he followed my instructions, I hooked a sharp left up Seventy-Seventh, then another sharp left around the northern end of the lake. Once out of the park and onto Thomas Road, I drove just over the speed limit—thankfully the lights were with me—until I reached the Pima Freeway, a mile east. Only when I'd merged onto the so-called high speed lane with rush-hour traffic did I chance a look in the rearview mirror to see if Brawny followed us in the work van. He hadn't, perhaps because then he'd have to leave the other boys alone without supervision, and God only knew what they'd tell the City of Scottsdale foreman about their illegal employment situation.

Attempting to relax the ashen-faced boy, I said, "Wasn't that fun?"

"I g...guess." His teeth were chattering.

"Are you okay?" This was the first time I'd taken a close look at him, and could now see clearly why his mother had been so concerned on his behalf. Clayton was at least an inch shorter than my five-eight, possibly more, and his pinched features hinted at a less-than-sturdy metabolism.

Still, he attempted to look brave. "Can't you go faster?"

"Not in this traffic." We were completely boxed in, not that I cared. The semis to my rear and right perfectly hid the Toyota from the view of anyone who might be following us. As long as I didn't make any stupid moves, we'd encounter no trouble with DPS, either.

Clayton didn't say anything else for the next few minutes, then, as I began cursing at a tail-gating Nissan, he asked, "Will I ever see my mother again?"

"As soon as she leaves the compound." A bit of a hedge, there. Once Darnelle had been driven to the isolated compound at Second Zion and assigned to a new "husband," her escape would prove much more difficult than Clayton's. Rosella being on the run would ratchet up the problem even further, with the anti-polygamists version of the Underground Railroad now minus one volunteer.

The desolate look in Clayton's eyes, as large and dark as his mother's, revealed that although he was relatively uneducated he wasn't dumb. "That'll probably be never. And Prophet Shupe doesn't let outcasts visit their families."

Outcasts. So that's what the lost boys and runaways were being called these days.

While we drove up the Pima Freeway toward the safe house I'd called the night before, Clayton loosened up enough to tell me about his two older brothers, twins Meshach and Laban, whom he hadn't seen in more than a year. When they'd reached eighteen, they'd been driven away from Second Zion and dumped in Phoenix, probably in the same run-down neighborhood where Jonah had been found. Clayton told me how hard his mother had cried over them, how he'd tried to be brave for her, assuring her she'd see them again in Heaven. From his wavery voice, I suspected he still cried over them, too.

"If I can't see Mother again, maybe I can find my brothers, like after I get settled. I've got it all figured out. I'll get me a good job, one where I don't have to carry so many heavy things. I can do math, too." His narrow chest swelled a bit with pride. "I can add and subtract and I know my multipliers all the way up to twelve. Mother used to drill me on them when nobody was paying attention. I can read good, too, so I'll be able to earn enough money to find my brothers, like she wants me to. When I find them, maybe we'll all go get her. If Prophet Shupe tries to stop us, we'll..." He trailed off, unclear as to what this small band of brothers would do then. His eyes blinked back tears, belying his courageous words.

"Sounds like a plan," I told him, heartsick over his naiveté. Maybe he was almost eighteen, but as far as his physical and intellectual level went, he was little more than a child, a woefully unsophisticated child, at that. "Don't worry, Clayton. There's a chance you can find them. And see your mother again. If you want..." I paused, well aware of the problems I might be letting myself in for. But what the hell. In for a penny, in for a pound. "If you want, I'll help."

"Really?"

"When you're ready, just let me know." I pulled a Desert Investigations card out of my vest pocket.

"What's this?" He didn't appear to know what a business card was. "My office phone number. All you have to do is call it. There's plenty of pay phones still around, mainly in front of Circle K's." Did he know what those were?

"The stores. Yeah, I've seen those." He glanced at the card again, then put it in his shirt pocket with the gentle care of a child protecting a valued baseball card. "What time of day can I call you?"

"Any time. If I don't answer, voice mail will..." Damn. He wouldn't know about voice mail, either. When I explained the function to him, his dark eyes grew wide with wonder.

"I got a lot to learn, don't I, Miss?"

For starters, the everyday aspects of twenty-first century life. But I gave him an encouraging smile. "You're smart. You'll get it down."

He fell silent until we'd exited the freeway and entered a residential area. As I pulled into the driveway of the large but anonymous-looking residence that served as a halfway house for lost boys, he touched me softly on the shoulder.

"Miss Jones, you don't even know me, so why you helping Mother and me like this?"

I had to swallow the lump in my throat before I could answer. "Because everyone deserves a chance at a decent life."

Even outcasts and discards.

Chapter Eighteen

"Thank God you're all right," Madeline said as I walked through the door to Desert Investigations. She and Jimmy were perusing a newspaper, and although neatly dressed in her more business-like uniform of pants suit and rabbit necklace, she'd either flubbed her eye makeup or wasn't wearing any. Her eyes looked swollen.

"Why wouldn't I be?" I hung up my heavy vest and lowered myself into a chair. "I just picked up Clayton and took him over to the safe house, no biggie." No point in telling her about Mr. Brawny and the outside chance he might have followed me. He didn't, so that was that. "Wait a minute. Have you been *crying*?"

Sniff. "You're pretty casual about risking your life."

"It's my job."

Madeline looked at Jimmy, who merely shrugged. "Forget it, Maddy. You can't tell her anything."

Maddy? I had never seen Jimmy take to anyone so quickly.

Before I could crack wise about the new nickname, Madeline thrust the newspaper toward me; it was open to the real estate section. "Changing the subject to something less worrying, did you know that houses in Arizona cost about one-half of what they do in New York?"

"Only for now. This downturn in our economy…" Then her comment sank in. "Wait a minute. Don't tell me you're thinking about moving here."

She tried for a smile. "Would you mind? I might turn out to be a terrible pest, always dropping by to borrow turpentine."

My face almost split from the wide grin it rearranged itself into. "When's the soonest you can move? Next week? Next month? Hell, I'll help! I'll fly back with you right now and help you pack, I'll…"

She held up her hand to stem my babbling. "I'm still at the thinking stage. There are a lot of loose ends I'd have to tie up, such as selling my house. Otherwise, I couldn't buy a dog house in a trailer park."

Then I remembered her family ties. "But your sister lives back there. You'd be willing to leave her?"

"Stella and her husband are moving to Sun City this fall. They want me to buy something near them."

"You? Living in a senior community that's enacted more rules and regulations than the U.S. Congress?" I had to laugh at the thought.

So did she. When we'd both settled down, she said, "Nah, those folks would ride me and my smelly turpentine rags out of town on a rail. Actually, I'm looking at the area outside Apache Junction. Jimmy says development begins to peter out beyond Gold Canyon Ranch, so I might be able to pick up some old handyman's special southeast of there, maybe with a large enough lot that I could build a separate studio. Before Brian got sick, he taught me some basic carpentry skills."

With Jimmy providing a sounding board, we talked property values and sweat equity for about an hour, while comparison shopping through the newspaper. By the time Madeline left for her gallery appointment, I was so excited I had to take a few breaths to collect myself. Little by little, it seemed I was accumulating a family—however unorthodox—and this realization led swiftly to another: I'd been lonely for a long, long time.

My relationship with Warren hadn't done anything to fix that, either. It wasn't his fault—God knows the man had tried—but like Madeline had reminded me earlier, foster children like myself often grew up with relationship issues.

Maybe foster children who *didn't* have relationship trouble were the exceptions. When you spent your childhood being transferred from one family to the next, you learned to wall off your heart. Attachment was the enemy when love and pain too-frequently marched hand in hand. I'd been funneled through, what, ten foster homes? Eleven? Twelve? I couldn't remember much about the first few, just a blur of welcoming faces that over time grew less welcoming. Yes, the bullet that had almost killed me had rendered me a problem child, and yes, those early foster mothers and fathers had tried their best to help, but until Madeline came along, every attempt failed. Which begged another question: why had I felt so safe with Madeline?

Again, easy answer.

Like most artists, Madeline was a societal outlaw, a person didn't follow the rules in either her work or her attitudes. Tell her to do something, she'd do the opposite. Tell her what to think and she'd laugh in your face. Even at the tender age of seven, I'd been able to recognize her as a kindred spirit, one untamed soul recognizing another.

Jimmy's voice brought me back to the present. "It's nice to see you happy for a change."

"I'm always happy."

"And I'm Eric the Red."

"What's that supposed to mean?"

"You've never been able to fool me."

Discomfited, I fussed around my desk looking for something to do. The phone rescued me.

"Lena, Nevitt's in the hospital! He's been there since last Friday, but we just found out early this morning." Angel. Calling about her stalker.

This was turning out to be a very, very good day. "Now that he's back in state custody, your troubles are over." Or at least until some idiot psychiatrist declared him well enough for release and he started his whole stalking routine all over again.

"You don't understand. He's unconscious and has been for days. Somebody beat the hell out of him, gave him a fractured skull and three broken ribs, plus a split lip and a broken nose. He lost a few teeth, too."

I winced. As problematic as Nevitt was, he didn't deserve that kind of treatment. "What happened?"

Her words held an undercurrent of panic. "Some skaters found him in Arroyo Seco Park Friday morning and called 9-1-1. He'd been lying there overnight and he'd lost some blood, but not enough to kill him. Anyway, he didn't have any I.D., which is why it took so long to notify me. But here's the thing. I got another one of those letters this morning!"

"Calm down, Angel. If you received another letter this morning, that doesn't necessarily mean anything. There's a reason it's called snail mail."

"I'm calm enough to know that even the U.S. Post Office isn't that slow. Don't you get it? The letter was postmarked in *Beverly Hills* late Friday afternoon, when Nevitt was already in the hospital. Sure, it took a ridiculously long time to get to my house—it might as well have been glued to a snail—but just because there was a screw-up at the post office doesn't change the fact that Nevitt couldn't have sent it."

If she was right, whoever had sent that letter had goofed big time. I offered one more possible explanation. "Maybe you've picked up another stalker."

"What a cheery thought. All the Nevitt-isms are there, the recent ones, anyway. Crappy spelling. A drawing of a hanged puppy. And a bonus present of a dead butterfly."

I wasn't yet ready to buy it. Perhaps the letter had slid behind something and not been postmarked until a day *after* it had been dropped in the mail box. If there had been a screw-up on the delivery, then why not in the sorting bins, also? Because, my suspicious nature told me, two mistakes with the same letter were unlikely.

"Read the letter to me," I told Angel.

Despite her fears, she read in a voice that revealed the disciplined actress. " 'Angel, since you don't listen I guess I'll have to send you stronger message. Look for a ticking package in the next few days. Better hope your little girls aren't home cause it's going to get real messy.' "

"Either he's accelerating or someone wants you to think he's accelerating."

"Exactly."

I made up my mind. "Get out of the house. Check into the Beverly Wilshire Hotel or some other security-conscious place, and don't tell anyone—I repeat *anyone*—where you're going. Not even Warren, do you understand? Call me as soon as you check in because I'm heading for the airport right now."

At her agreement, I slammed down the phone, and with a hurried explanation to Jimmy, rushed out the door. I didn't even bother to pack, but what the hell. Last time I checked, Beverly Hills had stores.

It was raining hard when the plane landed at LAX, so I bought a rain slicker, basic toiletries, and a tee shirt at an airport shop before heading to the Hertz counter. Still, when I arrived at the Beverly Wilshire Hotel, I looked so ragged that the valet smirked as he took my Ford Focus off my hands.

Angel was holed up in a suite that she immediately began apologizing for. "It's all I could get at such short notice."

Hollywood stars are different than us. The suite that so distressed her could have housed a Saudi prince and several of his wives. The elegant pearl-gray-on-charcoal living room/dining room combination was accented by two facing, down-filled silk sofas, the better from which to watch the fifty-inch plasma TV above the fireplace. But why bother to even turn the TV on, when from the every bit as elegantly furnished balcony, you could see all the way from Century City to the Hollywood Hills? In the rain, the vista had the blurry green and blue beauty of a Monet.

Fighting back a serious case of view envy—from my apartment over Desert Investigations you could see a Dumpster-filled alley—I sank into the sofa across from Angel. "Where's the Black Monk? Shouldn't he be hovering around somewhere?"

Shaking her golden waterfall of hair, she attempted her million-dollar smile, but her bitten nails gave her away. "He's setting up shop in the small bedroom. This thing with Nevitt, it's all screwed up, isn't it?"

"Sure sounds like it. One other thing. I did some thinking on the flight out here and I have to ask. Has Warren returned the twins yet?"

Her face hardened. "I don't want to talk about that."

In other words, the twins were still in Arizona and Angel had probably already been alerted that he planned to sue for full custody. Whose side should I be on? My lover's, or my friend's? For now, keeping Angel safe was my first priority. "We need to talk about the twins' situation, but first, did you copy the letter before you turned it over to the cops?"

She picked up a copy of *The Hollywood Reporter* from the coffee table, thumbed it to the centerfold, and drew out a smeary Xerox. I saw the same block printing, the same atrocious spelling as on the last letters.

ANGEEL, SINZE U DON'T LIZZEN, I GESS I'LL HAVE TO SEND U A STRONGER MEZZAGE. LOOK FOR A TIKKING PACKAGE IN THE NEXT FUE DAZ. BETTER HOPE YUR LITLE GIRZ AREN'T HOME CAUZ IT'S GOING TO GET REEL MEZZY.

It was all wrong, I realized. With a sigh, I said, "This didn't come from Nevitt, Angel. Neither did the others."

"What do you mean?"

We should have figured it out earlier. When Nevitt had begun writing Angel three years earlier, his letters had been poorly spelled; after all, he was dyslexic. But this wasn't the dyslexic spelling of a well-educated—albeit disturbed—young man, with letters and words reversed; it was the spelling of someone who wanted to *look* dyslexic but didn't really understand the condition. Before Nevitt had been hospitalized the first time, one of the tabloids had managed to get hold of one of his more rambling, illustrated letters and subsequently printed it, thus providing a template for a forger. But the forger had gone too far. Even in his wildest dyslexia-isms, Nevitt never wrote this badly, and he certainly never misspelled his beloved's name. And he had never threatened her or her children with harm; he wasn't that kind of stalker.

After explaining this to Angel, I asked, "Who's got it in for you?"

"No one!" She sounded shocked, as well she should. Considered one of the most dependable, least temperamental actresses in the business, she usually left a trail of adoration in her wake, not death threats.

"Everyone makes enemies. That's just the way life is."

"Not mine."

Time to address the elephant in the room. "We need to talk about Warren, Angel."

Her face closed down. "No, I told you. Now leave it alone."

I ignored her. "He's suing for custody, isn't he? Using Nevitt's so-called threats as the reason."

"So what if he has? It's no business of yours."

"Actually, it is." I felt sick over what I was about to suggest, but for now I was Angel's hired gun, so I put my Judas face on. "Warren misses the twins enough that he's even kept his house out here, so you need to open your mind to the possibility that he might go to other extremes to obtain full custody."

"Such as faking threatening letters? You're forgetting the fact that every one of them had a Beverly Hills postmark, even those that arrived when he was in Arizona."

"He could have hired someone to drop them in a mailbox here."

"What the hell's wrong with you, Lena?"

Plenty, but my shortcomings weren't the issue. "Just think about it. Moving on, Warren was your second husband, right? Or third?"

Heat came out of her eyes. "Third."

Hooray for Hollywood. "How are your relations with your other exes?"

"We parted as friends. And before you cross-examine me about them, Carl's been in an Idaho rehab facility for two months, and Rudy's filming in South Korea. Neither could have sent me those letters. Or had any reason to."

"Maybe not, but it won't hurt to check."

Outside, lightening streaked across the sky, followed by an almost immediate clash of thunder. The blue-white light made Angel's beautiful face appear ghostly. I hoped it wasn't an omen.

"Lena, I told you..."

She was interrupted by the thudding of heavy feet as the Black Monk hurried into the room. With his unshaven cheeks and just-as-stubbly pate, he looked more dangerous than usual. "We're all set up. Hi, Lena."

I waved a hello, but Angel beamed her gorgeous smile. "Give us a few more minutes alone."

"But she can't..."

Her face hardened. "Otto. Do as I say."

Otto gave her an anguished look, then reluctantly plodded back to the bedroom.

But not before I saw the scabs on his knuckles.

Because of the heavy rain, it seemed to take forever to drive to Boyle Heights, where Dean Orval Nevitt was being held in the psych ward of Los Angeles County-USC Medical Center. I didn't mind the rain all that much because the even worse than usual stop-and-go traffic gave me plenty of time to think. Two years earlier, when Nevitt's stalking behavior first escalated, Angel had hired Otto as her live-in bodyguard to keep Nevitt at arm's length when protection orders failed, which they all too frequently did. The Black Monk arrived with recommendations from other film stars he'd kept from harm. But Otto was human, and Angel was among the most beautiful of women. I couldn't help remembering last week's visit to her house. While we'd sat by the pool watching lit candles float by on fake lily pads, I'd noticed him moving his chair ever closer to hers as he sneaked glances at her slender hands, her full lips.

Why hadn't I realized then that he'd fallen in love with her? Just like Nevitt.

Would the Black Monk forge threatening letters in order to stay at her side? Or if he wasn't the culprit, would he—overcome with fear for her safety—have searched out Nevitt and beat him almost to death?

The scenery looked less and less Monet-esque the further east I drove, where glimmering green hillsides had been replaced by towers of steel and glass, which in turn were replaced by older concrete buildings not yet demolished. The faces I glimpsed hurrying on foot through the rain changed, too, from tanning-bed-gold to natural brown. Finally, the traffic allowed me to reach the massive, fifty-six acre hospital complex that tended to Los Angeles' knifed, shot, poor, crazy, and uninsured.

After I found the right building among the one hundred-and-twenty-three structures available to chose from, I bought flowers at the gift shop, then waded through a multi-lingual crowd to the reception desk. I identified myself as Dean Orval Nevitt's cousin to a harried young woman hunched behind a computer, who after several searches on her screen, gave me his room number. Before she could tell me he wasn't allowed visitors, I joined the throng headed toward a large bank of elevators.

My good luck stayed with me. When I stumbled off the elevator, the corridor was crowded enough to render me invisible, so I pushed my way through the herd toward Nevitt's room. The corridor stank of sweat, Lysol, and fear. Moans from the suffering cascaded over the nervous chatter of visitors. Although attempts had been made to repair the decades-old walls, the hospital's seventy-plus years revealed themselves in each gouge, each peeling-away section of paint. I counted no fewer than three custodians busily mopping away, but my feet still stuck to the aged tiles. Hard to believe that Norma Jean Baker, a.k.a. Marilyn Monroe, took her first sweet breath in this place.

Halfway down the corridor, a young woman at the nurse's station hailed me. "Wait, ma'am. Who are you visiting?"

I waved the flowers and repeated the same whopper I'd told the receptionist downstairs.

She glanced at her computer screen, then frowned. "You're not on the list. In fact, I can't seem to find any approved visitors for him."

"Bureaucracy just gets sloppier and sloppier, doesn't it? Myself, I blame computers. Garbage in, garbage out." Without waiting for her answer, I hurried down the hall.

Nevitt had a small room to himself, but this seemed little luxury, given the stout leather straps tethering him to his high-railed bed. The constraints hardly seemed necessary. His face, already marred by the port wine birthmark and badly-repaired cleft palate, was bruised black and swollen to twice its size. His blue eyes were so bloodshot they could have been bleeding. I pulled the visitor's chair closer to his bed and sat down.

"Hello, Mr. Nevitt. My name's Lena Jones. I'm a private investigator and if you're up to it, I'd like to talk to you about Angelique Grey."

He mumbled something I didn't quite get. "What's that, Mr. Nevitt?"

"My...my wife."

"No, sir, Miss Grey is not your wife." I accentuated the *Miss*. Angel wasn't his wife and never had been, although psychiatrists had failed to convince him of that. "She's the actress you've been stalking."

"Kept...kept marriage...s-s-secret." His cleft palate gave him trouble with sibilants. Nature had really done a job on the guy, and I had to fight back my pity.

Gentling my voice, I explained that with the writers' strike temporarily derailing *Desert Eagle*, Angel had accepted a supporting role in a film currently on location in Alaska. Since he was simply mentally ill, not stupid, I added, "It's one of those independent films, a Sundance type of thing, more arty than the commercial stuff she's used to. Oscar-contender stuff. Now listen to me, Mr. Nevitt. When Miss Grey returns to California, there's no point—once they release you from the hospital—of you hanging around her house. Do you understand?"

"Never hurt her. S-s-she's-s…my angel."

I noticed that he hadn't agreed to stay away from the object of his addled affection, but what did I expect, that I could succeed where a flock of psychiatrists had failed? Sighing, I took the copies Angel had made of the threatening letters and held them in front of his face. I shuffled them slowly, giving him time to read each one. "Mr. Nevitt, did you write these?"

"Vile," he whispered through his tears. "Vile."

"You didn't answer my question. Did you write them?"

"Love her. Why…why would I…Angel isss…isss s-s-s-*sacred*! Never hurt her. *Never!*"

"I need a yes or no answer, Mr. Nevitt. Did you write them?"

"*No!*"

"One more question. Who beat you up?" The Black Monk had appeared in so many photographs taken of Angel that I was certain Nevitt would be able to pick him out of a lineup. If it came to that.

"Di…didn't ss-see. Hit from behind."

"You saw nothing? Not even the fist coming toward your face?"

"No."

I stuffed the letters back into my vest pocket. Despite the fact that it would do no good, I delivered another warning. "Mr. Nevitt, you are not Miss Grey's husband, and if you continue to harass her, you'll wind up spending the rest of your life in state-run mental institutions. Is that what you want?" This was an exaggeration, of course, but only the direst threats would work in this situation.

"Angel needs me." His body trembled under the sheets.

I wanted to hate him for the pain he'd caused Angel over the years, but I couldn't. Instead, I found myself taking his hand.

"Mr. Nevitt, if you really love her, and I believe that you do, you'll do what is best for her. And that's to stay away. You're not a bad man, you're just confused about where loves ends and control begins. If you only…"

At that point, the door opened and a nurse built like a linebacker stomped in.

"Mr. Nevitt doesn't have any cousins." Her voice was sharp enough to cut wood. "He's an orphan."

She gripped my arm and hauled me out of the chair. Not wanting to create an even bigger scene, I didn't struggle, but as the nurse hustled me out the door, I snapped back, "Even orphans have family somewhere."

All we had to do was find them.

Chapter Nineteen

On my way back to the Beverly Wilshire Hotel, I did some hard thinking. The shock in Nevitt's eyes as he read the threatening letters had convinced me that he didn't write them. It was time to question Angel again.

When I hit the Beverly Hills city limits the rain slowed to a drizzle then stopped completely the minute I pulled up to the hotel. As another smirking valet took the keys of my cheap rental, a rainbow arched its way over Rodeo Drive. Miracles continued while I walked into the hotel elevator and saw that I'd be sharing it with actor Daniel Craig. He smiled, I slobbered. Unfortunately, we ended up on different floors.

My ebullience reverted to gloom when I saw that the Black Monk had rejoined Angel in the living/dining room for something that smelled like herbal tea. I needed to warn her about him, so I joined them at the big dining table.

"Chamomile, Lena?" Angel asked.

"I prefer drinks that are bad for me."

"Vodka, perhaps?"

"Not that bad. Look, I just interviewed Nevitt…" Here I sensed, more than saw, a posture shift in Otto's direction. "…and it's my opinion that he didn't write *any* of those threatening letters."

"What a load of crap." This, from Otto. "The guy's a wacko."

I ignored him. "Nevitt was unconscious when the last letter was mailed. Did you by any chance bring along some of his early ones, the non-threatening kind?"

She shook her head. "They're at the house. In the safe."

"Think back. How bad was Nevitt's spelling then?"

"He's dyslexic, so a lot of the characters were transposed. You know, l-v-o-e instead of l-o-v-e."

"What's that got to do with anything?" Otto again, sounding impatient.

I pulled the copies out of my pocket and spread them on the table. "Read these again, this time paying attention to the spelling, not the content. See any transposed characters?"

They both frowned as they read "Nevitt's" missives. Halfway through, Angel put her hand over her mouth. "Oh."

Otto was less delicate. "Aw, shit."

"You see? Whoever wrote these was trying to copy Nevitt's literary style, but he—or she—got it wrong. Like us, the cops were too focused on Nevitt to consider that someone else might be involved."

I snuck a look at Otto, but couldn't get a good view of his face, since his head was bowed. However, the tips of his ears were bright red. Angel had paled, but unlike her bodyguard, had no trouble meeting my eyes.

"Angel, I need to ask you some more questions."

"Bring them on."

"Who benefits if you don't show up on the set of *Desert Eagle* when they start shooting again?"

"Nobody, because I've never missed a call and I never will. Besides, that sort of thing is written into my contract, so unless I've been run down by a truck and have at least two doctors' affidavits to testify to near-fatal injuries, I'm obligated to show up."

"But if you were incapacitated, would *Desert Eagle* have to shut down production?"

"I *am* the desert eagle."

Angel was a nice person and she had a healthy ego; healthy enough that it sometimes blinded her. "You're not the only actress in the world. The Scully and Mulder characters were replaced on *The X-Files*, and when John Ritter died, the studio rewrote *8 Simple Rules for Dating My Teenage Daughter*."

"Both shows wound up cancelled, too," she shot back.

Correct. *X-Files* had limped along for a while with two new alien-hunters, but the network flushed *8 Simple Rules* almost immediately. "Financially speaking, what happens if *Desert Eagle* folds?"

From the conflict mapped across her beautiful face, she obviously had a difficult time envisioning America without her series, but she tried. "It would depend on the reason the show was cancelled. No show lasts forever, not even *Desert Eagle* or *The Simpsons*, which is why I pay close attention to my investment portfolio. I'm not one of those stars who lets their business managers make all the decisions."

"Very wise of you, too. Let's talk about the recent staff changes I've noticed on the show, especially one of the producers. Mid-season, Stuart Jenks replaced Brad Speerstra. That's pretty unusual, isn't it? Exactly what happened? Since I was in Arizona when it all went down, I didn't pay much attention. As long as my consultation checks clear, I'm happy."

A thin smile. "Getting the truth is difficult in this town, but there's a rumor going around that Speerstra's teensy cocaine problem became less teensy. There's another rumor that his girlfriend, you know, that brain-dead redhead who plays Kax on the 'reality show' *Sunset Slummin'* was pregnant and is refusing to get an abortion. Talk about stress, hm? So Speerstra's wife decided to divorce him and served him with the papers right on the set, for God's sake. Word is that his pre-nup isn't as cast-iron as it could be, too. Kudos to wifey's attorney, I guess. Anyway, right after Speerstra got served, he dropped off the face of the earth. Most of the cast thinks he's in Monaco auditioning a new girlfriend, but I happen to know that he's at the same rehab facility as one of my ex-husbands. Now Jenks is sitting in his chair at the head of the conference table, and the good ship *Desert Eagle* sails on. As soon as the writers' strike is settled, of course."

A palace coup, then.

"Do you know Jenks well, Angel?"

"Hollywood's an incestuous place, but Stu and I aren't close. Still, I've never heard bad stories floating around on the local grapevine. Nothing about women, nothing about money. He's Beverly Hills born and bred, USC film school, Loyola law, married, two kids in college, wife involved in a slew of charity organizations. Hardly a criminal background."

The Federal penitentiaries were packed with businessmen and women who, on paper, looked like saints. As soon as I finished here, I'd give Jimmy a call. If Jenks had so much as jaywalked in kindergarten, Jimmy would find out.

"Speaking of the local grapevine, Angel, last week's issue of *The Hollywood Reporter* ran a blind item saying that some agent was negotiating a contract for—let's see if I remember the wording—'a very blond star, who plays a much darker woman on her hit TV crime drama.' The item went on to say that the star was looking to double her salary. That item about you?"

"Since when have you started reading the *Reporter*?"

"Since Hollywood started writing me checks."

"Oh, all right. *Desert Eagle's* Nielsen ratings are through the roof, we're moving from cable to network, and Toyota just signed on as main sponsor. My agent thought it was time to negotiate. Like I said, I *am* the desert eagle."

So it was true; Angel was in the middle of contract negotiations, possibly to the tune of millions of dollars. "If you're right and nothing shady is going on, we need to explore other options. Who in your personal life might want to scare you, other than your ex-husbands."

Her answer came quickly. "No one."

"If I might add something here?" The Black Monk, silent until now, raised his hand. When I nodded toward him, he continued, "Angel's been having trouble with a neighbor. Is that the kind of thing you mean?"

Before Angel could wave him into silence, I asked, "What kind of trouble?"

"It's not a big deal, but the woman's been bitching that one of Angel's trees is killing hers."

A homicidal tree?

"C'mon, Otto," Angel said. "Nadine wouldn't resort to forging Nevitt's letters based on nonsense like that."

As far as I was concerned, most of Hollywood life was nonsense, but that didn't mean the natives didn't take it all seriously. I demanded details. The story that emerged was this: several years earlier, Angel had allowed her gardener to plant a pretty little thing called Tree of Heaven, which then proceeded to go forth and multiply itself along the southwestern side of her front yard. Angel had been delighted, because as the tree grew into a dense thicket, it hid the neighboring house, an ugly pink stucco belonging to Fifties film beauty Nadine Nedon. Unfortunately, the Tree of Heaven—which might more correctly have been named the Tree of Attila the Hun—invaded the aging film star's lawn by snaking out roots, one of which wrapped itself around Nedon's prized American sweet gum. Nedon's gardeners were now engaged in a battle to the death with the ever-growing green monster.

"She's suing me," Angel finished.

"For what?"

"Two million for lawn repair and tree replacement, another twenty-five million for pain and suffering."

I knew better than to laugh. Beverly Hills landscaping lawsuits were legendary. "Do you think she'd resort to sending you those letters?"

"Old bitch is crazy enough to do anything," Otto said. "But seeing as how you're looking at all possible suspects, I have another name for you."

We both turned to look at him. "Who, Otto?"

"Warren."

Angel stiffened.

So did I. I'd been prepared to deal with Warren later, but Otto had forced my hand. "What makes you say that?"

"He wants more visitation and Angel won't give it to him. If she went crazy, he could wind up with full custody, couldn't he?

I wouldn't put forging a few letters past the guy. Look at who his father was, the Porn King of North Hollywood. And wasn't Warren once implicated in some woman's death? I have friends who claim he did it, too. They say he..."

Angel jerked his cup of chamomile tea away, slopping tea across the table. "Say anything else about Warren and you're fired."

The Black Monk tucked his chin to his chest; it made him look like a sulking child, albeit a terrifying one. "Angel, do you mind if I speak to Otto alone?"

"You can flush him down the toilet for all I care." With that she glided off into the bedroom and slammed the door behind her.

I smiled at Otto as if he were my best friend. "Let's go down to the bar. We'll feel more comfortable there."

Within minutes, we were ensconced in a quiet chrome-and-wood lounge adjoining one of the hotel's restaurants. I sipped at my Coke while Otto belted bourbon and continued to revile my boyfriend. If I hadn't already noticed his feelings about Angel, his spite toward Warren might have shocked me, but now it only made me more alert. According to Otto, there'd been an ongoing series of blowups during the past few months between Warren and Angel over the twins. I found this interesting since Warren had kept me totally in the dark on the subject. According to Otto, Warren wanted the twins with him during the entire spring semester, but Angel had refused, holding him to the agreement set by the California court. The girls would stay with her during the school terms, with Warren only on weekends, summers, and every other Christmas and Thanksgiving. They were with Warren now only because of the threatening letters.

"Thanks to this mess, Warren might win the custody jackpot," Otto said, belting back another Jack Daniels, which made two doubles in the space of ten minutes. He ordered another double. The alcohol would put him off his guard, I hoped.

After he'd carried on about Warren for a few more minutes, mainly just repeating previous accusations, I leaned over and rubbed his bruised knuckles. "Wow, what happened here?"

"Bar fight."

"Which bar?"

"What's it matter?" When he looked at me, his eyes appeared almost as red as Nevitt's. Guilt?

"I'd like to run a theory by you."

"Don't give a shit what you do."

The bartender, who'd been wiping down the bar with a towel, threw him a worried look. At six-foot-four and weighing nearly three hundred pounds, Otto was one massive chunk of muscle. It's one thing for a woman to work out with weights and keep her karate skills honed, but Otto worked out, too, only with heavier weights and more lethal chops. He could probably even run faster than me. Still, a P.I. must do what a P.I. must do.

"Here's one way it could have gone, Otto. You may be putting the verbal smackdown on Warren now, but at the beginning, you might have thought the same thing the rest of us did, that Nevitt wrote those threatening letters. When not even the cops could find him, you felt helpless to do anything other than ensure he couldn't get close to Angel. When I came along and found the guy's stomping grounds, you could have driven over to Arroyo Seco, waited around until you saw him, then conducted a knuckle conversation.

"But maybe it went this way. Just a couple months ago, Nevitt didn't seem like a threat anymore. He'd been put back on his meds, and everything looked copacetic. Maybe Angel felt so secure that she decided she no longer needed a live-in bodyguard. Big problem for you, because you'd fallen in love with her. So you wrote a few letters yourself, making them look as much like Nevitt's as possible. After that, she needed you more than ever. The only puzzle is, if that's the way it went, why beat him up? Just for the thrill of it all?"

The whiskey glass broke in Otto's hand. After pressing something under the bar, the bartender came running over, towel flapping. "You've had enough, sir."

"Like hell I have." Otto's hand was bleeding but his voice remained perfectly calm. Not a good sign.

I slid off the barstool to give myself room. A chop to his nose might work if I delivered it quickly enough. While I considered my options, a man almost as large as Otto appeared from the shadows and placed his hand on Otto's shoulder. "The Beverly Wilshire thanks you for your business, sir."

Otto looked from the big man to the bartender to me.

"Fuck you all," he finally said.

And left.

When I got back to Angel's suite, she informed me that he was tending to his bloody hand. Interestingly, she didn't ask me how he'd been hurt, just sat there staring at me over the teapot as I called Jimmy and explained the situation and gave him the names I wanted researched. "Stuart Jenks and his wife. Bradley Speerstra, wife and girlfriends. Nadine Nedon, yes, *that* Nadine Nedon. Angel's husbands one and two—Carl Overstreet, and Rudy Monroe. Oh, yeah. And Otto Beasley, AKA The Black Monk. I'm especially interested in finding out if any of these folks' business or personal disputes have ever escalated into threats or overt violence." I would take care of the Warren situation myself; I could always tell when he was lying.

After I'd hung up, Angel said, "Otto would never pull something like that."

"Don't you want to be sure?"

"He'd give his life for me."

True. He loved Angel, which was precisely the problem. "I notice that you're not going out of your way to defend any of the others."

She stared at me for a moment, as if trying to figure out what to feel, then said, "Have some chamomile tea, Lena. Your hands are shaking."

"Otto's a scary guy."

"That's why I need him around."

I took the cup of tea that she handed me and sipped it. "Nice."

"And good for your nerves."

A couple of hours later, the Black Monk had recovered from his funk, and hadn't yet killed me. Jimmy hadn't called me back, and I'd decided that another day—at least—in Los Angeles was in order. Otto, Angel and I sat on the balcony watching a pink sunset streak across rain-freshened sky while she called the front desk and arranged for a suite one floor below.

"I don't need an entire suite, for God's sake," I said, aghast. Oh, the money. Oh, the horror.

"This is the Beverly Wilshire, not Motel 6."

Within minutes, a bellman arrived and escorted me to my suite. It wasn't quite as luxurious as Angel's, but the silk walls, mahogany woodwork and wheat-colored sofas still made me twitchy. This wasn't how P.I.'s were supposed to live.

After I'd tipped the bellman enough money to shop at Frugal Foods for a week, he exited. And I finally did what I'd been putting off.

I called Warren.

The conversation began pleasantly enough, considering the circumstances. "It's always nice to hear your voice, Lena, but don't you think we should have our 'relationship' conversation face to face?"

"This call isn't about us. It's about Angel. And the twins."

"Oh?"

Not mincing words, I told him. "So my question is, Warren, do you want custody of the twins badly enough to make Angel miserable like that?"

Silence.

Somehow I stopped myself from pleading, *Please don't hate me, I'm just doing my job.*

When he finally answered, his tone was flat. "The answer is no. And I'm deeply hurt, not to mention offended, that you needed to ask. So it looks like we don't need to have that 'relationship' conversation after all, do we? Time for both of us to move on. I'll always wish you well, Lena, and I want you to have a good life, but at this point I'm throwing in the towel. I'm just too emotionally exhausted to continue what's obviously a losing battle."

With that, he hung up.

An hour later I was grief-eating my way through the hotel's complementary fruit bowl, when my cell phone rang.

"Got the info you wanted." Jimmy.

"That was fast."

"What's wrong with your voice? You sound hoarse."

"Just a cold."

"You didn't have a cold when you left here this morning."

"It's raining and I got my feet wet. Can we hurry this up?"

"You sure you're all right? I mean…"

"Jesus, Jimmy, get on with it!"

"Since you put it that way, there's a *Twilight Zone* marathon on the tube and they're airing episodes I've never seen, so yeah, I'll get on with it. Stuart Jenks, Angel's new producer? He's in the deep brown stuff with one of the Vegas casinos, owes close to a half-million. Plus, one of the network execs has a brand new wife, an actress, of course, and she's been leaning on hubby to make her Angel's replacement. Word is he's been putting pressure on Jenks."

Not good. Not good at all. If Jenks was financially wobbly, he might cave to network demands. "What else?"

"Bradley Speerstra, the guy Jenks replaced? Angel's right. He's been in an Idaho rehab facility for the past sixty-five days, same one as Carl Overstreet, Angel's ex, so you can forget about the both of them."

I tsk-tsked. "At least they're getting help."

"Her other ex, Rudy Monroe, he's been out of the country for six weeks, which makes him a non-contender, too. As for Otto Beasley, the guy calls himself The Black Monk, I struck pay dirt there. Otto's had several assault charges lodged against him."

"Convictions?"

"All charges dropped."

"How long ago? Couple of years?"

"Try last month. Some guy got snotty with him at a bar. Otto walked him out to the curb and broke his jaw."

"And the charges were dropped? That's at least one count of aggravated assault, Jimmy. A felony!"

"Under ordinary circumstances, yes. But the witnesses who appeared at his preliminary hearing swore that Mr. Broke Jaw brandished a knife, making it a clear case of self-defense. Technically, Beasley's record is squeaky clean." When he paused, I heard a soft chuckle. "But that's not true of our lovely Nadine Nedon."

"Let me have it." Hollywood was beginning to look rougher than a prison yard.

His chuckle made me feel better. Not a lot, but some. "Over the years, Nadine Nedon, real name Josephine Gowland, born in Red Horse, Oklahoma, five years earlier than she admits, has been charged four times with shoplifting; twice for assault; once for forgery; and once for grand theft auto when she got drunk at a party, hot-wired somebody's Corvette, and wrecked it on Mulholland Drive. She was also charged with bigamy when she married her fifth husband without bothering to divorce her fourth."

"Seriously?" I couldn't believe that I was able to continue this conversation despite the huge lump in my throat.

"Seriously. The only reason she never served time is because the studio made everything go away. Of course, that was back in the good old days, when a star's naughty behavior was routinely hushed up. Today, she'd be left to dangle slowly in the wind."

By my estimation, Nadine Nedon was now at least eighty, too old to get in trouble. When I voiced that thought to Jimmy, he laughed outright.

"Oh, please. Currently, Nedon's being sued by her maid for hitting her so hard with a telephone that the maid lost a tooth. This supposedly happened last December, when the Christmas goose wasn't cooked to Madam's exacting specifications. Similar incidents happened with her last two pool boys, but neither of them brought charges against her. They just accepted payoffs and moved on to other pools."

I'd been so awed by Nedon's impressive list of misdemeanors and felonies that I'd almost let one go, the one that might matter most. "Give me the details on the forgery case."

"Back in the Dark Ages, when Ms. Nedon was seventeen…"

"Wait a minute. Juvenile records are sealed."

"You are such an innocent. No record is truly sealed when you know someone who knows someone who knows someone who lived in the same small town. As I was saying, Ms. Nedon was seventeen and still living at home with mama when she forged her father's will, making herself the beneficiary instead of Mommy Dearest, the rightful heir. Not that there was all that much to get excited over, just a small farm, a ramshackle house, and a beat-up tractor. Mommy Dearest was less forgiving than your enlightened Hollywood brethren, so little Nadine was shipped off to Juvie until she turned eighteen, when she split for Hollywood."

And now this elderly spawn of Satan was pissed at Angel.

After the day I'd endured, I needed a lift, so before I slid in between the high thread count sheets, I called Madeline on my cell.

"Sweetie, you sound so down."

"I'm fine."

"We're back to that again, are we? Is it your job? Your boyfriend?"

"Both," I admitted. "But mainly Warren."

"I thought so. Those packing cartons in your living room are as empty as they were the day I got here."

"The boxes are the least of my problems now. I think…I think…" I couldn't finish. The lump in my throat had grown too big. Just because you know endings are inevitable doesn't mean they don't hurt when they finally happen.

"Lena, you weren't ready. Some day you will be."

Thinking about the future depressed me even further, so I said, "Can we change the subject?"

"To what?"

"Anything. Just as long as the subject isn't my love life. Or lack thereof."

"Will do. Stop me when you get bored." With that, she described her day, beginning with her first gallery appointment, ending with the last. "I'm back in the game," she said, a well-earned note of pride in her voice. "Odd, isn't it, that Arizona galleries like my gloomy stuff."

I thought about the gaudy landscapes found in so many Scottsdale art galleries, the romanticized portraits of Caucasian-appearing Indians. Every now and then, though, the galleries were willing to showcase true talent. "They're not blind. But other than collecting oohs and aahs, did any of them offer you a show?"

"Tomorrow's appointment will be the second with Shadow Mountain Gallery. They're ready to talk dates."

Before I could gush my congratulations, she added, "Ah, something else is new on the horizon, too. Seems Jimmy has a cousin who owns ranch land just below Florence Junction. A couple of winters ago, a new arroyo formed on the southwest corner of his property, cutting off a triangular piece of land that measures out to about three acres. He can't do anything with it, and Jimmy says he might be willing to sell to the right party. We're driving down there tomorrow afternoon to take a look. Think you'll be back by then?"

Suddenly I felt a whole lot better. The thought that Madeline was serious about re-establishing her Arizona roots almost had me babbling. "Oh, I wish I could, but things are happening so fast over here it's doubtful I'll get back in time. You two go check it out, then call and let me know what's happening. If I don't pick up, leave a message."

Despite the roaming rates, we talked for almost an hour, and by the time we rang off, I'd regained my equilibrium. Madeline! A short drive away!

I was so happy that for a while I even forgot about Warren.

Celeste lay on the ground, surrounded by a circle of people. Some I recognized—such as Warren—some I didn't.

"Is she dead?" I asked the big man who'd finally stopped pistol-whipping her.

"Not yet," said Prophet Hiram Shupe, holding the gun out to me. "Finish her off and prove your loyalty."

"Why shoot her if she's already going to die?"

A tall woman who looked just like me but wasn't, left the circle to whisper in my ear. "It's just a game, to trick Abraham. Now close your eyes. Everything will be all right, I promise." She stepped in front of me to take the Prophet's gun.

"But he's not Abraham," I protested.

"Yes he is. They all are."

I looked again at the circle of people surrounding the dying woman and saw that she was right. The man I'd mistaken for Warren had shape-shifted into Abraham. So had everyone else, with one exception.

"I don't understand."

"You will," my mother told me. "Isn't that right, Madeline?"

Madeline, whose face had remained her own, said, "Eventually."

My mother handed me the gun. "Shoot Celeste now, Lena, so that she might live."

"But none of it makes any sense!" I screamed...

...as I woke up.

In the morning, Angel, Otto, and I shared a tense breakfast in Angel's suite.

"You're quiet, Lena," Angel said. "Anything wrong?"

"I'm fine."

"If you say so."

The Black Monk snorted. "If that's fine, I don't want to ever see her not fine."

When I returned to my room, I shook off the memory of last night's dream, and called Stuart Jenks' office. His secretary, who sounded a hundred years old, told me that *Desert Eagle's* producer was taking a meeting.

"Of course he is," I told her. "But tell Mr. Jenks that the script consultant Angel brought on board is a real-life private eye, not some scriptwriter's creation. Tell him he's been implicated in those so-called stalking letters she's been receiving. And then tell him that the real-life private eye will notify the police today if he doesn't…"

"Oh, my, the meeting's over already. I'll put you through to Mr. Jenks now."

Although I'd only sat through one meeting with Jenks, he'd impressed me as a smart man, if a bit on the weasely side, so I wasn't surprised when he listened carefully to what I had to say.

"That it?" he asked when I finished.

"If the letters stop, I'll forget the whole thing. If they continue, I'm going to the cops and I'll name names. Chief among them will be yours."

He didn't say anything for a moment, and when he did, his words were not unexpected. "I'll take what you've said into consideration, Ms. Jones. In the meantime, you're fired."

"Nice talking to you, too." Since Angel had insisted that my services be included in her new contract, I wasn't all that worried. If she won, I won. If she didn't, well, I'd be out of a job anyway, wouldn't I?

My next conversation needed to be face-to-face, so soon I was back in my rental, tooling down Wilshire Boulevard in haze-diffused sunshine toward Angel's house. Or rather, Angel's neighbor's house.

Nadine Nedon had built her thirty-two-room mansion decades before Beverly Hills land values soared into the stratosphere, but she hadn't kept up repairs on the pink monstrosity. On the side nearest Angel's property much of the stucco had crumbled, leaving uneven patches of dirty white. Most of the clashing green shutters were missing louvers, giving the wall an abandoned appearance. The front elevation wasn't much better, although someone had at one time attempted to match the original pink in a sloppy patch-up job, so now the house looked polka-dotted.

The landscaping, however, was glorious.

As I picked my way along the disintegrating cobblestone walk, I passed through a veritable jungle of flowering bushes a-flutter with butterflies and bees. Despite my concerns about facing down the old battle ax, I smiled at this tropical profusion of color. Bright red poppies nuzzled a lavender-bloomed wisteria. A few yards away, green and white caladium circled a yellow ginkgo tree, themselves surrounded dazzling beds of bearded iris, pansies, begonias, and gladioli.

Among all this botanical beauty stood the alleged victim of Angel's rapacious Tree of Paradise: a sickly American sweet gum tree, its branches drooping, its five-lobed leaves in the process of falling unseasonably to the ground.

"Who the hell are you and what the hell do you want?" a raspy voice called.

I looked away from the dying sweet gum to see a tiny woman, her face smeared with green goo, standing on the doorstep, arms akimbo.

"My name's Lena Jones and I'm a private detective. May we talk for a moment?"

"Whatever it was, I didn't do it, and you couldn't prove it if I did," she snapped. "Now get the hell out of my yard before I sic the dogs on you."

If she owned dogs, they'd be barking by now, but I approached her carefully, one rickety cobblestone at a time. "My client Angel Grey has been receiving…"

"I don't care if Ms. Grey's been receiving smallpox. I want her out of this neighborhood, her and those ugly twins of hers. What are they, albinos?"

I had no problem with people insulting me or even Angel, but they'd better not insult those two precious girls. "They're natural blondes, actually." I pointed to her own dark-rooted goldilocks. "Unlike you. What's the matter, miss your touch-up appointment at the salon? Or did the last check you wrote them bounce?"

To my surprise, she laughed. Her teeth were her own, although yellow. "I like a woman with spirit. Care to step in for a chat and a nice cuppa hemlock? I'd love to hear about Ms. Grey's grievances. In sordid detail. Other people's unhappiness makes me feel so much better about my own."

The old bat was growing on me. "I'll pass on the cuppa, but I'm up for the chat."

After its exterior, the house she led me into came as a shock. It was spotless and in museum-perfect condition, furnished in an assortment of antiques most dealers would kill for. Eclipsing all that splendor, a large painting of a youthful Nadine, looking ravishingly beautiful and completely untrustworthy, hung above a fireplace big enough to roast an entire cow.

"Wow," was all I could say.

"Don't be too impressed. I'm selling off everything, one piece at a time. With any luck, I'll be dead before the Jacobean armchairs go. Sure you don't want a drink?" She held up a crystal decanter. "I've been drinking down the wine cellar so this stuff calling itself merlot is nothing but cheap plonk, but any plonk in a storm, huh?"

I declined this gracious offer and lowered myself into one of the armchairs, which was as uncomfortable as it looked. Her own drink poured, Nedon sat down in the matching armchair across from me, and raised her glass. "Here's to trouble." She took a drink, sighed. "Now let's hear the threat."

"Threat?" I hadn't yet mentioned the letters.

"Oh, c'mon. Nobody drops by just to pass the time. You're here to threaten me either with police action or a lawsuit, possibly both, so kindly spell it out. Be warned, though. Whatever crimes I've committed, the statute of limitations elapsed long ago."

She seemed so forthright I decided to test her. "Did you forge your father's will?"

"Of course I did."

"How about shoplifting?"

"Ten times more often than they caught me for."

"Hitting your maid?"

Her face took on a sly look. "Since that's part of an ongoing lawsuit, I cannot comment at this time."

"Did you write threatening letters to Angela Grey?"

"Don't be an ass. Why would I do something like that?"

"Because you're angry about that ailing American sweet gum tree of yours, and what Angel's Tree of Heaven might be doing to it."

"To paraphrase that big-eared alien in that stupid space opera, there is no 'might be,' there only *is*. One day phony Indian Maiden Ha Ha is going to come out and find every last goddamn root of her murderous plant chopped up into one-inch pieces." She took another drink, a larger one this time. "Look, Miss Jones, if that really is your name, the only thing I have left worth caring about besides my portrait and my Jacobean armchairs, is my garden. Screw with it and you screw with me."

The woman was indomitable, but I hid my admiration. "Give me a yes or no, Ms. Nedon. Did you send threatening letters to Angel?"

She crossed her arms over her scrawny chest and said, "That's for me to know and you to find out."

Once back at the Beverly Wilshire Hotel, I related my findings while Angel listened attentively. "Both Nedon and Jenks had reasons to write those letters. So did…" I flicked my eyes toward the Black Monk, who glared at me from his seat at the dining table. "So did Otto." Hating myself, I added, "And maybe Warren."

She didn't looked as shocked as I'd wished. "Because of the custody thing?"

"Yes."

"I know him better than you, Lena. Warren wants the twins, but there's a limit to how far he'll go. With him, there's *always* a limit. Hey, what's wrong now?"

"Nothing."

The Black Monk made a disgusted sound. "Can we get on with this?"

I cleared my throat and continued. "As for Speerstra, you're right, he and your ex haven't left that Idaho rehab facility for weeks. And your other ex is still in South Korea. I've scared Nedon and Jenks off, I believe, so what do you want me to do now? Take my findings to the police?"

She shook her head. "No. Maybe whoever's been sending the letters will stop now that you've outed them as forgeries. If they don't stop, then we'll see. I'll tell you this, though. I'm moving back home first thing tomorrow. As for Warren, I'll fight him to the bitter end. I want my babies back." Her voice trembled slightly; talking about her little girls always made her emotional.

"If I may make one suggestion?"

"Suggest away."

"Get rid of that Tree of Paradise."

She managed a smile. "I'll call the gardener now."

Flouting Hollywood convention, Angel and I shared an early dinner in the hotel restaurant while the Black Monk looked on with no apparent appetite. Angel was more relaxed than I'd seen her in some time, and it was fun going over new script ideas now that *Desert Eagle* might be moving to one of the networks. If the writers' strike ever ended.

"You'll get a raise," she said. "Networks pay consultants more money than cable."

The amount I was already getting seemed astronomically high for doing nothing more than reading scripts and flying out to L.A. once a week to point out their errors. Then I remembered something. "Jenks told me I was fired."

"Doesn't he wish. But I've made it clear that you're part of my package—if I'm the *Desert Eagle*, you're the *Desert Eagle's* baggage, so to speak. Who else has enough balls to sit at a conference table and tell the writers that revolvers don't eject shell casings?"

"Women don't have balls," the Black Monk grumped.

Angel laughed. "The hell they don't."

<><><>

Two hours later, while I was returning my rental car to Hertz, my cell phone chirped.

Jimmy began shouting even before I got the phone to my ear. "Jesus, Lena, why haven't you been answering your phone? I've called a dozen times!"

"I was busy doing interviews, so I turned it off and only a few minutes ago realized I'd forgotten to turn it back on. How'd the trip out to the Florence Junction property go? Did Madeline make an offer?"

"There was no trip, because someone broke into your apartment last night. Jesus, Lena. There's blood all over the place. And Madeline's missing."

Chapter Twenty

Scottsdale detectives Bob Grossman and Sylvie Perrins, with Lieutenant Dagny Urich listening carefully, were interviewing Jimmy when I arrived at my apartment. As he had told me over the phone, blood spattered the living room, most of it located near the door.

"There's not enough blood to indicate fatal injury." Dagny's voice was unexpectedly gentle. Maybe because it wasn't my blood.

Jimmy's own voice reflected a combination of fear and pride. "Madeline put up a hell of a fight, didn't she, Lena?"

The television, its screen shattered, lay on the floor. The coffee table, tossed all the way to the other side of the room, now had only three legs; the fourth had come to rest against the opposite wall. Papers, books, and Madeline's slides littered the carpet. Everything, including the door frame, was smudged with fingerprint powder.

"Looks like whoever did this was wearing gloves, but if we lift anything promising, we'll run it through AFIS," Dagny said. "We have your prints on file, Lena, and Mr. Sisiwan's. Has there been anyone else up here lately we need to rule out?"

"Just Madeline. And Warren, my ex-boyfriend. He was up here a couple weeks ago."

Her eyes sharpened. "Acrimonious break-up?"

There being no point in going into the details, I shook my head. "No worse than usual. But he'd never do anything like this."

After a noncommittal grunt, she thrust a baggie toward me. Secured inside was a block-printed note that said, MIND YOUR OWN BUSINESS OR SHE DIES. "This was on your kitchen table. Any idea who wrote it?"

I opened my mouth, but for some reason couldn't make a sound.

Before I could wave him away, Jimmy guided me to the sofa, sat down beside me, and slipped his arm around my shoulders. "Put your head down between your knees. Take deep breaths."

How could I, when I couldn't breathe at all?

"Lena!" Jimmy pounded me on the back with his fist.

Air rushed back into my lungs, and with it, bile rose in my throat. Covering my mouth with my hand, I staggered to my feet, and stumbled toward the bathroom. I almost made it.

"There goes the crime scene," Dagny muttered as I fell to my knees and heaved all over the carpet.

"No prob," Bob Grossman replied. "Techs finished testing that area fifteen minutes ago."

"We can get prelim results as early as tomorrow," Dagny said. "Blood type, anyway. DNA'll take weeks. If we're lucky, this might not all be the victim's blood. When the final results come in, CODIS might be able to identify the perp."

Would Madeline's medical records still be at the hospital where she'd been treated for breast cancer so many years earlier? Before I could ask, another bout of nausea hit me. This time I managed to make it to the bathroom, Jimmy trailing behind. When my brain began functioning again, I realized he'd never left my side. Once finished emptying my stomach, I threw cold water on my face and gargled. Somewhat refreshed, I ran back to the living room, grabbed my vest, and charged out the apartment door.

"Lena! Where are you going?" Jimmy called.

"To the compound. Those bastards are responsible for this."

He caught me in the stairwell and stopped me before I made it to the street. "They won't let you in."

"Then I'll climb the goddamn fence!"

"I already filled Lieutenant Ulrich in on everything. She decided there's probable cause for a search warrant. It's in the works right now."

"On what grounds?"

"Before you got here, I told the lieutenant about Darnelle and what I saw on the monitor Tuesday night. Assault. Possible rape. I even gave her a copy of the tapes. You can see Prophet Shupe back-handing Darnelle, clear as day, blood on her mouth, him dragging her toward the house. Everything he said's as clear as a bell, too. And I made certain *those* tapes were legal."

"By the time Dagny gets her warrant, if she does, Madeline could be..." I couldn't say the word that scared me the most. "... could be hidden away at some compound in Mexico." Figuring I could make it to the one in Scottsdale within ten minutes if the traffic lights were with me, I started out the door. This time my rush was interrupted by a herd of cops thundering down the stairs behind me.

"Headquarters just radioed that the warrant came through," Dagny said, as she trailed me down the sidewalk. "We're on our way to the compound, but you have to stay here. The last thing we need is for you to muddy the waters." To Jimmy, "Hold her down."

"Yes, ma'am," my friend and my traitor answered, taking hold of my arms so firmly that I couldn't follow as Sylvie and Bob rushed past.

Helplessly I watched them disappear onto the street, listened as sirens wailed into the night. "You bastard," I said to Jimmy, while trying to figure out a way to knock him down the stairs. A knee to the groin?

He released me. "They're gone now, but I want to drive. You're in no shape."

How could I have doubted him? We ran to the parking lot and jumped into his pickup. Fortunately, it was a weeknight and traffic was light because we blew through a few red lights without getting killed. On the way to Ten Spot Construction, my panic settled into a white-hot calm.

"Leave your .38 in the truck," Jimmy said, as he rolled to a stop behind several blue-and-whites.

I didn't argue. If I'd learned one thing from my years on the force, it was that rage and guns were a lethal combination. In my mood, I was as apt to shoot a cop as I was Madeline's kidnapper.

Dagny hadn't stationed any uniforms outside the compound, so we were able to enter the house in time to see a thunderous-looking Prophet Shupe finish reading the search warrant. When he handed it back to Dagny, he gave Ezra a venomous glare that would have poisoned a weaker man.

"Is Ms. Madeline Grissom on these premises, Mr. Shupe?" Dagny asked. I noticed she didn't call him "Prophet."

He blinked, but didn't answer. Ezra just looked scared, as did the other men grouped in guard formation around him: jackals protecting a lion. One of the jackals had a freshly-bandaged ear.

As I was considering the import of that, Dagny caught sight of me. "What are you doing here?"

"You have to ask?"

She looked at Prophet Shupe, then back at me. "Step onto the porch and let us do our job."

As the cops spread out through the house on their search, I could hear sleepy children's voices supplanted by those of frightened women, among them Darnelle's and Opal's. Doors opened and closed, closet doors slid back. Yes, the cops were doing their job, and doing it well. I nodded at Dagny, and as she'd requested, backed onto the porch, Jimmy acting as my shadow.

"Let's make sure the outbuildings are checked," I whispered. "The construction company, too."

"Already on it," he whispered back.

But the cops were already covering the other buildings. Their voices drifted toward us on the cool night air, overpowering the whisper of wind, the disgruntled mutterings of awakened nightbirds. After watching them come up empty time after time, I realized that Madeline would not be found here. They'd taken her somewhere else.

I remembered the legal problems that sometimes arose with search warrants, which by their nature, were necessarily limited in scope. "Jimmy, that search warrant Lieutenant Ulrich was able to wrangle?"

"What about it?"

"It's probably just for this address, this property. Since Madeline hasn't been found here, there's no legal foundation for the cops to collect DNA from those men without a court order, and you know the lieutenant, these days she does everything by the book."

"Unfortunately." He sounded as depressed as I felt.

"I have an idea."

Mind made up, I trotted back to the house.

Although the noise from other rooms proved that the search continued, the glum expression on Dagny's face revealed that she wasn't expecting our luck to change. She didn't even seem angry when she said, "I thought I told you to wait outside."

"You did." My only satisfaction came from seeing that Prophet Shupe's protective God Squad, apparently once more smug in their ability to evade the law, had relaxed their guard over him.

With a sigh, Dagny turned away from me and back to the men. "I'll ask you once again, gentlemen. Have you ever…?"

She never finished, because with a loud screech intended to show I'd lost my mind—and maybe I had—I charged Prophet Shupe, and with my right hand, slashed him across the face. My fingernails were short, but long enough to do the job. Before the jackals could close their protective circle again, I slashed Ezra with my left hand. Then, when Band-Aid Man muscled me away from his holy men, I bit him hard enough to draw blood.

Mission accomplished, I stopped my screeching, and in a normal voice, said to Dagny, "It might be a good idea to check my victims' I.D.s, since I'll now be prosecuted for assault, right? You need to know for certain who I assaulted."

The alarmed look that passed between Prophet Shupe and Ezra showed they understood what had just happened.

So did Dagny. Her voice held less outrage than I'd expected when she said, "That's the way it works, all right. Bob, bag her hands and cuff her. Sylvie, get the victims' identification. When you get the assailant down to the station, have a crime tech check her out and take those DNA samples. For the future assault case, of course." Her next words, directed toward the men, sounded harsher. "We prosecute lawbreakers around here."

Then, my mouth and fingernails loaded with polygamist DNA, I listened to the sweetest sound I'd heard in the past hour: my old pal, Sergeant Robert Grossman, intoning the Miranda as he snapped cuffs around my wrists.

But it wasn't over. Just as he was about to lead me away, I heard a strangled sound, followed by a thud. I turned to see Prophet Shupe on his knees, arms outflung, his eyes rolled back so that only the whites showed. His body was twitching so violently that two of his men put their hands on his shoulder to stabilize him.

"Elohim, Elohim, Lord God of Highest Heaven!" Spittle flew from Shupe's mouth. "Smite the whores and their associates, smite the unbelievers! As you promised in your covenant with me, together we shall bring about a great awakening and a great slaughter, and...and a...and a..." His mouth moved silently for a moment. Then he began to drool.

"A Revelation!" Ezra cried. "The Prophet is having a new Revelation!"

He sure was. Spittle flew as Shupe continued his rant. "...and a great crying of condemned souls from the flames of Hell and a...and a..."

"Go on, Prophet," Band-Aid Man urged, his face aflame with religious fervor. "We hear your words and as your obedient servants, we will obey."

Dagny was less impressed. "Epilepsy, is my guess. Or a brain tumor. Whatever the problem, he needs medical care, not a pulpit. Want me to call 9-1-1?" She directed her question to Ezra, who gave an angry shake of his head.

"You are witnessing a holy moment, Unbeliever."

Dagny sniffed. "Whatever."

"...and a rising of saints up to...into...Heav...Bazeiel Alamoama Gramael..."

As the assembled police officers stared in disbelief, every member of the God Squad fell to their knees and bowed their heads. Thus loosened from their steadying hands, Shupe slumped all the way to the floor. His twitchings became convulsions, but this didn't stop the words streaming from his foaming mouth. He was now in full Speaking-In-Tongues mode, the spate of names—or whatever they had been—degenerating into nonsense syllables. The more he raved, the more fervent his witless followers became.

"You are truly the Living Presence of God on Earth!" Ezra called out, his voice choked with emotion.

"Verily!" Band-Aid Man agreed, tears streaming down his face.

"...hakimo walzeribab uleeria nizheilrak..."

"Enough of this crap," Dagny snapped. "Bob, take Lena down to the station and book her ass. In the meantime, I'm calling 9-1-1."

Just after midnight, Jimmy made my bail. As I was being processed out, Bob Grossman stopped by to tell me that the Living Presence of God on Earth, who'd recovered from his seizure by the time the EMT's arrived, had refused medical treatment. No surprise there. Unlike the average person who suffers from epilepsy, Shupe, like his father before him, was also a lunatic. Regardless of his very obvious mental problems, his followers continued to turn over their lives—and the lives of their wives and daughters and sons—to him. Compared to Shupe, Dean Orval Nevitt was sanity itself.

Bob had more immediate news, too. "The early results just came in from the blood spatters in your apartment, Lena. Female, type 0 negative; male, type AB positive. You think that guy with the bandage on his ear is Mr. AB?"

"The odds are strong."

"Just so you know, we have the plate numbers on all the vehicles at the compound, including a couple of cars that were parked there last week when we did the welfare check on those kids. An Aerostar van is missing and Lieutenant Ulrich's already sent out an APB on it. Anything pops up, I'll let you know."

I gave him a peck on the cheek, my thanks for him being so gentle with the handcuffs, then waved everyone goodbye.

"What now?" Jimmy asked, as we drove out of the cop shop parking lot into the deep night. A gentle rain had started to fall. Reflections of street lights glimmered off blacktops.

"We go back to my apartment and wait."

"But…"

"There's no point in driving up and down the streets of Scottsdale looking for Madeline. Prophet Shupe isn't stupid, and he won't have told the God Squad to stash her anywhere near the compound. Now that they're aware Band-Aid Man can be I.D.'d as one of her kidnappers, Shupe will order the bastards to let her go." In other words, he'd decide that the kidnap conviction of one of his believers was preferable to a homicide conviction.

For the next few hours, while awaiting news from the cops, Jimmy and I kept ourselves sane by straightening up my apartment. I mopped up blood and vomit, he hammered the leg back onto the coffee table. After flattening all my empty moving cartons—who needed them now, anyway?—I put them in a large pile, then reorganized Madeline's slides. Jimmy dumped a pile of ripped-up magazines on top of the moving cartons. We both drank coffee until our hands shook.

"I can't stand this," Jimmy said, replacing a sofa pillow as pale sunlight began to filter through the blinds.

"Neither can I."

"We've got to do something. Just thinking about Maddy…"

"We are doing something. We're waiting."

"Hell."

"You got that right."

We began straightening again, repositioning tables, chairs, pillows, and magazines. By the time we gave up, we'd rearranged the furniture four times and vacuumed the carpet twice. Despite my attempts with Resolve, the bloodstains remained.

"Have to get a new carpet," I mused aloud.

"Berber or pile?"

"Berber's pretty."

Jimmy stared at the ruined rug. "I like the way pile feels on my bare feet."

"Pile it is, then."

"Not that I'll be running through it barefoot or anything."

"That would be a sight."

"Then again, there's wood planking. They're using wood from demolished barns now. Bet that looks great."

I shook my head. "Wood flooring isn't appropriate for a second-story apartment. Too noisy."

"The only thing below you is Desert Investigations, and I won't complain."

"You never complain about anything. Except, maybe, me."

"That's not fair. I…"

The phone rang.

Jimmy and I almost knocked each other down getting to it. Elbowing him away from the receiver, I picked up the phone.

It was Madeline.

Chapter Twenty-one

The cops and the EMT's had long since beat us to the biker bar where Madeline had turned up. Gringo's Knife & Gun Club, located off SR-86, halfway between the town of Sells and the Mexican border, had—like most biker bars—a reputation for unseemly doings. It was possible that the God Squad, when dumping Madeline in the desert nearby, believed that if she somehow made it to the bar, the bikers would finish what Hiram's men had started. If so, they'd miscalculated.

Bikers have mothers, too.

When I ran into Gringo's, it took a moment for my eyes to adjust from the bright desert morning to the dim interior light. Stale beer, cigarettes, coffee, and another sharp but unidentified smell assaulted my nostrils. On the jukebox, Bob Seger growled something about running against the wind. As my eyes adjusted, shapes coalesced from the darkness: women with too-knowing expressions, men with the faces of medieval torturers. They looked like they'd been partying all night.

"There she is!" Jimmy shouted, pointing.

At the end of the long bar I saw a conglomeration of cops, EMTs and rough-looking men standing around the table where Madeline sat, puffy-faced, wrapped in a baby blue blanket. As the EMTs took her vitals and a cop talked into his radio, an enormous bald man clad in leather and tattoos leaned over her solicitously. "Ready for more hot coffee, hon?"

Madeline nodded a head that was now as bald as the biker's. "Thanks, Snake."

When I rushed forward, the biker looked around. "You the daughter?"

I nodded, put my arms around her, and leaned onto her breastless chest. She smelled faintly of bleach.

"Don't cry, Lena. I'm fine. These nice folks've been taking good care of me."

"I'm not crying. I'm just cold."

"Liar."

While giving Madeline a cup of coffee that had been handed along the bar in a biker-style water brigade, Snake explained, "She stumbled in here naked a couple of hours ago, told us she'd been kidnapped, drugged, and dumped in the desert. When she came to, she said, she wandered around until she heard our jukebox. Greasy Ed over there had just bought a blanket at the swap meet down the road, so we wrapped her up and poured hot coffee down her. Looks like she'd been out there half the night in the rain. Shitty way to treat a lady."

Madeline must have seen the question in my eyes, because she said, "I wasn't raped, just force-fed some pills, and God only knows what they were. But tell me this. Why did those men have to strip me down, shave my head, and douse me in bleach? Wasn't hitting me over the head and drugging me enough? Damn pervs."

Once I was certain I could talk without making a further fool of myself, I answered, "They did it to get rid of everyone's DNA but yours." Quick study, that Prophet, not that bleach was guaranteed to wash away DNA—just blood. I wanted to rage against him, but the detective in me asserted itself. "Before you passed out, did you get a good look at any of them?"

She shook her head. Not only was it bald, but it had been shaved by someone who obviously wasn't used to doing it, because her scalp was covered in nicks and scrapes; the whole mess was crowned by a large purple knot. Lower, I saw a bruise forming near her eye, and scabbed-over cut on her jaw. If it hadn't been raining, she might have sported bleach burns, too. Band-Aid Man had better hope he never ran into me again.

Oblivious to my revenge fantasy, Madeline answered, "Sorry to disappoint you, but when those guys, there were three of them, broke into your apartment, they were all wearing masks. The Halloween type, you know? Like I told the deputies, there was Wile E. Coyote, Tweety Bird, and Batman. It was all pretty confusing, what with them yelling stuff about you needing to keep your nose where it belonged, and tossing around all your pretty furniture. I remember thinking that the masks were a good sign, that it meant they probably didn't plan on killing me. I'll tell you this, though. I got my own back by biting the guy wearing the Tweety Bird mask on the ear. Boy, you should've heard the sissy scream. But then they crammed those pills down me, jammed the pillow case over my head, and the next thing I knew I was in Dreamland. When I woke up I was freezing my ass off in the desert."

At that point, after letting me have Madeline to myself for a few moments, Jimmy thrust himself forward and she rewarded him with a hug, cooing, "What a nice boy you are, worrying about me like this."

"Geez, Maddy, we thought..." His voice on the verge of breaking, Jimmy shut up. But he didn't let go of her hand.

The Pima County deputies, silent until now, began asking me questions. I answered truthfully, right down to the details of my arrest for misdemeanor assault. The deputy in charge, his badge said ASHTON, seemed amused. "Interesting way of collecting DNA evidence. I might try it some time. From that bleach smell on her, though, it looks like they figured out why you did what you did. But there might not be any uncontaminated DNA left, what with the bikers fussing over her. And, considering all the hugging that's been going on, yours and Mr. Sisiwan's DNA will have added to the soup."

I reminded him that because Madeline bit Tweety Bird on the ear, there was a chance one attacker's DNA remained lodged between her teeth.

"Washed down by a gallon of biker coffee. But we'll see."

At the end of a brief interview, the EMT's loaded Madeline onto a stretcher and wheeled her out to the ambulance. I climbed in with her, and after finding out which hospital we were headed for, told Jimmy to meet us there. At one point during the drive, which to Madeline's child-like excitement was conducted with the siren screaming, I gave some thought to the location.

Prophet Shupe ran a big compound in Mexico, where given the Federales bribe-friendly practices, his followers were seldom bothered. But that didn't necessarily mean anything. The Prophet was cagey enough to misdirect the authorities by having his men drive Madeline south, dump her, then turn around and head north to Second Zion or even one of his compounds in Canada. Regardless of which way he'd worked it, we might never see Band-Aid Man again.

"You're about to break my hand, sweetie," Madeline said, interrupting my thoughts.

I relaxed my fingers. "How are you feeling?"

"Like those women in Picasso's *Demoiselles d'Avignon,* all twisted around. I've survived worse, so comparatively speaking, last night was no big deal. But…" A crease of worry crept between her bloodshot eyes. "But you look more upset than ever. What's wrong?"

"Nothing."

I'd just realized that loving me could be harmful to others.

After a variety of tests, Madeline was pronounced sound enough to leave the hospital. As we headed for the parking lot, we were waylaid by a camera crew from a Tucson TV station. Clad in borrowed scrubs, she submitted to a brief interview, which made me proud of her courage, but I was frustrated by her seeming calm. Didn't she realize how close she had come to getting killed? Didn't she want to go back to my apartment, shower, crawl into bed, and cry for an hour? Or ten?

I sure did.

After she waved the press a cheery goodbye, Jimmy hustled her into his truck. Madeline seemed drowsy during the ride, perhaps because of the lingering effects of whatever drugs her abductors had given her, but when we reached my apartment and she saw her slides on the coffee table, she came alert.

"Oh, crap. I missed this morning's appointment at Shadow Mountain Gallery. Guess I'd better give Perez a call and tell him what happened. I'll be damned if, on top of everything else those pervs did to me, I let them screw my chances for a show."

Despite my protests, she called the gallery, gave the director a highly expurgated version of the night's events, adding that if he didn't believe her, to watch the five o'clock news. Then she listened for a while, and when she hung up, a smile warmed her battered face.

"Perez says he'll have a contract ready for me to sign tomorrow, and he might even be able to arrange an opening as early as next month. I guess what they say is true—there *is* no such thing as bad publicity."

Chapter Twenty-two

"Hey, Country Boy. You know sumthin' 'bout this?"

Jonah had always tried to tune out his talkative cellmate, but now Crazy Al rattled the newspaper right in front of his eyes. If he did that one more time, Jonah was going to…going to… going to what? Fucker was *huge*. "Don't know nothing about nothing," he grumbled. "Take that thing away."

"Can't read, can you, Country Boy? So I'm gonna read it *for* you, let you know what kinda shit your friends been up to."

Jonah tried to close his ears but found it impossible. Crazy Al's voice was too loud, and if truth be told, too scary-big to hit.

In a voice almost as large as his physique, Crazy Al intoned, "Headline says '*Artist claims kidnap by polygamists.*' Now we move onta the story, Country Boy, and you better be payin' attention, 'cause it's all about you folks. My woman Tracy delivers newspapers and brings me a leftover every time when she visits, like this morning. She's one smart woman, got her GED and startin' college next fall, gonna get a big degree, gonna make something of herself. 'But don't you forget your Al,' I told her. 'Don't you be thinkin' you're gettin' too good for him, 'cause…'"

Kidnap? Polygamists? Despite his fear of the big man, Jonah interrupted him. "If you're gonna read the damned newspaper, get to it. I'm not interested in your woman."

Crazy Al snorted. "Not interested in *any* woman, is what I hear."

If anybody else had said that, Jonah would have knocked him through the wall, but the man had at least a hundred pounds on him. And wasn't he in for attempted murder? Almost tore some guy's head off with his bare hands or something? "Just read, okay?"

Smiling an evil smile, Crazy Al read.

"Tucson—AP. *Artist claims kidnap by polygamists.* Oh, yeah. Tracy told me that AP stands for Associated Press, that another paper wrote the story but they let this one had it. Weird, huh?"

Jonah closed his eyes. "If you say so."

"Where was I? Ah. *Madeline Grissom, 62, an artist visiting Scottsdale from New York, claimed she was abducted by three polygamists on Thursday and dropped off in the desert near Sells sometime late Friday morning before turning up at a biker bar. In an interview with a Tucson television station, Grissom said that a northern Arizona polygamy leader known as Prophet Hiram Shupe might have orchestrated the kidnapping, and had it carried out by a group of local polygamists presently residing in Scottsdale. She added that her abductors wore Halloween masks of Tweety Bird, Wile E. Coyote, and Batman.*

"When asked to comment on Grissom's claims, Lieutenant Dagny Ulrich, of the Scottsdale Police Department, said that an investigation was ongoing, in concert with the Pima County Sheriff's Office.

"'We did find evidence that a crime may have been committed, but at this point, we're still waiting on test results,' Lieutenant Ulrich said.

"An unnamed police source said that the apartment from which Grissom was allegedly abducted is owned by Scottsdale private investigator Lena Jones. When contacted, Jones refused comment.

"Grissom, a former resident of Phoenix, was at one time known for her colorful abstract paintings, and used to be represented by Brent Goodson Halworth Galleries. She has not shown her work there for several years."

"'Tastes in art change over time,' said Brent Goodson Hallworth. 'Ms. Grissom came in here a few days ago looking for representation

again, but I had to tell her no, her work was dated. When an artist falls out of favor, they sometimes resort to publicity stunts to put them back in the spotlight. I'm not saying definitely that's what Ms. Grissom has done here, which would be slander, but stranger things have happened. This business about the Halloween masks and the polygamists, for instance. That's exactly the kind of tall tale an out-of-stater looking for free publicity might dream up. Anyone who lives in Scottsdale these days knows quite well we don't have polygamists.'"

As soon as Crazy Al stopped reading, he shoved the story toward Jonah again. "So what you got to say 'bout this, Country Boy? Is that what you polygamy folks're into now, grabbing women right off the streets? What, you guys ain't got enough women of your own?"

When Jonah remained silent, Crazy Al slapped him across the face with the newspaper. "Answer me, Country Boy!"

Jonah took the abuse for a while, then, his mind made up, twisted out of Crazy Al's reach and ran to the cell door.

"Guard!" he yelled. "I got to talk to somebody!"

Chapter Twenty-three

Jail food must have agreed with him, because Jonah looked healthier than the last time I visited. Three squares for seven days had filled out his face, and his withdrawal tics had eased. After telling me about the compound's installation in Scottsdale almost a year earlier, and how he and a cousin had wound up on the Phoenix streets, he launched into a long tirade about Hiram and Ezra Shupe.

"I musta been as stupid as people been saying I was, because I really believed Prophet Shupe was The Living Presence of God on Earth 'cause he says he is, but after a few days in here and hearing what other people got to say about shit like that, I been thinking it's all a crock. Ain't no God, least not one here on Earth, just liars trying to get everybody else's women and money. Brother Ezra, he's just as bad, even meaner than the Prophet. Maybe he's the one killed my mother. Otherwise, how come my little shove killed her? Yeah, I shouldn't a shoved her, and anybody who hurts his momma needs to go straight to Hell like I'm gonna go, but after she fell down, she got right up and seemed okay, wasn't even bleeding. Maybe Crazy Al's right, that it takes a lot more than a shove to kill somebody, even a woman. Is he telling the truth, Miss Jones?"

Since I didn't know Crazy Al, I couldn't trust his interpretation of how much force it took to kill someone, but I trusted the medical examiner's findings enough to reassure Jonah of his innocence. "The M.E. found wood splinters in your mother's head, so the chances that you killed your mother just by pushing her down are slim to none. When I found her, she'd been beaten repeatedly. Remember, you may have given her that shove in front of the compound, but I found her body a half-mile away."

He shook his head. "That ain't right. Last time I saw her, she was going through the gate, back to that pig Ezra."

"More proof that you didn't kill her."

"You swear?"

I raised my right hand. "Swear."

I gave him a few minutes to cry it all out. Even though his cold-hearted mother had rejected him, Jonah still loved her. His language might have taken on the roughness of the times, but deep down he was still little more than a scared kid who belonged in a remedial reading class, not hustling his ass on the streets. As soon as his tears subsided, I repeated my previous offer of assistance. All I needed was a statement from him that I could take to his court-appointed attorney.

"You tell me what all you want me to say, and I'll say it."

I held back a sigh. When someone was raised on lies, they lost the capacity to distinguish between fact and imagination, so for the next few minutes I held a crash course on the differences between "I saw" and "I think." "Tell me *only* what you actually saw with your own eyes. Then we'll go into what you've heard and you suspect. For starters, who might have had a grudge against your mother?"

He looked appalled. "Ain't no one hold a grudge against her! My momma was the kindest, sweetest person ever lived!"

To my way of thinking, kind, sweet women didn't abandon their children just because someone ordered them to, but I wasn't about to say that to Jonah. He felt miserable enough. "Even mothers can have enemies. How about Ezra? Or the rest of the God Squad? She ever have a run-in with any of them?"

"Mama always did what she was told. She stayed sweet, like a good wife should."

Stayed *sweet*, a polygamist's term for an obedient woman. For all his recent experiences on the street, Jonah still saw the world through a polygamist's eyes. As for the *wife* bit, according to Arizona law, Celeste was no man's wife. She'd never actually been married to either Prophet Shupe or his brother Ezra. Polygamists didn't bother with little details like marriage certificates and state-sanctioned ceremonies, which was why they were usually able to evade bigamy charges. Not that Jonah knew the difference. All he knew was that when the Prophet gave a girl to a man, the girl was that man's wife—until the Prophet changed his mind again, which he so frequently did.

"How did your mother get along with her sister-wives?"

"Perfect."

"No spats?" I remembered Opal, and her heavy-handed rule over Darnelle and Josie. "Say, over cooking oil?"

"What goes on in kitchens is women's business, not men's."

"Let me be more specific. How'd your mother get along with Opal?"

"Perfect."

"With Darnelle?"

"Perfect."

"Josie?"

"Perfect."

It was hopeless. The boy remembered only what he wanted to remember. Now that Celeste was dead, he had transformed his mother into an impossibly perfect creature who'd never drawn a disagreeable breath. A woman myself, I knew what hogwash that was. The situation reminded me of the Kurosawa film, *Rashomon*, the story of a rape and murder told through the individual points of view of the people involved: the woman, the bandit, the woodcutter, and with the help of a psychic, even the murdered man. Each person related the events differently, and in the end, the audience was left to puzzle over the ancient question—what is truth?

I brought the conversation back to Ezra, his mother's putative husband. There I struck a nerve. Jonah ranted about Ezra's treatment of his women and children, pausing at one point to describe a particularly nasty beating after Darnelle inadvertently spilled a glass of milk. If Jonah was being straight with me, and I believed he was, he'd witnessed enough violence to support charges of domestic abuse. The women would probably deny they'd been beaten, but the tape Jimmy had made of Prophet Shupe hitting Darnelle might mitigate those denials. In this state, a woman didn't have to press charges against her batterer for the state to prosecute. Of course, getting a conviction when the woman refused to testify was always problematical.

More promising were the names Jonah gave me of the companies that regularly used Ten Spot Construction, and by doing so, employed underage workers. That would bring the Feds in, and the Feds were always interested in prosecuting sources of illegal income.

The best part of my jailhouse visit was in securing Jonah's promise to start cooperating with the investigation. "I'll even talk to the cops right now if you want," he said.

"Let's hold off on that for a while. I want to call your attorney first and relate this conversation. Then we'll work on getting you out of here."

Before bringing the interview to a close, I attempted to engage the boy in a discussion about his après-jail release, where he might go, where he might stay. His plan, he told me, was to return to the apartment where he'd been staying with a cousin and several other young men. When I pressed for an address and his cousin's name, he turned cagey.

"Ain't about to bring Mesh...him into this mess. He got enough trouble. I been helping take care of him, and I'm gonna keep on doing that."

While Jonah's loyalty to his cousin was admirable, it wouldn't fly with a bail bondsman. I knew there was no apartment, no real address. According to the cops, he'd been squatting in an abandoned building with a group of other street hustlers. When I explained this to him, he just shrugged.

"I'll come up with somethin'. Last time I saw her, Mama told me, 'Jonah, you're old enough and smart enough to take care of yourself.'"

Later, when emerging from the fluorescent-lit jail into the soft twilight, I realized that the more I learned about Celeste, the less I knew her.

But I'd already decided this much: I didn't like her.

Chapter Twenty-four

"You sure this is the right time to be doing this, Maddy?" Jimmy, crammed into the back of my Jeep as we cruised along SR-60, couldn't get over the fact that only two days after Madeline had been kidnapped, she was determined to drive out to the property near Florence Junction.

"The desert is a natural tranquilizer," she answered.

"Bet you didn't feel like that when you woke up naked out there," I said, sharing Jimmy's concerns. Madeline needed to be back at the apartment recovering her senses. Not that her senses appeared addled. To the contrary, she exuded a Zen-like calm, as reflected by her tee-shirt-of-the-day which proclaimed, "WHATEVER." Its orange background clashed hideously with her turquoise wig.

We were headed toward the property Jimmy said his cousin might consider selling to "the right buyer." In Arizona-speak, that meant he'd sell only if the prospective buyer was an un-annoying type who loved the wide open spaces as much as he did. As we sped along, tall saguaros whipped past us, their arms lifted skyward. In the distance, lavender mountains thrust themselves from the wild-flower dotted desert floor. The March rains had encouraged a profusion of blooms, and vast fields of beavertail cactus sprouted their gaudy pink flowers as a carpet of yellow cream cups and purple owl flower crept toward them.

"Looks just like a painting," Madeline said.

"Not *your* paintings," Jimmy grumped from the back. "All those grays and browns. Talk about muted." He'd only seen Madeline's recent work, not her earlier bright canvases.

Still that beatific smile. "My palette might be broadening soon. Especially if I move out here."

A while back, we'd passed a desert nursery, where various species of cacti uprooted by storms and construction were stored until they could be sold. Other than that, we hadn't seen any signs of human habitation for miles, unless you counted the big E-Bar-B Ranch sign and the barbed wire fencing that snaked along its perimeter.

Just as I began to think we might have passed the sale property, Jimmy called out, "There! That dirt road up ahead on the left. Pull in."

I saw only a faintly-visible double rut ending at a deep arroyo. "But it peters out at the wash."

"Which is why Ernest wants to sell."

"To the right buyer," Madeline amended.

I pulled onto the abandoned road. After we'd descended from the Jeep, we stood there enjoying the sweet desert air and spectacular view, which except for a large barn at the far end of the property, continued unhindered all the way to the mountains. The property was as pretty as Ernest had described it over the phone. Saguaros, prickly pear, and cholla dappled the ground. By a happy chance of nature, even more wildflowers bloomed here than at any of the spots we'd passed, perhaps because cattle never got the a chance to gobble up the seedlings.

"Paradise Lost," I said, thinking of all those hungry cows.

Madeline laughed. "For me, it's Paradise Found."

"*If* you don't sleepwalk into that arroyo and break your neck." Jimmy walked over to the edge of the new ravine carved out by last winter's unusually torrential rains. Ending at a culvert under the highway, the deep fissure began several hundred yards to the northeast, where it had been birthed by the main arroyo that snaked to the west. Between those two sometimes-rivers lay this isosceles triangle of land with the highway at its base. Both ravines looked so perilous that Jimmy's cousin had erected a double thickness of barbed wire to keep his cattle from falling in.

As I scanned the landscape, I noticed the lack of houses, trailers, or any other signs of human habitation. "It's awfully lonely out here, Madeline. Would you feel safe?"

A wry smile. "There I was in your apartment, in the middle of beautiful downtown Scottsdale, minding my own business, and thus—at least theoretically—perfectly safe, when all of a sudden three masked men broke in and…"

I sighed.

"You see, Lena? Safety is relative, not absolute. Now let's check out that barn. It's the right size for a living space-cum-studio."

In a phone call the evening before, Ernest Sisiwan had told Madeline that the barn, which he'd built last spring, had originally been meant for hay storage. But then the rains came, cutting it off from easy access to his ranch. One-and-a-half stories high and with a good-sized loft, the barn was now little more than an empty rectangle resting on a cement foundation.

"It even looks like a studio," Madeline said. It was obvious her mind was already made up.

A few minutes later we were in the sprawling living room of the E-Bar-B ranch house as Madeline went over paperwork with Ernest and Bess Sisiwan.

"No new construction," Ernest said. "All you can do is fix up what's already there." Due to his Anglo mother, his face wasn't quite as dark as Jimmy's. His children's faces—I counted five, ranging from a toddler to a pre-teen—were even paler, due to their own Anglo mother. Bess Sisiwan, a cheerful thirty-something with auburn hair, appeared thrilled at the prospect of getting rid of the unusable tract, especially given the amount of money Madeline was prepared to pay. Contingent upon the sale of the New York house, of course.

"I need lots of glass on the barn's northern exposure."

"Sounds reasonable to me," Ernest rumbled, making a note on the contract. Like Jimmy, he was a big man with a soft voice.

"And I'll want to put sealant on the wood siding to keep it from rotting."

"As long as you don't paint it purple, you have my blessings." Another note.

The property turned out not to be as isolated as we'd thought. The Sisiwans' ranch house was less than a mile away, although hidden on the other side of a gentle rise and further disguised by a row of cottonwoods. If for some reason Madeline ran into trouble, help was just down the road. And if she became lonely, the Sisiwans said she could drop by any time, although she might get drafted to haul around a few hay bales.

"To the side of that desert nursery you passed on the way here, there's a small coffee shop where the locals get together," Bess added, pulling a fussy toddler onto her lap.

Madeline looked up from the contract she was studying. "What locals?"

Bess smiled. "Oh, you'd be surprised how many of you artist types live out here."

At that, Madeline signed the contract without further ado.

After dropping Jimmy off at his trailer on the Pima reservation, Madeline and I continued on to my apartment above Desert Investigations. Within minutes she was on the phone to a New York real estate broker friend. While they talked, I realized it was time for me to straighten out my own living situation.

The relationship with Warren being effectively over, it was time to return the few things he'd left in the bedroom closet: a pair of jeans, two tee shirts, an expensive-looking silk sport coat. Then there was the key to that damned Paradise Valley house; it still dangled on my key ring. I folded Warren's clothes into one of the unused packing boxes I hadn't yet carted down to the Dumpster, started to punch in his number on my cell, then killed the call. Just looking at the sport coat brought a lump to my throat. Best to get things over with.

I called out to Madeline, "Be back in an hour."

She look briefly, gave me a wave, then returned to her phone conversation.

The sun reached its zenith as I steered up the narrow road leading up to the house. Pool parties were in full swing, including—as it turned out—at Warren's place. But no children's voices floated over the pool fence to me, just those of several raucous adults. Were the twins inside? I'd miss them, I belatedly realized. Well, it couldn't be helped. Perhaps I'd be able to see them after one of *Desert Eagle*'s production meetings.

I shifted the carton into one hand and used my key to open the pool gate. "Warren, I brought…"

I stopped.

A bikinied blonde with impressive breasts lounged on a chaise next to Warren. The fact that she vaguely resembled me didn't make the moment any less painful.

When Warren's eyes met mine, there was no apology in them nor any accusation. He'd already moved on. It was time for me to do the same.

"I brought your things," was all I said.

"Including the key?"

I held it up.

"Good. Leave everything there."

I started to say something, then stopped. Warren's love life was his to handle as he pleased, but I hadn't realized he'd get started again so quickly.

.

Chapter Twenty-five

Madeline slept in Monday morning so I kept the bedroom door shut as I dressed for work, which in my case simply meant pulling on a clean black tee shirt, a new pair of black jeans, and my photographer's vest. While eating a hasty bowl of Total in front of the TV, my gloomy mood lifted somewhat when CNN announced that an agreement ending the screenwriters' strike had finally been reached.

An hour later I was on the phone to Angel, who as Hollywood folks go, was considered an early riser. "How soon before you start filming again?" I hoped it would be a location shoot somewhere in Arizona, which would help keep threatening letters away.

"First thing next week, so be ready to attend a production meeting this Friday, same place, same time. Oh, and there's other good news. The judge signed an emergency order transferring Nevitt to an in-patient mental health clinic, where he's going to get the treatment he needs."

I murmured that that was indeed good news, especially since the letter writer would now have to stop. I had my theory as to the writer's identity, but no proof. It didn't matter. Halting the letters was the important thing. If they ever started up again, which I doubted, I'd share my suspicions about Stuart Jenks with the police. I thought about telling Angel, then decided against it. She still had to work comfortably with the sonofabitch, so the less she knew, the better.

"But I was saving the best news for last," Angel continued, happily oblivious to the truth about her business associate. "Warren brought my babies back!"

My mouth fell open. Only a few days ago he'd been talking about suing for full custody. "When did this happen?"

"Late last night. He just showed up at my house with them in tow, and after they'd toddled off to their rooms, explained that he'd suddenly become too busy to give them the time they deserve."

What made him so busy; the new blonde? But perhaps I was being unfair. "Did he explain what changed?"

"Apparently he's come up with an idea for another documentary. About stars and their stalkers."

Oh, Jesus. "How do you feel about that, Angel?"

A low laugh. "At first I was shocked, but the more I thought about it, the more I realized it was a story that should be told. He's bringing over a film crew next weekend and will start the project with my interview."

Hooray for Hollywood, where personal trauma and film projects merged into one. "Well, good luck." Just as I was about to ring off—after all, I'd see her again at Friday's production meeting—something she'd said finally registered. "Wait a minute. You said he came by your house. Does that mean you're out of the Beverly Wilshire already? How does the Black Monk feel about that?"

Her voice took on a hard edge. "How Otto feels doesn't matter."

Poor Otto. I wondered if she knew he loved her, then decided she probably did. Angel didn't miss much, except when it came to villainous producers.

I sighed. "See you Friday, then."

And I rang off.

While I was still digesting our conversation and the sharp turns my own life had taken over the past couple of weeks, the phone rang. It was Jonah's attorney. Although murder charges might still be pending, the judge was cutting the kid loose for now.

"He'll be through Processing in about an hour. The bonds-man you set up for him gave him a strong talking-to, but he'll forget it in a New York minute if he goes back to his old haunts. Didn't you say you'd found a possible placement for him?"

True. We made arrangements for me to pick Jonah up at the jail, and less than two hours later, I delivered him to the same safe house where I'd taken Clayton.

Bernie, a volunteer with a careworn face, said Clayton was in his room studying, and while he went off to get him, Jonah and I settled ourselves in the large day room, which had been furnished entirely by donations. As usual in such cases, the room was a polyglot horror of styles, with the early Sixties represented by a massive kidney-shaped coffee table; the Seventies by a U-shaped, screaming-gold velour sectional; the Eighties by a green-plaid La-Z-Boy armchair; and the Nineties by two ersatz Laura Ashley-flowered love seats. This millennium was represented by a thirty-seven-inch flat screen TV tuned to the Discovery Channel.

"Man, this is classy," Jonah said.

Saving me from a reply, Bernie arrived with Clayton. The surprise reunion between the two was so emotional that we left them to it. After all, boys don't cry—at least not when someone's watching.

While the two blubbered over each other, Bernie took me into his office, which was no more stylish than the day room but considerably smaller. Photographs of the safe house's "graduates" covered the wall. Smiling boys stood with their arms around new families. Other boys posed in front of college dorms. In one of the photographs, I recognized ASU, my own old alma mater.

After taking a seat on a rickety chair, I went into more detail about Jonah's time on the Phoenix streets.

"Drugs? Well, of course the kid's using," Bernie responded. "How else do you think he could stand his life? He needs a treatment program. There's an opening in a state-funded rehab facility that I know of, and if he agrees, we'll take him over there tonight. When he completes treatment, he can come back here, and we'll start him on the same remedial education classes track Clayton's in. Speaking of Clayton, by the way, it's going to be a while before he'll be ready to take the GED test. His education's too deficient, especially in history, science, and economics—not to mention the fine arts. Fortunately he's emotionally healthy, mainly because you got to him before the street did. Jonah's a different story. That boy's going to have a rough road ahead, but having his friend here will help."

"Actually, they're half-brothers. Same father—Hiram Shupe—different mothers."

Bernie grunted. "Jonah's taller and heavier, but now that you mention it, they do have similar features. What else can you tell me about their background?"

"Not much, I'm afraid. Just the usual polygamy upbringing. I've met Clayton's mother and she seems like a nice person. As for Jonah's mother Celeste, I never met her. While she was alive, that is."

"Par for the course in these cases." Bernie already knew that Celeste had been murdered, and that I was the person who found the body.

My inability to tell Bernie anything about Celeste started me thinking about all the problems I'd had getting information. Prophet Shupe certainly wouldn't talk to me about her, and neither would Ezra nor Opal. It was doubtful that Josie, with her limited capacity, could shed any light on the matter, and Jonah's view of his rejecting mother was more colored by guilt than fact. Even Clayton...

Wait. When I'd driven Clayton away from the work gang, I'd been so concerned about getting him to safety that we'd not discussed his family situation. I wasn't even certain he knew Celeste was dead. Time to rectify that.

Misty-eyed happiness still radiated from both boys when Bernie and I went back to the day room. Although Jonah tried to disguise his up with a manly scowl, he still looked like a kid on Christmas morning.

"Jonah, Bernie needs you to fill out some forms. Do you mind?"

A quick nod. "See you in a few, bro," Jonah said, giving Clayton a friendly fist-bump.

As soon as the older boy followed Bernie down the hall, I settled myself next to Clayton on the sofa. "How much do you know about Celeste?"

He looked down. "My mother told me that she's gone to see our Father in Heaven."

At least I wouldn't have to break that news to him. "Did your mother tell you what happened?"

A shrug, which I took to be a yes. "How well did you know Celeste?"

He looked at me in shock. "I don't know nothing about her! Brother Ezra don't allow the women to mix with the men, so I just mainly saw her when she was serving breakfast and dinner. But I'm sure none of the family ki...uh, did that to her."

"She never argued with anyone?"

He twisted his hands, a tell that he was about to lie. "Oh, no. She kept sweet."

Kept sweet. There was that damned phrase again.

"No woman 'stays sweet' all the time."

"Our women do."

And I'm an aardvark. "C'mon, Clayton. I can tell that you know more than you're saying."

He sighed. "Well, okay, I guess she did argue with Opal once. It started off kinda funny."

"Funny how?"

"It was over food! Opal was in the kitchen with all the other women, making up the shopping list, and Celeste wanted her to add a bag of potato chips. Opal said no, but Celeste kept on begging, saying that she needed them, that she was having strong cravings, or some such. When Opal heard that, wow, she hauled off and smacked Celeste across the face."

"You actually saw this?" Opal sure as hell didn't 'keep sweet.' Cravings weren't abnormal for a pregnant woman, but apparently Opal felt little sympathy.

"Naw, I just heard it. So did Brother Ezra. We men was eatin' supper at the time, and all that screaming and crying really got him mad, so he went into the kitchen and it sounded like he slapped everybody in there."

One perpetrator, mass punishment. Ezra liked hitting women. Before I could ask another question, Clayton leaned forward, a worried look on his face. "Uh, Miss, now that we're talking, maybe you can help me with something that's been bothering me. Since you brought me here, I been watching a lot of TV, and it's most always turned to the Discovery Channel. Yesterday they was doing this program on geenics…"

"Genetics," I corrected.

"Yeah, geenics. Anyway, they was talking about this family out in Tennessee or some place, and this family was all the time marrying between themselves, and there was a lot of things wrong with the kids. Cripples. Retards. Stuff like that."

No mystery to where we were headed. "Studies have shown that when closely related men and women marry, their children run a high risk of birth defects. Profound mental retardation is just one of them."

"Is that what happened to Josie?"

Josie, the pretty but blank-faced young woman I'd seen with Opal and Darnelle at Frugal Foods. "Were her parents related?"

He had trouble meeting my eyes. "First cousins."

This was hardly surprising, given that most people in the polygamy compounds were related to each other by one degree or another. "Distant cousins can marry and not have problems, but if first cousins marry, or brother and sister, or uncle and niece, grandfather and granddaughter and whatever, birth defects are a distinct possibility."

He looked down at the scuffed linoleum floor. "Prophet Shupe and Opal is brother and sister."

Hoping I hadn't heard right, I asked, "*Full* brother and sister? Or half, like you and Jonah—same father but different mothers?" Not much better.

The tips of his ears glowed red. "Same mother, same father. And they got several kids can't even talk, just grunt. That's why they was all left up at Second Zion. The Prophet only wanted healthy-looking folks down here. Or at least, people that didn't look any worse than Josie."

Polygamists don't view congenital defects as problems, but not because of any compassion they might feel toward those afflicted. No, it all came down to money. Although the government had curtailed straight-out Welfare payments to several years total per woman, *not* per child, genetically-damaged children continued to draw monthly SSI payments for the rest of their lives. But since incest brought so much extra government money into the compound, something confused me.

"If Shupe and Opal—his sister—were able to have so many children with birth defects and get all that government money, why did he reassign her to Ezra?"

"Oh, The Prophet always does that when a woman is getting close to, uh, the end of her, you know." He looked away in embarrassment.

"The end of her periods, as in menopause?"

"Yeah."

In other words, once Shupe's cash cows dried up, he was through with them, and his hand-me-downs became his brother's wives. "Your own mother—Darnelle—is still young. I happen to know she used to be with the Prophet, so why'd he reassign her to Ezra?"

"Because of the First Revelation."

I thought back to what little I knew about the Bible, and vaguely remembered a story about a wife being passed from one brother to the next. As I recalled, it was because the first brother died. Then again, maybe I was mixing that story up with another.

"Maybe you'd better tell me about that First Revelation, Clayton. My biblical knowledge is pretty much zilch."

"When the Old Prophet died…"

"Wait a minute. Which prophet are we talking about here? Hiram's father?"

From the research I'd necessarily done on Arizona's polygamist compounds, I knew that Jeremiah Shupe, who'd been reputed to be even crazier than his crazy son, had reigned over Second Zion for almost forty years. Prone, like his son, to fits that seemed more epileptic than divine in nature, he'd delivered revelation after revelation, most of them on that favorite topic of fundamentalists everywhere, the End of Days. But his revelations were invariably followed by new "commandments," such as the one his followers had to turn three times in a clockwise direction before going to bed in order to "slip free of demons." Another ordered that no one, not even children, drink anything after sundown; another directed the women to...

Oh, there were just too many commandments to keep up with.

"Yes, Miss, Jeremiah was our Prophet's father. After Prophet Jeremiah ascended into Heaven, God told our new Prophet to reassign all the women and kids, even the babies. And Prophet Shupe always follows the word of God."

"Did God tell Shupe *why* he needed to reassign all the women and children?"

"To atone for what his daddy done. You know, Prophet Jeremiah."

I felt more bewildered than ever. "What did Jeremiah do?"

"Causing all them people to get sick, you know. Babies died. And the men, after they got sick, some of them couldn't give their wives any new babies. Surely you heard about that."

It all came back to me then. After emerging from one of his many seizures, Prophet Jeremiah had called an emergency meeting of everyone at Second Zion. He said God had revealed to him that the U.S. government was using tainted medicine to wipe out of people of Second Zion. That was the reason so many of the children were sickly, because they were the issue of mothers and fathers who had held out their arms to clinic needles and gave their babies any medicine handed them by the

Satan-influenced medical establishment. Jeremiah then ordered his followers to bury all their medications, even their aspirin, to stay away from the county health clinics, but most importantly, to stop having their children vaccinated.

If a child fell ill, Prophet Jeremiah promised, God would provide the cure.

Nothing serious happened for several months, but eventually German measles swept through the compound, followed by an outbreak of mumps. When children started dying, Prophet Jeremiah mysteriously disappeared. His followers claimed he'd ascended into Heaven, but the polygamy grapevine muttered that he'd been shot to death by a grieving father. Whatever the truth, Prophet Hiram Shupe ascended the throne. Hiram, more intelligent—if not more sane—rescinded his father's No Inoculation Commandment, but not before a total of twelve children had died and an undisclosed number of men had been rendered sterile.

Suspicion nudged at me. "How old is Ezra's youngest child?"

I could almost hear the gears grinding away in Clayton's uneducated brain. "Lemme see. Mark is almost thirteen. No, Eleanor just turned twelve and she's his youngest. Brother Ezra sent her up to Second Zion a couple months ago because she was about ready to, well, you know."

Because she was almost ready to be bred. "If Eleanor is Ezra's youngest child, who's the father of all those young children I saw at the compound?"

"They're kids who were reassigned to Brother Ezra. Four of them are Fawn Burr's children. Prophet Shupe's punishing her for tryin' to run away from her husband, and he said with Brother Ezra not being able to make any more babies, there was plenty of room for them."

Poor Fawn. "It's interesting what you said about Ezra not being able to have any more children, because Celeste was pregnant when she was killed."

"A miracle from God!" His face shone with religious fervor.

Miracle wasn't the word I'd use. "You're certain that none of those other children belong to Ezra?"

At my sharpened tone, his face closed up. "Wait a minute. Miss, you ain't thinking that, uh..." Clayton was no rocket scientist, but he was a long way from being dumb.

"That Celeste was having sex with another man? It's a possibility."

"She stayed sweet!"

If I heard that phrase again, I'd throw up. "Well, they do say that God works in mysterious ways."

"He sure does!" Clayton nodded furiously, apparently unable to believe the obvious truth.

"Did you like Celeste?"

He threw me a wary look. "She was okay, I guess. Like I said, I didn't know her that much."

"Did you two ever have a personal conversation?"

A line appeared between his eyebrows, but at least his ears didn't catch fire again. "Personal? Like what?"

"Did she ever tell you how she felt about Ezra, say, or Prophet Shupe?"

"Jeepers! Why would a woman talk to me about something like that?"

Because a woman liked to share her sorrows, and an innocent young boy about to get kicked out of the compound might be considered a safe confidant. "Maybe I should rephrase the question. Did you ever hear Celeste complain about anyone?"

"Just about Opal. She didn't like her."

Who did? "When did she tell you this?"

"She never told me, Miss. I overheard it."

"When?"

"One night I was out in the yard chasing crickets, I heard her on the porch whispering to my mom. I don't think they knew I was out there."

"Did Darnelle and Celeste have a close relationship?"

"Sister-wives are always close, ain't they? And they tell each other things. Anyway, lots of times I heard them talking."

I was beginning to suspect that Clayton spent many evenings 'chasing crickets' but I knew better than to accuse him of snooping. "What kinds of things did they talk about?"

He darted a glance around the small office, as if afraid someone might be listening. Then he leaned forward and whispered, "Mainly 'bout Opal and Ezra. But…but one night I heard Celeste whispering that she was thinking 'bout runnin' off, that she had a friend who would help get her set up, somebody on the outside."

At this bombshell, it was a struggle to keep my voice level, but somehow I managed it. "A friend on the outside? How'd she meet this person?"

"Don't know, Miss. Maybe they talked through the fence, like you did with my mom."

Someone at the Kachina, then? "Did you ever hear her friend's name?"

He frowned. "Yeah, but I can't remember it. But it was a man's name, maybe a nickname. For sure, not from the Bible."

I cast my mind back to the renters at Kachina 24-Hour Storage and tried to come up with a likely prospect. The elderly man with the *Arizona Highways* magazines? A member of the rock band? Someone I'd not yet seen?

"Try to remember, Clayton. It's important." To jog his memory, I offered several currently popular, non-Biblical names. "Chad? Dennis? Keith? Brian? Maury? Harry? Scott? Charlie? Art? Ian? Eric?"

Suddenly he beamed. "I got it!"

"Which one?"

"You said 'Eric.' But that's not exactly what she called him."

"What, then?"

"It was when you said 'Eric' that I was able to remember."

I wanted to strangle him for drawing it out so long, but he was relishing his moment in the spotlight, and in his brief life, he'd been given so few chances to shine. "I knew you could do it, Clayton. You're a bright boy."

Now he positively glowed. "Thank you, Miss."

"So give me his name."

With a sigh of satisfaction, he relinquished his moment. "She called him 'Little Rick.'"

Chapter Twenty-six

The interesting thing about life is that just when you think you've got it all figured out, you realize you don't know jack shit. Who had recognized Celeste from the picture I'd shown him? Little Rick. Who had pointed me toward Frugal Foods? Little Rick.

But who, in retrospect, seemed the least likely of all possible Romeos? Little Rick.

One of the first things any good law enforcement officer learns is to not judge people by their appearance. The handsome, well-spoken Ted Bundy had been a vicious serial killer with a more-than-passing interest in necrophilia. Wyatt Earp might have paid undue attention to his wardrobe, but he'd won the shoot-out at the OK Corral. And Little Rick? Just because a man was married, middle-aged, badly overweight, and squinted at the world through Coke-bottle glasses didn't mean he couldn't fall in love. Or that someone couldn't fall in love with him.

After bidding Clayton and Jonah farewell for now, I hopped back into my Jeep and drove down to Little Rick's You-Store-It. This time I was greeted by an elderly woman in a wheelchair who sat behind the front desk. As she checked the application just completed by two young men wearing ASU tee shirts, I noticed how thin her arms were.

"Third lane on the right, fifteenth unit down," she told them "If you have trouble finding it, just ask my husband Rick for directions. Can't miss him. Real big guy, cleaning an empty unit right behind the office."

When the young men stepped outside, she looked up at me through eyes milky with cataracts. From the door, she'd appeared to be at least twenty years older than Little Rick, but close up, I noticed taut skin and lack of age spots. Her small, sharply-defined features hinted that she'd probably been pretty before disease had taken its toll.

"Looking for a storage unit?" A young woman's smile in a ravaged face.

I flashed my I.D. "I just want a word with your husband."

The smile disappeared. "About what?"

With a merciful lie, I said I'd been hired to look into a series of burglaries at a nearby self-storage company and was checking other places to see if they'd had trouble, too.

Her pale eyes narrowed, then raked my face and body. Was she, perhaps based on past incidents, sizing up the competition? "The only problem I've heard about was over at the RV storage place, and that was nothing but taggers. Kids with too much time on their hands."

Just as I started to soothe her with another lie, the back door opened and Little Rick thudded in. Although the day was unseasonably cool, his plump face shone with sweat. "Annie, did you…?" Catching sight of me, he stopped.

I repeated my original lie, then added, "Maybe we could talk outside?"

He swallowed. "Good idea." Hooking a beefy arm around mine, he hustled me out the door before his wife could object.

The layout of the storage facility was identical to that at Kachina, with approximately ten paved lanes comprised of facing units, which ranged from tiny to room-sized. Out of habit, I turned toward the right, where at Kachina my own unit would be located, but was checked by Little Rick, who hauled me to the left.

"Less crowded over here," he explained, between gasps for breath. "More long-timers. And not many's doing business there right now."

I complied with all this hustling and hauling until we reached a quiet area between lanes seven and eight, then planted my feet. "Okay, Little Rick, this is far enough. Time to come clean about your relationship with Celeste King."

The only people around were a depressed looking middle-aged couple at the far end of the row loading what appeared to be a household full of furniture out of a U-Haul trailer and into their unit. Victims of foreclosure? Or a mere redecorating job? Whatever the reason, their proximity made me feel secure.

Little Rick's voice came as little more than a whisper. "What relationship are you talking about?"

If the subject hadn't been so serious, I would have laughed in his face. "Celeste was pregnant when she was murdered."

He pretended to watch the couple, who were now dragging a worn sofa into their unit. Foreclosure, probably. When you're redecorating, you don't save junk.

Eventually Little Rick looked back at me, making a feeble attempt to seem unconcerned. "I read in the paper that she was one of those polygamists. Those women get pregnant all the time, don't they? That's their job."

Nice parry, but it didn't work. "I've acquired information that casts doubt on the possibility of her husband being the father. You need to know that during the autopsy, the medical examiner took DNA samples from the fetus, a boy. The results should be back any day now. Want me to give Scottsdale PD a call, tell them to come over here with a swab kit for a possible match? Or would you prefer to answer my questions?"

"Why should I be worried about some DNA test?"

"Because you're the father."

"You're crazy." His voice carried no conviction.

I slipped my cell phone out of my pocket and flipped it open. "I know I've got Scottsdale PD somewhere in here," I muttered.

Before I could punch up the menu, he yelled "Stop!" so loudly that the U-Haul couple turned around in astonishment. Little Rick ignored them. "Why is this any business of yours?"

I closed my cell but didn't put it away. "Because her son's about to be charged in her murder."

"Oh, God." He hung his head. "She...She was so beautiful."

And, unlike his wife, healthy. "Did you first meet at Frugal Foods? Or somewhere else?"

"She was loading groceries into a van and dropped a bag. I helped her gather everything up. She...I've never seen eyes that blue."

"Wait a minute. Are you saying that Celeste was alone?"

"They used to let her do the grocery shopping all by herself. That was before..."

"Before what?"

"Before that Opal bitch started getting suspicious."

Funny how Opal's name kept popping up. "Just go ahead and tell me everything, how your relationship started and what you planned to do about it. If I have to keep asking questions like this, we could be here all day. Myself, I have plenty of time, but I'm figuring your wife's a bit on the suspicious side."

Guilt swept across his face. "Don't judge me."

"If I used up my energy judging everyone, I'd be too tired to get out of bed in the morning."

"You promise not to say anything to my wife?"

"Seems to me she already has enough trouble. Now start talking."

He took a deep breath, then let it out in a long sigh. "I love Annie. I always have. But I loved Celeste, too, and I wanted to help her. She was..." He trailed off.

"She was what?"

Another sigh. "Desperate." He clenched his big fists and fell silent.

I reached for my cell again. "Boy, I really hate to do this."

"Okay, okay. But let's go sit over there, 'cause this'll take a while and my feet are killing me." He walked toward a picnic table set up under a mesquite tree at the end of the row. Since it remained in the sightline of the U-Haul couple, I followed. He'd been too full of surprises for me to take his seeming harmlessness for granted.

We settled ourselves under the mesquite, frightening away a group of sparrows that had been singing from its branches. Judging from the bird droppings on the table, the serenade had been a long one. I lay my cell on the table, but made a mental note to scrub it with alcohol as soon as I got back to the office.

Rick eyed the cell. "You won't need that. Like I said, I met Celeste at Frugal Foods about four months ago. After I helped her put the groceries in the van, we started talking. At first she was kinda shy, but after meeting a few times, she loosened up and told me about her life, all about the polygamy thing, how it was beginning to wear her down. She was only thirty-six, but she'd had twelve kids already. Not all of them lived, though."

"The ones that died. Were they boys?" Baby boys had a strangely high death rate in polygamy compounds.

"How'd you guess?"

I waved the question away. "Continue."

"Anyway, she told me her youngest, a girl named Eleanor, had just been shipped off to get married in some compound up by the Canadian border, and what with all her kids gone now, there was no reason to stay on, so she was thinking about making a new life for herself. She hated her husband. Said he was mean, real mean."

That sounded like Ezra, all right. "Did she ever talk about Jonah?"

"Who's that?"

"One of her sons. He was thrown out of the compound last year, when he turned eighteen."

"Really? She never mentioned him."

"Never talked about Jonah at all?"

"No."

"She didn't seem worried about him?"

"I told you, no."

The woman described as "maternal" by Rosella, "the kindest and sweetest" by her throwaway son, and "unhappy" by Little

Rick, had long ago stopped thinking about anyone other than herself. Maybe she never had. Maybe she'd just been a good actress, willing to assume any role that helped her survive an increasingly unhappy life.

A sweet whistle made me look up. The sparrows had begun drifting back to the mesquite, and Little Rick made a big show out of watching them sidle next to each other on the tree's branches.

I was less entranced. Instead, I was wondering why men couldn't see through manipulative women. "Sounds like your relationship was developing like a house afire."

"You don't need to sound so cynical, Miss Jones. What's the matter? Don't you believe in love?"

"We're not talking about my love life, just yours." I tapped my fingers on my cell phone.

"All right. Somewhere along the line, Celeste and I fell in love. To give us more time to be together, I started helping her do the grocery shopping. She'd give me half of her list and I'd run around, grabbing things off the shelves. Afterward, we'd carry the groceries out to the van and sit there and talk for awhile. One thing led to another, and…" His face pinked up. "And, well, the van was big enough to, well, you know."

"How often?"

He shifted his great bulk in discomfort, and wiped a beefy hand across his eyes. "I don't see why…" Seeing my hand reach for the cell again, he continued. "Every week for about two months. Then that bitch Opal must've started getting suspicious, because she stopped letting Celeste shop by herself anymore. But she'd always leave a note for me underneath the apples, telling me when I could meet her over by the construction yard fence, you know, Ten Spot Construction. They all lived at that house in the back. We never had long to talk, and of course we couldn't, uh, get together. So we began making plans to change that."

"What kind of plans?"

Although the day wasn't that warm, he began sweating even harder. "I found her a small apartment over in Phoenix and put some furniture in it that I'd salvaged from an abandoned storage unit. And I was going to hire her to do some work here, just easy filing and stuff. Maybe cleaning out empty units. She was stronger than she looked."

"You didn't worry that your wife might get suspicious?"

"Annie's been feeling worse lately, MS, you know, and I told her it might help if she took some time off. Until she felt better." From the tone in his voice, he knew Annie was never going to feel better.

"Were you going to leave Annie for Celeste?"

He looked shocked. "Why would I do something like that? Annie needs me!"

Men and their so-called loyalties. All I could do was shake my head in disbelief. "Did Celeste know you were married?"

"Of course. And she didn't mind."

Hardly surprising, since any woman raised in a polygamy compound was used to sharing her man. "Exactly how long after you started having sex did Celeste ask you to help her get set up on the outside?"

"Why does it matter?"

Because gullibility, thy name is man. "Answer the question."

"I know what you're thinking, that she was taking advantage of me, but that's not it! She never asked me to do anything for her, I just offered! But I guess it was about after the second time we, uh, had sex, maybe even the first time. Hell, I wanted to help her because she was so desperate."

And manipulative. "So you rented her a Phoenix apartment and offered her a job. How was she supposed to get to work? Surely you weren't going to shuttle her back and forth."

"I'm not stupid, you know. She told me she'd always dreamed of having a blue car to match her eyes, so I was going to buy her one, a blue Mazda or Hyundai."

What a sap. Then again, love made fools of us all. "Getting back to basics, Little Rick, when did Celeste tell you she was pregnant? Or did she ever?"

"I didn't know." He mumbled something I didn't quite hear. Even after I asked him to repeat it, I still had to lean close enough to feel his breath to hear his reply. That's when I saw the tears in his eyes.

"I...I was going to have a son." His broken voice was filled with love, longing, and regret.

One man's throwaway was another man's treasure.

Chapter Twenty-seven

The strain of the past few days must have caught up with me because I arrived at Desert Investigations feeling emotionally exhausted, not yet ready to sort through what I'd learned. I buried myself in paperwork until Jimmy gave a startled yelp. "We just received an email from Rosella!"

In my haste to get to the computer, I spilled papers all over the floor, but I didn't care. "Oh, crap. I told her not to contact us, that it's too dangerous." But I was glad to know she was still alive.

"Don't worry," he said, pointing at the screen. "She took precautions. It's from an Internet cafe. Here, read."

FROM: ROSERUNNER

TO: DESERTINVESTIGATIONS.COM

K & I still on move. Read thru scottsdalejournal.com bout M. Happy 4 reunion but hope shes fine after stuff p-men put her thru. They otta be boiled n oil but prob get away with it—always do. Gotta go. Send U email n couple days. Be good or be careful. K sends her luv & me 2. R

"She sounds all right, don't you think?" Jimmy asked.

"Yep." I didn't trust myself to say anything else, just walked back to my desk and began picking up the papers I'd dropped so he wouldn't see my face.

"Are you okay, Lena?"

"Why wouldn't I be?"

"Because you sound…"

I kept my head down. "Weren't you working on something?"

With a grunt and a click, he killed Rosella's email and went back to doing whatever he'd been doing.

Paperwork is the bane of a P.I.'s existence, but it does have its merits. For instance, it can keep you from obsessing about the safety of your friends. I worked on a group of case notes and invoices until Madeline walked in and announced that Glenda, her real estate agent, had called with the news that the New York house was already in a bidding war.

"How can that be possible," I asked, "when you just talked to her yesterday?"

She gave me a smile that perfectly matched today's GENGHIS KHAN IS MY HOMEBOY tee shirt. "New roof, new furnace, two bedrooms, one-and-a-half baths, attached studio, carpenter's workshop, wooded lot, and within bicycling distance of the Catskills. Glenda said two different artists viewed it this morning—they've both made offers. Plus, a sculptor and a book designer are scheduled to see it tomorrow."

The news cheered me considerably. "If you sell it by the end of the week…"

"Escrow could close in thirty days," she finished.

"Way to go, Maddy!" Jimmy enthused.

We spent the next few minutes celebrating Madeline's good fortune, doubly welcome because of her kidnapping ordeal. Nietzsche, the German philosopher, said that what doesn't kill us makes us strong, but I knew better. For many people the opposite was true: too much terror, too much heartbreak, and they were wounded for life. This sad realization tore me away from the celebratory moment with Madeline and back to the sorrows at hand: damaged Jonah, murdered Celeste.

I had a strong suspicion as to the identity of Celeste's killer, but before I took my theory to Scottsdale PD I needed an answer to one final question. The only person who might be able to give me the answer was Darnelle, the dead woman's confidant. Contacting her would prove difficult, but the conversation with Little Rick had given me an idea.

"Jimmy, I hate to break up this love fest, but since tonight's the night the sister-wives do their shopping at Frugal Foods, I need someone to drive over there and pass a note to Darnelle. Opal knows what I look like, so we need a fresh face. Any ideas?"

Madeline immediately volunteered, but I turned her down. "I'm not risking you again."

Over her protests, Jimmy came to the rescue. "Heather would be perfect."

I drew a blank. "Heather who?"

"Don't you remember? The pretty woman I met when we were on the way to lunch at Malee's."

"The yuppie from Chicago? You've been *dating* her?"

"A couple of times. Well, maybe three or four, actually. And we meet for lunch every now and then."

My partner's easy rapport with women never failed to amaze me. "Bringing a stranger into this…"

"Hear him out, Lena," Madeline said, before I finished dismissing the idea. "He's told me about Heather and he may be on to something."

Jimmy threw her a grateful look. "Heather's bright, and since she works with people she knows how to handle difficult situations."

"Works 'with people'? In what capacity? Cosmetic salesperson at Neiman Marcus?" Although I'd seen the woman only once, I remembered her sleek good looks and perfect makeup. She probably spent more on lipstick than I did on rent.

He frowned. "Heather's a conflict resolution specialist."

So much for stereotyping.

Madeline could see that I still wasn't convinced. "With her professional background, she'd be able to read Darnelle's body language—as well as that of the other two women—which means she'd find the perfect moment to pass a note. I vote yes."

"Since when is this a democracy?" At their combined frowns, I tried a final argument. "Well, it's nice that Jimmy wants to volunteer his girlfriend for such a touchy assignment, but she'll probably turn him down flat, as well she should."

I lost that argument, too. Jimmy picked up the phone and dialed the resort where Heather was staying, and within seconds, secured her excited agreement. When he hung up, he said, "She told me it sounds like more fun than settling the usual corporate squabbles."

Fun wasn't the word I would have chosen.

The workday ended with me composing a note to Darnelle, asking her to meet me at the fence Tuesday night after the others had gone to bed. I handed the note to Jimmy, and he headed off for an early dinner date with Chicago Heather, Girl Detective.

Jimmy arrived at the office the next morning saying that Heather had passed her assignment with flying colors. "Once she caught Darnelle's eye, she tucked the note in the middle of the apple display. Then she moved over to the pears and fussed around until Darnelle retrieved it. Told you so."

I'd spent the night in a jangle of nerves, reading the Celeste King case file over and over again to make certain I hadn't skipped anything. The file included the medical examiner's report, everything the police had told me, the events surrounding Madeline's kidnapping, and my interviews with Jonah, Clayton, and Little Rick. Putting all this together with the information Rosella gave me before she'd been run out of town, I'd charted a loose timeline of Celeste's life that extended all the way back to her years with Hiram Shupe in Second Zion.

It still wasn't enough.

Somehow I managed to get through the day. Madeline was full of excited chatter about turning the empty barn into a home, listing all the elements she'd need to order, including insulation, drywall, flooring, and kitchen and bathroom fixtures. And those were just for starters. Her plans for her upcoming show at the

Shadow Mountain Gallery were moving forward, too. An artist friend was nailing together the packing crates necessary for shipping fine art, and promised to have the job completed by the end of the week.

This kept my mind busy until eight, when I filled a thermos full of coffee, slipped on my many-pocketed vest, and departed for the unit at Kachina 24-Hour-Storage. Once there, I was pleased to discover that Jimmy had reinstalled the spy camera and monitor before he'd headed up to the Boulders for another date with Heather. All I needed to do was relax on my chaise and wait for Darnelle to make her appearance at the fence.

For whatever reason, the Kachina was extra busy tonight. Until just before eleven, the aisle outside my unit jingled and rattled with the sounds of opening locks and accordion doors. Pieces of conversation drifted toward me, revealing bits of interrupted lives. The only note of cheer came from the potter two units away, who'd turned up her CD player as she worked, and the retro sounds of the Beach Boys drifted toward me in the rapidly-cooling night air: songs of sunlit beaches, teenage dreams, little deuce coupes. Had life ever been that innocent?

When the potter, the last person on my aisle to leave, finally pulled her accordion door down, locked it, and walked away, I went over the case again and again, double- and triple-checking to make certain my assumptions were right. Despite popular belief, "stranger murders" are rare, because in most cases, people tend to be killed because of who and what they are. This doesn't mean that victims deserve their fates—no victim does—only that they had inadvertently put themselves in harm's way through business dealings or personal relationships. The amount of overkill Celeste had suffered meant that no stranger had killed her, she'd been killed by someone who either loved her or hated her.

Who?

In the beginning, I hadn't believed that Prophet Shupe could summon up the passion necessary to personally kill Celeste. After all, he'd pawned her off to another man without a second thought. As for Ezra, all he cared about was carrying out his elder brother's edicts. Opal seemed to exist in the same emotional vacuum, and while she was violent, I doubted she would keep hitting Celeste once she'd stopped moving. But this was *before* Celeste became pregnant. Afterward, the dynamics in the compound could have shifted.

If Ezra realized his wife had been unfaithful, he could have been angry enough to order his henchmen to carry out an act of Blood Atonement. However, Blood Atonement usually called for a clean bullet to the head, followed by a body dump in the desert, not right down the street. Had Opal guessed about the pregnancy? Clayton had told me she once flew into a rage when Celeste mentioned something about "cravings." But, again, would she have kept hitting Celeste once she was dead? Probably not enough passion. For sheer passion, Jonah was the obvious subject, and he'd already confessed to the crime. Abandoned on the street to survive as best he could, his feelings of rejection could have temporarily eclipsed a son's love for his mother. It was easy to visualize someone in his situation clubbing, clubbing, clubbing an already-dead woman.

But one more person had come to mind. With any murder case, once you rid yourself of preconceived notions about who could kill and who could not, you came away with a plethora of suspects. Gentle Clayton, for instance, appeared incapable of hurting anyone, and wasn't that the perfect disguise for a killer?

Getting involved in a murder case sure played hell with your ability to trust.

As I sat in the storage unit mulling over the various possibilities, the silence outside and increasingly stale air in the storage unit soon had me fighting sleep. Finally, at twenty minutes after midnight, a pale face appeared on the monitor: Darnelle. Moving quickly, I left the storage unit and tiptoed up to the fence. Her pale blue dress gleamed under the full moon, which also revealed something different about her face, a firmness in her demeanor that hadn't been there before, a determined tilt to her chin.

Before I could say anything, a flurry of whispered words tumbled out of her mouth. "Miss Jones, thank God you contacted me. You have to help me get out, just like you did Clayton. I want a new life, one where I can see my baby whenever I want. Could you take me to one of them safe houses for women in my situation?"

That's when I noticed the Frugal Foods shopping bag on the ground next to her. It overflowed with clothing, reminding me of earlier years, when I'd moved my own paltry belongings from foster home to foster home.

"I'm not sure you can make it over the fence with that bag, Darnelle." I gestured toward the razor wire coiled across the top of the fence.

Moonlight glimmered off her smile as she opened her hand, revealing a key ring. "They're to the gates. I stole them from Ezra's pocket when he was finished with me tonight. He sleeps like the dead."

Probably because like any true sociopath, he never felt guilt. With a heavy sigh, I said, "All right. I'll take you to a safe place tonight, if that's what you really want."

"I do!"

Within minutes, Darnelle had slipped through the compound's gates and was waiting for me at the curb as I exited the Kachina. As soon as she settled herself and her grocery-bag luggage in to my Jeep, she made another demand. "I want to see Clayton. *Now.*"

"But it's after midnight!"

The determination never left her face. "I need to make sure my baby's all right."

Mother love. Although the quality had been effectively quashed in most polygamy women, it burned strongly in Darnelle. Against my better judgment, I pulled away from the curb, and while I headed for the freeway, phoned Bernie at the half way house. He picked up just as the answering machine kicked in. Shouting over his recorded message, he agreed, but just this once. From now on, he told me, Darnelle better remember that visiting hours didn't run this late, he'd have to drag Clayton out of bed, which would disturb the entire house. Furthermore...

Before he could finish his litany of complaints and possibly change his mind, I thanked him profusely and rang off. Then we headed up the Pima Freeway's entrance ramp, leaving south Scottsdale—and all that would soon transpire—behind us.

Although I hadn't yet questioned Darnelle, she was so looking forward to seeing her son that I realized it would be pointless to try now. Instead, I just let her sit beside me, imagining her new life we sped along the nearly-empty freeway to north Phoenix. It was too loud for conversation, anyway. A freshened wind blew straight across the windshield and into the Jeep. I saw Darnelle shiver, so I yelled at her to reach behind the seat for the flannel jacket I kept stashed there. The jacket proved too small for her to zip up completely, but at least it kept her arms warm.

The trip, uncluttered by heavy traffic, took only twenty minutes, and when we arrived at our destination, we found Bernie waiting on the porch. Without a greeting, he led us into the dimly-lit day room where Clayton waited, sleepy-eyed, on the sofa. Darnelle's face glowed as she threw her arms around him, and amidst kisses and caresses, told him her plans for their future. During all this, the poor kid remained half-asleep. Would he even remember this meeting in the morning?

Darnelle's ecstasy at being with her son triggered more memories from my past: my own mother—the biological one—sitting beside me on the white bus, whispering those last words before her gun ended my childhood.

"Oh, my baby, my baby, always remember how much I love you."

Mothers. Lost children. In a perfect world there would be no such goodbyes.

But we don't live in a perfect world. We live in this one.

I turned away from my past and listened to the words of a different mother. "And then I'll get an apartment, Clayton, and a job. You'll come live with me, and you'll go to college, and someday you'll get married to a girl *you* choose and you'll have children no one can ever take away from you."

I could hardly stand to hear so much joy, underpinned as it was by a lifetime of farewells. So I stared at the wall and pretended

I was back in my small apartment, back where Madeline waited for me and a newer, happier, life was about to unfold. Pretended that I couldn't hear Darnelle's promises.

When the meeting reached the half-hour mark, Bernie cleared his throat and tapped meaningfully at his watch. "Clayton has a big day ahead of him."

So would everyone involved with Celeste's case, but he didn't need to know that. As gently as possible, I said to Darnelle, "Time to go."

Some of the joy slipped from her face. "So soon?"

"It's almost two, and growing boys need their sleep." Now I was talking about Clayton as if he was still a child. In a sense, he was.

Darnelle gave her son one final kiss. "Mama will see you again just as soon as she's set up, all right?" He didn't reply, just gave her a perfunctory peck, and shuffled back to bed. Tears glistened in Darnelle's eyes, but the glow remained.

Bernie's scowl followed us to the door. "Six to eight p.m., those're the standard visiting hours. Anything else, call at least several hours in advance. And *never* in the middle of the night like this again, okay?"

I didn't foresee a repeat of tonight's visit, but I readily agreed. Before he opened the door, I asked as an afterthought, "How's Jonah?"

"In rehab. If you're a praying woman, offer up a couple for him."

The last time I'd prayed had been a couple of years ago, when I'd been stranded in the desert, near death from heat and dehydration. Perhaps my prayers had helped, since I was still alive. Then again…"I'll give it a try, Bernie."

He nodded, then locked the door behind us.

The wind had pushed a cloud across the moon, inking the sky. As Darnelle and I walked to the Jeep, the temperature felt like it had dropped several more degrees. My turn to shiver.

"Oh, I'm so happy," Darnelle said, as we drove down the dark street. "You'll never know how much this all means to me, Miss Jones. I can't thank you enough."

During her conversation with Clayton, I'd made the required phone call and set things in motion. Before I dropped Darnelle off, I still needed to question her, but since the wind hadn't subsided—it roared past us stronger and louder than ever—I decided to wait until we exited the freeway. What I hadn't counted on was the time.

Bars in Arizona close at two a.m., and as soon as we entered the same freeway that had been nearly empty an hour earlier, the Jeep became sandwiched between three drivers who hadn't received the memo about designated drivers. To my left, a blue Mazda filled with teen girls proved that contrary to popular belief, girls are no more cautious than boys. On the right, a middle-aged man in an aged Buick held a cell phone in one hand, a beer can in the other, and steered with his knees. Ahead of us a Chevy pickup drifted from one lane to another, keeping me from speeding up to leave this gaggle of fools far behind.

Disgusted, I pulled my cell phone out of my vest and alerted DPS while I slowed the Jeep to a barely-legal snail's pace and let the drunks pull ahead.

"Will the police stop them?" Darnelle shouted into the wind.

"Before they kill themselves, I hope," I shouted back. "You still cold?"

She shook her head, but pulled the flannel jacket tighter.

The rest of drive was uneventful. When we took the off ramp onto Indian School Road, the wind quieted enough for me to ask my questions. "When we talked last time you were unhappy, but you didn't say anything about wanting to leave the compound for good. What changed?"

Darnelle didn't answer, just stared out at the buildings we were passing. Due to the hour most of the condominiums were dark, but a few lights remained on in a large apartment complex popular with the under-thirty crowd. Strains of music drifted to us through the thin night air. Rehashed Dylan or Nickleback? The sound was so distorted I couldn't tell.

"Darnelle, what changed?" I repeated.

She wiped at her eyes. Tears, or the wind? "At dinner tonight, Ezra told me that Prophet Shupe's reassigned me to a man up in Second Zion, and that he was sending a van down tomorrow to pick me up."

This explained some of her urgency, but not all. "At least at Second Zion you'd be able to see your other children."

The sound she made could have been either a laugh or a sob. "After Clayton ran off, Prophet Shupe decided to punish me for not keeping him in line, so he had them all reassigned to that compound in Canada. I'm not even sure exactly where it is, just up in the mountains somewhere, so I'll never see them again, anyway." She uttered another half-laugh-half-sob, and added, "My new husband is Brother Gorman. The flames of Hell would be more merciful."

"Gorman Green?" I hoped there was another polygamist Gorman, not the one Rosella had once told me about.

"Yeah, him."

Green, an eighth-generation polygamist, was a man so given to violence against his twenty-two wives that even Ezra seemed gentle in comparison. Darnelle was right. She was definitely being punished, and yes, Hell would be easier to bear. The loss of her children, her reassignment to an even more vicious man, they all explained her sudden desperation. I felt for her—what woman wouldn't?—but if I wanted my curiosity satisfied, now was the time.

"Did Ezra know Celeste was pregnant?" I asked.

As Darnelle stared at the condos slipping by, her face grew puzzled. "I don't think so. If he had, he'd of killed her." Realizing what she'd just said, she clapped a hand over her mouth. "I didn't mean that!"

The effects of compound brain-washing ran deep. With all the reasons Darnelle had to hate Ezra, she still felt it necessary to protect him. "How about Opal? You told me she slapped Celeste when she said she was craving potato chips, so she must have known about the pregnancy."

"Of course she did. One morning Opal caught her throwing up in the bathroom, and there was a big scene. I was walking past on my way to the kitchen and heard everything."

A woman could hide pregnancy from a man for a while but not from another woman, especially when that woman was as alert as Opal. "What did she plan to do about it?"

"Tell Ezra, I guess. She'd have to."

Hiram Shupe had reassigned Darnelle to Gorman Green because she hadn't controlled her soon-to-be-throwaway son, a boy no longer necessary to the compound's financial well-being. Although Ezra took care of the compound's business interests, it was Opal's job to keep the compound's women in line, and Celeste's pregnancy would have been proof that she'd failed at her job. What fresh hell would Hiram and Ezra Shupe have dreamed up for Opal then? Would she, too, be reassigned to Brother Gorman? Or just shot in the head and buried in the desert?

"Had Opal told Ezra about the pregnancy yet?"

Darnelle started to shake her head, then, with fresh excitement on her face, said, "Maybe she killed Celeste so she wouldn't have to tell him! Oh, Miss Jones, that's it!"

As we approached the notoriously accident-prone raised intersection at Indian School and Hayden roads, I eased off on the Jeep's accelerator. Running under the intersection was the southern end of Indian Bend Wash, Scottsdale's miles-long green belt, where egrets, blue herons, coyotes, and other wildlife served as witnesses to car-crumpling wrecks. I slowed even more as I considered my passenger's words. Her proposed solution to the murder may have sounded reasonable, but I knew it wasn't true.

I turned to her and said, "Opal didn't kill Celeste. You did."

Chapter Twenty-eight

The streetlights illuminated Darnelle's shocked face. "What do you mean, *I killed Celeste?*"

I'd already switched on the tape recorder I'd stashed in a vest pocket. But before I could coax Darnelle to say anything else, two cars—a burgundy Infiniti wobbling through a left turn and a blue Geo speeding from the opposite direction—slammed into each other in the middle of the intersection. To avoid the tangled mess, I hit the brakes and held my breath as the Jeep slid across the asphalt, stopping mere inches from the Infiniti's rear bumper. The drivers climbed out of their cars and began cursing drunkenly at each other. Within seconds, their curses evolved into a fist fight.

As I pulled out my cell phone, Darnelle took advantage of the confusion by bailing from the Jeep. Blue dress whipping in the wind, she fled past the brawling drivers and onto the winding path that descended into Indian Bend Wash below. Within seconds, she had vanished into the darkness.

I couldn't leave the Jeep to block the only clear spot in the intersection. Nerves twitching from frustration, I pulled around the crumpled cars and to the curb, stopping under the NO PARKING sign. Although my feet itched to follow Darnelle, my police training made me do the right thing: alert the authorities. But before I finished dialing 9-1-1, another car swerved around the wreck and came to a stop several feet from me. His own cell was already in his hand and, over the still-brawling drivers, I heard him report the incident.

I repocketed my cell and sprang from the Jeep. Darnelle might be a killer, but no woman, especially a woman wearing a movement-hampering long dress, should be left alone at this hour in the Wash, where predators—both animal and human— could lie in wait.

By now, she had a good head start on me, though, so rather than take the meandering pathway she'd followed, I made up time by sliding on my butt straight down the steep grass verge to the Wash twenty feet below. The maneuver saved me only seconds, and by the time I'd clambered to my feet, I couldn't even hear her. Had she run north, toward the lagoon? Or through the dank tunnel that passed under Indian School Road and opened onto the southern end of the Wash.

As much as I hoped she'd turned north—it would be so much easier to catch her by the small lagoon—the alarmed squawk of a heron on the other side of the tunnel convinced me she'd fled south. Perhaps some sort of homing instinct was leading her into south Scottsdale and the compound that had served as her home. Did she expect help from Ezra, the "husband" who was handing her over to another man? The chances of that were doubtful since the only woman he'd ever shown the least bit of loyalty to had been Opal, a woman as heartless as he. If by some miracle Darnelle did managed to reach the compound, it was more than likely that he would shoot her himself, then dispose of her in the desert.

"Darnelle, stop!"

The echo of my voice bounced through the tunnel, but no one answered. I only heard the drivers on the street above, the Good Samaritan attempting to calm them, and the wind as it rushed through a stand of reeds. That meant she'd probably left the path and was headed out across the lake-studded Continental Golf Course. Fortunately, I was a good runner, and unlike Darnelle, I was wearing jeans and Reeboks. Without another thought, I darted into the tunnel.

Golf course or no, the Indian Bend Wash was a big piece of wild in the middle of the city. A quarter-mile wide and twelve miles long, it had been built by the Army Corps of Engineers to redirect the flash floods that plagued Scottsdale during our infrequent but often heavy rains, and the Wash did its job well. During the last monsoon, the area had lain underwater for a week, and even now the tunnel stank of wet, decaying things. As I pounded through the pitch black with my arms outstretched to keep me from hitting the walls, ground squirrels—or, worse, rats—squeaked in alarm as they scurried down the tunnel ahead of me. When I finally emerged into the clean night air, my sight-line improved somewhat, but not enough to spot Darnelle.

Miles of lakes and green belt stretched before me, dark from the cloud-covered moon. But at the top of the Wash's eastern edge, the grass was eerily lit by the ambient glow of an all-night McDonald's drive-thru.

The light was too far away to help me. Down here, tall olean-der and bougainvillea thickets hugged the shores of a large lake, adding even deeper shadows to the night. As I pressed forward, though, my eyes began to accustom themselves to the darkness, and eventually I could make out the cement culverts designed to feed excess water into the lake. Wondering if Darnelle had taken shelter, I walked over to the nearest one.

"Darnelle! No one's going to hurt you! The police just want to talk, to find out what really happened."

Other than the annoyed quacks of waterfowl, I heard noth-ing. I plucked my Mag-Lite from my vest and clicked it on, but discovered that the only thing staring back at me was a startled mallard. Clicking the light off to save the battery, and I began to circle the lake, repeating the same routine at each culvert. By the time I reached the last one, I'd pretty much given up. Darnelle was frightened, and frightened women tend to flee— not hide. As I straightened up after yet another fruitless search, a siren cleaved the night, signaling the arrival of a squad car. I thought for a moment of running up to the street to hail them, then decided against it. The wreck would necessarily be the cops' first priority, not chasing after some lost woman. I abandoned the lake and headed at an angle across the golf course, and the smell of fishy water evolved into the tang of mown grass.

The soft green cushioned my feet. Aided by the crisp air, my breath came without a hitch. So did my long stride, shortened only when I had to detour around a gopher hole. For the next few minutes I ran easily, flushing panicked wildlife from their hidey-holes, until the cloud that had earlier covered the moon finally parted, and revealed the silvery shimmer of a blue heron gliding straight across the green. The scene would have been peaceful if not for a nearby coyote, which was dragging a still-alive Canada goose along the ground. As I circled him, the coyote growled a threat, but he kept his jaws clamped around the thrashing bird's neck. I didn't interfere. For all its beauty, nature is seldom gentle. Death for the goose meant survival for the coyote.

Unwilling to witness the goose's final agony, I turned my eyes away, and in that moment saw another pale flicker as the heron changed course and flew into a stand of mesquite.

No. Not a heron.

It was Darnelle, the flutter of her pale blue skirts mimicking the outstretched wings of a large bird.

"Darnelle! Stop running! It's over!"

She didn't answer, not that I expected her to. Her blue skirt danced back and forth between the trees until she'd disappeared. Had she run through the thicket and come out the other side, or was she lying in wait, a hastily caught-up weapon in hand? A limb, maybe, or a rock. Under normal circumstances she was probably no more violent than the average woman, but another obstacle to her reunion with Clayton might turn her vicious again. Now, instead of me being the savior who'd saved her son, I was the devil about to part them.

I stopped at the edge of the mesquite thicket and made certain my pocket recorder was still running. The light glowed red.

"Give it up, Darnelle," I shouted, pointing the mike toward her. "I've already told the police, and they're waiting to talk to you. There's nothing to be afraid of. They know you didn't plan to kill Celeste, and that'll make a big difference in court. You just lashed out at her with whatever was at hand." I didn't mention the part about her continuing to hit the woman. "That kind of thing is called a crime of passion, and judges treat them much more leniently than they do cold-blooded murder. Why, you might even get off on probation." This was a stretch, but she didn't know it.

"What…What's probation?" Her voice, breathless from her run, drifted from a mesquite so old its branches drooped to the ground.

"Probation means you just report to a social worker instead of going to prison."

"Are you sure?"

I hated to keep lying, but even more, I wanted to deliver her safely into the arms of Scottsdale PD, where detectives Sylvie Perrins and Bob Grossman waited, having been alerted by my earlier phone call from the halfway house. If she kept running around the Wash in the dark, something bad could happen. Javelina, with their bad tempers and sharp tusks, had been known to travel up the Wash.

"Why don't you tell me everything? It had something to do with Clayton, didn't it?"

"Y-yes."

Honing in on her voice, I edged closer to the thicket. Once I had her talking, I planned to make a dive for her, handcuff her, and take her back to the Jeep.

"Darnelle, I understand the extremes a mother will go to for her child." Three women had taught me all about that; Rosella, Madeline, and my biological mother—whoever and wherever she was.

The genuine sympathy in my voice must have made an impact, because after she'd taken a deep breath, she said, "You don't blame me?"

"No." It was almost the truth, but even a woman like Celeste had a right to live.

"I didn't mean to kill her, Miss Jones."

"Of course you didn't. But what happened? What made you...do what you did?"

Once she'd hitched her breath again, she began to talk so intently that she didn't notice me moving closer, the handcuffs out and ready to snap around her wrists.

"Celeste and me, we was out in the yard looking at the stars. Opal wasn't feeling good that night so she'd turned in early. Clayton, I think he had the same bug Opal did, he was asleep, too. Ezra was in bed with Josie. Celeste started talking about this guy Little Rick, bragging that he was in love with her and had found her an apartment, a job, and was even buying her a blue car to match her eyes! I begged her to take me and Clayton with her, that we'd both of us get jobs, but she looked at me like I was crazy. She said no, that she wasn't about to let me and Clayton mess up her new life."

"That's when you hit her?"

"I hit her after she told me I needed to toughen up, that she'd let Ezra get rid of Jonah and good riddance to him, so what made me think my puny little punk—that's what she called him—was any more special? Then she *laughed*, Miss Jones! I was crying so hard and she laughed. Laughed at me, laughed over Clayton being so scared! That's when something ugly happened to me inside, like I became a different person, or some kind of animal. We was standing right next to this stack of two-by-fours left over from a construction job so I grabbed one and I hit her, then hit her again. All I wanted was make her stop laughing."

By now, I'd almost reached the thicket. Her blue dress was visible again, almost within reach. As she talked, I kept moving.

"I'm not a killer, Miss Jones. I..."

The moon glinted along the handcuffs.

"Wait a minute! What's that in your...?"

With a shriek, Darnelle charged out of the other side of the mesquite thicket and across the green. At first I thought she was making for the compound again, but moonlight soon revealed that she was headed straight for the largest and deepest of the green belt lakes. I didn't waste my breath trying to call her back; I started running.

By the time I reached the rocks at the edge of the lake, she'd already made it off the shore and was sloshing her way through a morass of lily pads. Her long dress was already weighted down with water. Was she trying for the other side? Or…Afraid that I knew the answer, I shrugged off my heavy vest and waded in after her, but almost immediately thick mud sucked at my running shoes, slowing me down.

"Don't be an idiot, Darnelle!" I yelled, as she widened the distance between us. I pulled my feet away, leaving my Reeboks behind in the mire. "Suicide won't solve anything!"

"I don't want to live without my baby!" With that, she ducked her head under the water, but came up gasping. Seconds later, she ducked under the water again and this time she didn't resurface.

Barefoot now, I leaped forward and swam with strong strokes to the area where I thought she'd gone under. I took a deep breath and dove. Even though I kept my eyes open, the water was too murky for moonlight to penetrate but I stayed under, grasping at reeds, at anything that signaled movement until my burning lungs forced me to the surface. Then I took another breath and dove again. And again.

On my third try my outstretched hands bumped into something soft and warm. I felt my way along Darnelle's arm, grabbed a fist full of dress, and pulled upward with all my strength. While we rose into the moonlight she didn't struggle. Her body remained limp even after I'd hooked my left arm around her neck and towed her toward the shore.

As soon as my feet touched mud, I shifted my neck hold and grasped her around the waist. Then I pulled her through the reeds to dry land.

"Darnelle!" I screamed.

Nothing.

When I felt her neck, her pulse was still. I started to begin CPR, then remembered what I'd recently been told by an experienced EMT, a man who'd brought three toddlers back from the brink of death after near-drownings. *"A for airway, B for Breathing, C for circulation—but get that water out of the victim's lungs FIRST."* So I hauled her upright, bent her over, and positioned my fists under her diaphragm. Then I performed the Heimlich maneuver. With a great rush, water spewed from her mouth.

The second time I received only a trickle. Now that her lungs were as clear as I could get them, I lowered her to the ground and began CPR to the beat of the BeeGee's "Stayin' Alive," an aptly-titled song that perfectly mimicked the downbeat of a healthy human heart. When I made it to the second verse, Darnelle gave a big hiccup, then began to breathe on her own.

Chapter Twenty-nine

Although my efforts to save Darnelle had broken two of her ribs, no one at the hospital blamed me since she was conscious, crying, and telling everyone who'd listen that she really, really didn't mean to kill Celeste. Most appreciative of my efforts—and Darnelle's continued verbosity—were Sylvie Perrins and Bob Grossman, who'd arrived at the Emergency Ward during her babbled confession.

"I thought you were bringing her in for questioning, not joining her for a moonlight swim," commented Sylvie, as she watched a nurse administer Darnelle an antibiotics shot.

"Two drunks got in my way."

Bob cleared his throat. "Which reminds me. That wreck? Your Jeep got towed right along with the other cars."

"What?!"

"You shouldn't have parked on the sidewalk," said Lieutenant Dagny Ulrich, who'd made the trip with them. She was back to her old self, gleeful at catching me in the wrong. Somehow I found comfort in that.

Darnelle's eyes searched mine. She was still covered in mud and weeds, but sadness had replaced the wildness in her expression. "Promise me," she whispered.

Touched by her anguish, I said, "What?"

"Keep an eye on my baby. Make sure he's all right."

I didn't even have to think about it. "Whatever it takes, Darnelle."

"Thank you." With that, she covered her face with her hands and didn't say another word, not even when the hospital released her into the waiting arms of Scottsdale PD.

Four hours later, Jimmy and I—armed with a wad of cash, driver's license, car registration, proof of insurance, and other official papers—stood waiting for the impound lot in an industrial section of Mesa to open. The day promised to be a warm one, with the sun already blazing down from a cloudless sky. Although I still hurt over what I'd had to do to Darnelle, the realization that law officers now swarmed the polygamy compound—the scene of the crime—helped ease the pain. Polygamists didn't like people knowing their business, so chances were good that Prophet Shupe would call them all back to Second Zion. That was the good news. The bad news was that Second Zion, and its multitude of sins against women and children, would continue to prosper.

Some day, though...

"Can you see the Jeep?" I asked Jimmy, as we peered through the impound lot's chain link fence.

"Just a couple of big dogs. We'd better step back."

I ignored his suggestion until two Dobermans rushed the fence, fangs bared. What made them even scarier was the total silence in which they moved. They weren't out to frighten, they wanted dinner. I muttered, "There better not be any scratches on that Jeep."

Jimmy shot me a look. "Cars can be fixed."

"Meaning?"

"Meaning that people sometimes can't. What you pulled last night was pretty stupid, driving around at two a.m. with a murderer." He raised his palms in a gesture of exasperation.

"The chances that Darnelle would try to hurt me were slim, but if she did, I knew she was no match for me. Not without a two-by-four handy, she wasn't."

"Still..."

"Still, nothing. I was perfectly safe, whether you believe it or not."

"She could have had one of Ezra's handguns hidden somewhere in that dress."

"No pockets. And if she'd strapped a gun to her thigh, don't you think I would have noticed when she hiked up her skirts to run?"

A grunt.

The Dobermans, frustrated at not being able to chew our legs off, began snapping at each other. We watched in silence until the larger Doberman intimidated the smaller one into slinking away. The winner of this face-off then returned to the fence and flashed triumphant teeth.

"Such a nice doggie," I said.

Nice Doggie wagged his stump of a tail.

Jimmy managed a resigned laugh. "You always did have a way with animals."

"Too bad it doesn't extend to men."

With that, we fell silent and watched Nice Doggie scratch himself. After a few minutes, the vanquished Doberman shuffled up and sat a few feet away from the other. Nice Doggie snarled, sending him scuttling back under a rusted '92 Seville.

A few minutes later, after the interplay between the Dobermans grew boring, Jimmy said, "How'd you know?"

"Know what?"

"That Darnelle killed Celeste. It's not like you had any proof."

"She's the only person it could have been." As opposed to other cases I'd worked where I'd finagled access to suspects' homes and businesses, the polygamy compound was a closed site. None of its residents, other than Darnelle, would talk to me, so I'd had to rely solely on my knowledge of victimology. In the end, that had been enough.

Jimmy still didn't get it. "Why not Ezra? Or that monster Opal? Or any one else at the compound, maybe even the guys who kidnapped Madeline."

"Darnelle was the only person with the means, opportunity, and *passion* to beat Celeste to death. None of the others cared enough."

Now several other drivers had formed a line behind us: a jittery brunette with a squalling baby; a Hispanic man dressed in mechanic's overalls; an elderly man leaning on a walker; and several twenty-somethings. The twenty-somethings all looked defiant; the rest looked scared.

"Passion?" Jimmy's disbelief brought me back to his original question.

Keeping my voice low enough that the others couldn't hear, I said, "Yeah, passion, but not the kind you're thinking about, just a mother's passion to keep her son safe. Women have killed for their children before, and they will again." My own mother's face flashed into my mind. *Had she killed for me?* "Darnelle's tragedy was that she asked the wrong person for help."

At one time, I believed, Celeste would have been the right person. She'd helped Rosella and KariAnn escape from Second Zion. But time changed people, often in terrible ways.

"People who have no power—women especially—learn to use manipulation to get what they want," I explained, "which is what Celeste did to survive. Her father told her to marry Prophet Shupe, so she did. When Shupe sent her daughters to other compounds, she acquiesced, but she got her revenge by helping other girls escape. When Shupe reassigned her to Ezra, she acquiesced again. By then the damage was done. Even Darnelle said that she seemed somehow 'different' after she'd been given to Ezra."

"If that's true, why'd Darnelle ask her for help?"

"There was no one else to ask. And remember what I said about manipulation. Celeste had learned to survive by hiding her own feelings, kowtowing to Opal, always smiling—and 'staying sweet'—for Ezra. She probably encouraged other women to confide in her because it reminded her that she wasn't the only miserable person around. But after those first adventurous years up in Second Zion, when she ran her own small version of the polygamy Underground Railroad, she stopped helping anyone. She was so far gone that when the day came, she even stood passively by when Ezra's goons drove her own son away and dumped him on the street like garbage."

Once a woman allowed her heart to be numbed, her soul soon followed. By the time Darnelle approached Celeste for help, she'd long been deaf to other people's pain. So in the end, her own heartlessness killed her.

"It's a rough life, polygamy," Jimmy said, after I'd voiced my thoughts.

"Yeah. That poor woman."

He gave me a questioning look. "Which one?"

I thought for a moment, then answered, "Both of them."

Author's Note

If one man can have ten wives, nine men will have none.

While recent events at the YFZ (Yearning for Zion) compound in El Dorado, Texas, may have familiarized the public with some of the more onerous customs of the Southwest's polygamy compounds (child marriage, incest, brain-washing, etc.), a major problem area remains largely unexplored: what happens to polygamy's surplus boys?

By order of the reigning prophet, those surplus boys are being systematically culled from the compounds where they grew up. Between the ages of fourteen and eighteen, these surplus boys—now termed Lost Boys—are loaded into vans and dumped out on the streets of St. George, Utah, Flagstaff, Arizona, or larger cities to make their way as best they can. They are not allowed to contact their families again or return to the place of their birth.

In a *New York Times* article dated Sept. 9, 2007, Paul Murphy, an assistant Utah attorney general who has worked with these boys, said, "In part, it's an issue of control. If you're going to have plural marriage, you need fewer men."

Making this culling practice even more tragic is the fact that many boys (and girls) raised in polygamy compounds are so undereducated that their reading and math skills test out at the second grade level. This makes the boys uniquely unsuited to the challenges of modern life. Ultimately, many fall prey to crime and drugs. To feed themselves, some even turn to prostitution.

Fortunately, some Arizona and Utah charitable groups, such as the HOPE Organization, the Diversity Foundation, and the Child Protection Project have stepped in to stem the tide of misery.

In an article published by the *Deseret Morning News* on May 28, 2006, Elaine Tyler, founder of the HOPE Organization, which provides food and shelter for these culled children, said, "We try to just cover their basic needs. They're coming out with nothing. The Lost Boys are living out of cars."

In an interview that ran on National Public Radio on April 11, 2008, Tyler went into further detail. "They don't know how to handle money, how to get a library card. We're seeing seventeen-year-olds who can't even read the menu at McDonald's." She also adds that many of them have been subject to sexual abuse. "Building trust with these boys takes a long time. They're burdened with a sense of guilt and shame. So this is not a quick fix."

Two of the most notorious polygamy compounds, Colorado City, Arizona and Hildale, Utah, were—until recently—run by FLDS prophet Warren Jeffs, convicted on two counts of rape as an accomplice, and who is now serving two terms of five years to life in Utah; he is awaiting trial on further felony charges in Arizona relating to the sexual abuse of a minor. Estimates are that during Jeffs' reign, between five hundred to one thousand boys were ejected from his compounds in order that Jeffs' chosen followers could have multiple wives. Long before the boys' expulsions, however, Jeffs forced these children to drop out of school between fourth and eleventh grades and work without pay in Jeffs' various businesses, where workdays averaged ten to twelve hours.

Although this is in flagrant defiance of child labor laws, testimony before the U.S. Senate on July 24, 2008, revealed that Jeffs' companies included New Era Manufacturing, which has a Department of Defense contract for aircraft wheel and brake manufacturing worth $1.2 million. Another is JNJ Engineering, which has an $11.3 million deal with the Las Vegas Valley Water District. A third of Jeffs' companies, Paragon Contractors Corporation, has been fined more than $10,000 by the U.S.

Department of Labor for employing twelve-to-fifteen-year-old boys and not paying them.

These financial malpractices caused U. S. Sen. Harry Reid, in a Senate hearing on the matter, to label Jeffs' FLDS church a form of organized crime where the FLDS has "wrongfully cloaked themselves in the trappings of religion to conceal crimes such as bigamy, child abuse, welfare fraud, tax evasion, massive corruption, and strong-arm tactics to maintain what they think is the status quo."

Although at the date of this writing Jeffs remains in jail, his hand-picked deputies still control the compounds at Colorado City, Arizona, Hildale, Utah, and El Dorado, Texas—where girls as young as thirteen are given to elderly men to serve as "multiple wives" and surplus boys continue to be expelled onto the streets of neighboring cities.

When *Desert Wives: Polygamy Can Be Murder* (Betty Webb, Poisoned Pen Press) was published in 2002, few readers knew that polygamy was still being practiced on American soil. Even fewer were aware of its many human rights abuses. The Author's Note to that book quoted Linda Binder, former Arizona state senator and a vigorous anti-polygamist activist, as stating, "We have a situation here that is unconscionable. We have the Taliban in our back yard."

The Taliban is still here.

Resources

For more information about polygamy:

Organizations

The Child Protection Project—*www.childpro.org*

The HOPE Organization—*www.childbrides.org*

The Diversity Foundation—*www.smilesfordiversity.org*

Articles

"Polygamy in Arizona: The Wages of Sin," by John Dougherty, Phoenix New Times, April 10, 2003.

"Seeking Shelter in a Storm: Amid Flurry of Controversy, Girls Flee Polygamist Enclave," by Betty Webb, East Valley Tribune, January 15, 2005.

"Polygamy's Lost Boys Need Not Walk Alone," by Brooke Adams, Salt Lake Tribune, August 1, 2004.

"Lost Boys: Polygamy, Prostitution and Rape in the Name of God," by Ben Williams, Salt Lake Metro Magazine, November, 2005.

"Polygamist Leader Quietly Awaits Trial in Jail," by Felica Fonseca, Washington Post, February 14, 2009.

"Evidence Reveals a Paranoid Jeffs," by Paul A. Anthony, San Angelo Standard Times, February 15, 2009.

Books

Lost Boy, by Brent W. Jeffs and Maia Szalavitz. Broadway Publishing

Under the Banner of Heaven, by Jon Krakauer. Doubleday

The Secret Lives of Saints, by Daphne Bramham. Random House

Church of Lies, by Flora Jessop and Paul T. Brown. Jossey-Boss

Stolen Innocence, Elissa Wall, Lisa Pulitzer. William Morrow

Escape, by Carolyn Jessop and Laura Palmer. Broadway Publishing

Documentaries

Banking On Heaven: Polygamy in the Heartland of the American West. An inside look at the compounds and their people. Over the Moon Productions

Polygamy Diaries: 2001 to the Present. A series of televised reports by Arizona journalist Mike Watkiss, of KTVK-TV. To access, check *http://intentionalfamily.org/polygamy/documentaries.htm*

To receive a free catalog of Poisoned Pen Press titles, please contact us in one of the following ways:

Phone: 1-800-421-3976
Facsimile: 1-480-949-1707
Email: info@poisonedpenpress.com
Website: www.poisonedpenpress.com

Poisoned Pen Press
6962 E. First Ave. Ste. 103
Scottsdale, AZ 85251

LaVergne, TN USA
10 November 2010
204264LV00003B/14/P